Also by
Barbara Whitehead

THE CARETAKER WIFE

Quicksilver Lady

Quicksilver Lady

BARBARA WHITEHEAD

1980
Doubleday & Company, Inc.
Garden City, New York

ISBN: 0-385-12779-0
Library of Congress Catalog Card Number 79-7457

LONDON

Routs, Riots, Balls and Boxing matches,
Dowagers and Demireps, Cards and Crim-con,
Parliamentary discussions, Political
details, Masquerades, Mechanics, Argyle
Street Institution and Aquatic Rooms, Love
and Lotteries, Brookes and Bonaparte,
Exhibitions of pictures with drapery, and
women without; Statues with more decent
dresses than their originals, Opera
singers and Orators, Wine, Women, Waxworks,
and Weathercocks . . . Evening Squeezes, and
Public and Private Parties . . .

Byron, July 1807

Quicksilver Lady

Chapter One

"Pray do, Mr. Welby!"

The girl who had just spoken was standing near the window which looked out on to the tree-bordered drive of Curteys Court; with her simple white muslin dress and attitude of expectancy, she looked poised as though about to take flight. In that room soft with autumn sunshine she had all the hope and eagerness of spring.

Richard Welby was still standing just inside the door. He discovered that his sister-in-law's eyes, when not alight with mischief, could be uncomfortably beseeching; he twiddled the letter he had just received between his fingers and looked across doubtfully at his wife.

"Caroline—what do you think, my love?"

She looked up at him laughing, for she was holding their baby son, and one of his jumps for joy had nearly carried him out of her arms. In that case he would have landed on top of old Pug who, after a lifetime's experience of the Welby children, was wary of this sixth and youngest and, seeing his danger, snuffled away in the sulks, settling half under a chair.

"What? Go to London? Take you to London, Arabella? Oh, Richard, you know what a country mouse I am . . ."

Her husband had crossed the room and was bending over her, tickling Baby Charles. He murmured, for her ears alone,

"A country bird, my dear, a little wren," but she went on with her train of thought, with just a sweet smile up at him.

"Being a town mouse comes hardly to me; are there not enough conquests in Linchestershire, Arabella? Have you not set enough hearts alight in Melton, at the balls and assemblies? Will nothing content you, but Almacks and St. James?"

"Nothing, sister! Do say we may go."

For a few seconds nothing more was said, and Baby Charles' chuckle was the only sound. Then Arabella tried again.

"You will want to see that Welby House is still safe and sound, now that the rich family from the West Indies have got their daughters launched in Society, and left it, do you not?" she said persuasively.

"I have no fears on that score," replied Caroline. "They have been excellent tenants. I own that I have some curiosity to see the saloon, which they have redecorated in the Egyptian manner. But such an emotion would hardly take me from home for a season."

Arabella tried another approach.

"It would be such good practice for you! When Lucy and Martha are Out, you will be taking them to Town; and you can try your prentice hand on me, and be quite experienced for the more delicate task of guiding them. After all, Lucy is now eleven."

"And will hardly be Out for another five years; and I would not take her to London for at least six."

But Caroline had noticed that Richard was not seconding her in her opposition to her youngest sister's notion. She glanced up at him, and wavered. It had occurred to her lately that it was a pity that a child so graceful and musical as Lucy should not have the advantage of the best masters for music and dancing. And if Richard had a mind to go . . . Caroline deposited young Charles on the carpet, where he took the opportunity to crawl over to Pug and bang him over the nose with a coral and silver rattle. His mother stretched her arms and turned to look out of the window.

"Soon we will be dining by candlelight—it is almost too dark at dinner-time now to see our meat. Well, Arabella—if you have Mr. Welby's support, and by his look I think you have—" he smiled, but said nothing—"we'll go up for some weeks. But mind, weeks only! We're not taking up residence in Town. Through this winter, perhaps, but as soon as spring promises, no London for me, balls or no balls, assemblies or no assemblies . . . Shall we reply to Mr. Watts, Richard, and tell him we will come? As soon as it may be arranged. Goodness, child, you will tread on the baby!"

For Arabella, she of the jaconet muslin and primrose slippers, who had stood still until she could stand still no longer, could only express her delight by dancing down the length of the lovely, faded room. The young woman of twenty-one looked more like the impulsive schoolgirl who had once, in this very room, dealt the dignified Mr. Watts a blow over the knuckles with her fan.

Too late, Richard and Caroline thought of imposing conditions.

"You will show proper respect for the old, particularly the dowagers?" said Richard.

"You will move and speak quietly?" added Caroline.

"Show that you have been brought up to appreciate elegance and propriety?"

"Be ladylike?"

But Arabella had caught up her small nephew from the floor, and danced with him out of the room. She was taking him upstairs to his nurse, and only the patter of her feet, and the distant sound of her laughter, answered them.

It was easy to write to Mr. Watts, of Waveney and Watts, their man of business and dear friend, to say that they would come to London. It was not so easy to leave Curteys Court as it lay dreaming in the gentle light of late September.

Richard had all the business of the estate to settle. Since Trafalgar—that battle fast passing into legend—and his return to Curteys, he had gradually recovered from the loss of his arm, and his health was now excellent. But he felt so isolated from events, here in the country! There was no longer fear of invasion; but on the Continent Napoleon was laughing at the forces brought against him. England had joined forces with Portugal and Spain, but the French Emperor had declared to his troops that the Leopards of the Allies would soon be devoured by the Eagles of France. Even now, Bonaparte was on his way to a meeting at Erfurth with Emperor Alexander of Russia and Emperor Francis of Austria; a momentous meeting, which would be well canvassed in the lively London coffee shops, and among any of Richard's old friends of the Navy who might be ashore. But here in the country no one had any interest in it. Life flowed on, and perceptions had narrowed for the time to local affairs.

In his brisk way Richard walked cross country—as riding was now something of a trouble to him—over every field of his estate, and through every wood. There were coverts to inspect, and shooting rights to arrange; tenants to visit; repairs to put in train, which the busy summer had left undone, but which were needed before the onslaught of winter; fencing to put to rights, and hedges for laying.

"What about next year's crops?" he said to Fred Wilson, the bailiff. "The rotation should be turnips this year in Hollin Meadow . . ." And there were the cattle, gradually building up in quality and quantity; he told Fred which bull he had in mind, and he bought a new tup from Squire Grey, which had to be introduced to the little harem of sheep.

On a wet day Richard watched the threshers at work and said, "Mind you get those ricks thatched, first fine day we get!" "We will that," said the men cheerfully. And there were the geese— how many would need to be slaughtered to be sent to Town at Christmas?

When Caroline and Arabella were alone, Caroline had taken the opportunity of saying, rather hesitantly, "You surprise me, Arabella, wanting to leave Linchestershire. I had thought you and young Wilberfoss were going to make a match of it."

Her sister turned her head away, so that Caroline could no longer see her face.

"He went to London himself, in the summer, and brought a bride back with him: an heiress. It is quite the thing, you see, Caroline, to go to London for one's marriage partner."

Caroline had not heard, and she was at a loss for a comforting word. For surely comfort must be needed. Arabella's name had certainly been linked with that of the young man, and he was suitable, if not rich. She knew that Arabella would flinch from a kind word. From what she could see of the averted face, she guessed that the happening had wounded her sister . . . her pride, if not her heart, must have suffered . . .

"To be sure," was the only remark she made. But her opposition to the scheme, if it had still remained, was now quite ended. Society and distraction were obviously the best cure.

Around Curteys Court, the great forest was turning to russet and gold, and when the children of the house took their morning exercise on horseback, yellow leaves were drifting down into the clearings through the early mist, and they came back with dew spangling their hair.

Arabella's thoughts and feelings ranged from hurt to happiness. Sometimes they raced ahead to London, its entertainments and shops; sometimes she was depressed and distrait. But all was forgotten when she was out riding. She loved to gallop whenever she could, and it was when she reined in her horse and paused, that she felt the exquisite melancholy of the season as some prospect of distant landscape unfolded before her. The undulating fields and hedgerows, the patches of trees and thickets of bramble, misty and veiled: she caught her breath at their loveliness, and a dreamy solemnity visited her when she came across the barrier of some little brook. Normally a placid obstacle, but now swollen with the autumn rains to twice its normal size, it rushed down its course decked with twigs and leaves as though enwreathed for a carnival. Then for a few minutes she forgot to feel impatient at their delay in setting off on their journey.

For they were not yet ready, even though Caroline too had discovered reasons for wanting to visit London. These reasons were connected with cabinet makers, upholsterers, and various little replacements she was planning in the furnishings at Curteys, and a surprise gift she had in mind for her second sister, the married one, Sarah Tibbel . . . but she could not set off without satisfying herself that every last corner was in order. Rooms that were not to be used in their absence must be wrapped in holland; carpets must be taken up; silver and china either packed to take with them, or locked away. And the human beings of the household— so much less easily ordered than the goods and chattels——

"You would think they had grown roots!" wrote Arabella, to this same sister Sarah, "and that I was setting about tearing them up in a most merciless and violent manner! I have been angelic, sister, quite angelic! I have run here, and run there, at everyone's bidding; I have broken the news to William, our invaluable servant, that the visit was to take place, when even Mr. Welby did not like to do it, on account of William being in love with Hannah, the little dairymaid, whom we will have to leave behind, for I tell Carrie that she will have no need of a dairymaid in London, though the cows cannot do well without her here. William, they insist, they must and will take with them; so I told him myself, and his face fell to the length of father's old fiddle, but all he could find to say which would delay our departure was that the carriage needed painting, which no doubt it has done these ten years, but no one would bother. So Mr. Welby has agreed, and they are busy with it now. We are wasting more days which I could be spending in buying muslins and hats, ready for visiting, and silks, for parties and balls . . ."

Of their servants, the Welbys relied more than any on William Pigeon. Thomas Snow, who had come from her father's service when Caroline married, had grown so old that she had bought him an annuity and let him go to live with his married daughter. Old Bundle, the coachman, was no longer active, and just tottered out each day leaning on his stick, to scold the stable lad; William's father, old Walter, could cope with a garden all put to bed for the winter quite nicely, but they did not need or want him in London.

"You've got Joel Tomkins," Arabella had remarked. "He's young and active. Why is William so indispensable?"

"Joel will look very handsome standing in the hall in London, with his hair powdered, and his best livery on," replied Caroline, "and he will keep Richard admirably turned out in the way of well-brushed coats and burnished boots, none better; but as for anything that involves head, you know, or intelligence, or being helpful in a crisis—well—let's just say we want to take William. Poor man! How he will miss his Hannah! I wish she would make up her mind to marry him, even though it would mean finding a new dairymaid."

The carriage had been dragged out into the stableyard so that William, in his painting, which he did very well, as he did most things, could work more conveniently. He could also keep his eye on his pretty Hannah as she worked around her dairy; and Mr. Bundle, leaning on his stick against the wall of the coachman's house, could keep his eye on William.

William had done all he could, in his two-and-a-half years of courting. He had joined those people called Quakers, for Hannah was of that persuasion; daily he wooed her with little gifts, finds which he shared with her: the first primrose; a sky-blue egg abandoned on the grass by a bird; a bright, scarlet autumn leaf. Always she thanked him, with her clear, innocent eyes childlike, and her lips just curved in a smile . . . and still she evaded him. And another thing—how could he leave his beloved garden? But Mrs. Welby had said he was to go with them, and that was that.

"You are coming, William," she had said quietly, when he had rushed to her full of protests, on being told by Arabella. How could he bear it? His brush slowed, and he looked in the direction of the dairy.

"You've not done yet, surely, William?" said Mr. Bundle, and Hannah, passing with her pails of milk, said, "Now, Friend, see thee attends Meeting regular in London, for I've heard it's a wicked place, and full of temptation."

"Oh, it is! It is!" and William resumed his painting, a little heartened at the thought that she did not want him to run into temptation . . . but perhaps that was only for the honour of the Society . . . and his brush slowed again, imperceptibly . . .

A week had gone by in these preparations, and Arabella began to think another two days might see the end of them, when Dick put the cat among the pigeons.

He was fourteen now, the oldest of the children, and he had been nerving himself to it for some time. It was the move to London which brought his courage to the sticking point, and he arrived at the study door and flung it open, just as his father and Caroline were finishing their accounts.

"I will not come with you to Town," he announced.

Arabella was crossing the hall, and heard him with astonishment. The twins were playing on the stairs, rolling a ball from step to step; they stopped, letting the ball bounce unheeded down into the hall, and pressed their faces against the banisters to see what was going on. Lucy and Martha who had been sitting just inside the drawing-room door, waiting to be called into the dining-room to eat, came to the door when they heard his raised voice, and added their ears to the others.

"What do you mean?" said Richard. "Will not come?"

The boy went on, in a lower and less nerve-racked voice, now that he had made his throw.

"I do not wish to come with you and Mama and everyone else to spend the winter in London."

"Do not wish is one thing, but will not is another. I'll have you know, Dick, I will not tolerate insubordination."

Richard Welby was a kind, nay, an indulgent father; but he had been for many years an officer in His Majesty's Navy, and before that tone in his voice many a seaman had quailed.

"Please, sir . . ." Richard saw with astonishment that the boy was on the verge of tears, and he fourteen. Many a youngster had been at sea four years or more, by Dick's age.

"You must have a reason, Dick," interposed Caroline, "apart of course from a dislike of our company, which I do not think we can suspect you of. Come, what is it?"

"Must I go to London?"

"You can hardly stay here on your own."

"Can I go somewhere else?"

"Where would you go?" the two adult voices spoke together.

"Dick is being a bad boy," remarked Kitty to Henry on the stairs.

"Will he get a walloping?" whispered Martha in Lucy's ear.

The first task over, Dick nerved himself to the second. "Edward Palmer has gone to a tutor to be prepared for Oxford," he said.

"So that's it!" Caroline was relieved. Edward was the grandson of their neighbours, the Gregorys, and there was a fierce friendship between the two boys. Edward was the more self-contained; he had not Dick's compassion for the small and weak, but to compensate for that, he was not plagued by the apprehensions which sometimes worried the more sensitive boy.

Richard's face cleared, and Martha's anticipation of a walloping for Dick receded. She and Lucy turned back into the drawing-room and began reading one of Martha's picture books together, and the twins on the stairs wondered what had happened to their ball.

Arabella sidled into the study after Dick and shut the door.

"He said we could do as we liked, but he would not come," exaggerated Arabella later, while writing to Sarah. "We had a fine to-do; but after some talking, it was agreed that he is to go to the tutor his friend is with. Caroline thinks it is a good idea, but that any man is a fool who agrees to have Dick and Palmer's boy in the same house for less than twice the money this man is asking. Joel Tomkins was sent over with a letter, and it is all fixed. So as soon as possible, when they have got his clothes in order, and Caroline has finished his new shirts, Mr. Welby will be riding over with him, and our departure will be that much nearer. We have sent one of the farm wagons off to London, to Welby House, with a load of apples, and another with potatoes and turnips, so wish me luck, dear sister; perhaps the next letter you have from me will be from Town. So long as Mrs. W. does not intend to feed fashionable ladies on turnips and potatoes . . ."

Caroline was in the dining-room when Arabella joined her.

"I believe the most fashionable collation at present is turkey salad and champagne," she said airily to her eldest sister, worried about the turnips.

"Indeed!" Caroline shot her an expressive look. "Is that what you recommend for our rout, just supposing we have one?"

"Perhaps—or chicken—sweetbreads—oysters——"

Caroline thought for a minute. In spite of the war and its disruptions, oysters were, she knew, still arriving daily at the oyster warehouse at number two Giltspur Street. She decided that William French should have her order for a barrel of the native Miltons when she should entertain. But she did not mention this to Arabella, or there would have been a little transport of joy to live through, and Arabella would have been convinced that she was getting her own way in the matter of luxurious entertainment. Although Caroline was prepared to go as far as oysters, with fine flour at seventy-five to eighty shillings the sack, costs were going to be watched very carefully.

"It is a pity Pattie has asked to stay here with her Aunt. She makes excellent custards. I do not believe they could be bettered by all the pastrycooks in London."

"What a good idea, Carrie, to employ a pastrycook," said Arabella, with a kind of innocent artfulness.

"I did not suggest such a thing, Arabella! But we will have to employ extra people. I wish we had more fruit from the garden. The nuts are poor this year, and the pears will not be worth offering for a dessert for as long as usual."

"You can buy things, sister. In London, so I have heard, you can buy anything at any time of the year. Oranges, grapes."

"Buying at Town prices has cost this family dearly once and I have no intention that it should do so again. We do not buy anything that our wagon can carry up for us. But I was thinking, Arabella, of a maidservant for you. Have you read Father's letter?"

They had written to Charles Hill, the father of Caroline, Sarah, and Arabella, to ask his permission for Arabella to accompany them to London. It was a polite formality, as they knew he would not object; they did not actually say that she had wheedled and coaxed until they had submitted, but Charles Hill had not lived with his youngest daughter for one and twenty years for nothing. He sent a handsome draft on his bank, so that she should not be an expense to anyone but himself, an affectionate brief note to Arabella, and a rather more explicit letter to Caroline.

"What!" he wrote, "so you have been cajoled into taking my butterfly husband-hunting! I wish you well of the expedition—rather you than I, dear Carrie. You have no idea what a dance she leads me, although when she is away I miss her, I must confess. The house is quiet and life is dull without her. But young folks must have their fun, and a dull life is the best for a rheumaticky old gentleman, no doubt you will agree. My knees are bad at present, and Mrs. Hunt has to help me on with my socks and slippers, and give me her arm when I rise from my chair, which I do as little as possible—I am no company for Arabella, and she is best away while young Wilberfoss is flaunting his new bride all over the county.

"Don't mention my rheumatism to her, for she has a good heart, for all her flighty ways, and she would be coming back to look after me, and tease me to death by her attentions."

This part of their father's letter, Caroline had kept from Arabella; but she had passed the rest of it on to her to read. Apart from local gossip, it contained one item of news which might be useful.

"You remember my housekeeper, Mrs. Hunt, talking of her niece, Phoebe," wrote Charles Hill. "It appears that at present she is out of a place. She is here on a visit to Mrs. Hunt, and seems a very good, quiet, civil-spoken sort of young person, and a lady's maid, so I hear; so if you have room for her in your household, she and her aunt would be grateful."

"I have wanted my own maid, this long while," said Arabella hopefully, in reply to Caroline's question. "And Phoebe has been in good service, in London, too, I understand. I would be glad to have her."

So Joel was dispatched on another errand, this time to fetch Phoebe, so that she could travel with them. It really seemed as though the preparations were almost at an end. Dick was safely installed with his tutor, the other children, Lucy, Martha, and the twins, Henry and Kitty, had already gone ahead in the charge of Betty, Caroline's maid. There remained only themselves and Baby Charles. When Joel returned with Phoebe, they could be off.

Joel had gone, obediently, without any feelings of anticipation. But when he saw Phoebe, neatly cloaked, waiting for him with her little box, he was immediately affected by her. Such a slender thing! So demure! She looked up at him submissively, and he was lost.

It took some minutes, with Mrs. Hunt fussing round her niece, and Charles Hill hobbling out to see that all was well, to organize the box and Phoebe on to the pillion, but with straps and patience it was managed, and they started the return journey, going rather slowly, because the horse must be considered.

It was delicious to Joel to feel Phoebe's arms round him, and hear her soft high voice in his ear. She was full of questions about the family, and all their affairs, and the house in London. Joel told her what he could, but he had never been to Welby House, so his information was limited.

"All that's been arranged by Mr. Watts," he explained.

"Cornelius Watts?" asked Phoebe.

"I believe that is his name," said Joel. "How did you come to hear of him?"

"At the place I was living before; Cornelius Watts, that has the bastard daughter."

"Oh, no!" cried Joel. "That must be another man. There's no one more respectable than our Mr. Watts!"

Behind him, Phoebe smiled quietly to herself.

"Then it must be someone else I was thinking of," she said. "I've muddled him up with someone else. Now what were you saying about Miss Hill?"

Arriving at Curteys Court, Joel helped Phoebe down as though she were a princess, and led her into the house with the air of bringing in something more precious than all the rubies in Christendom. Arabella looked at her with some curiosity as she entered. This girl, hired unseen, was to be in the intimate relationship of Maid to Mistress . . . she saw a slim, narrow-waisted, modest-looking girl; dark hair drawn back under a white cap; eyes dropped, under heavy white lids. Joel hovered protectively in the background, and Arabella noticed him, amused.

"We have heard a great deal of you from your aunt, Mrs. Hunt," she said gently, thinking that the other girl would be feeling shy and ill at ease.

"Yes, Miss Hill," replied Phoebe, and somehow, it seemed to Arabella that through the polite response she could hear another remark, "and I have heard about you, too," and in the girl's glance she read something that made her wonder if the report had been favourable. She shook off the silly fancy, and felt surprised at herself for indulging in such imaginings, trying to regain her previous clear pleasure in having her own maid at last.

"We set off in the morning," she said, "at eight o'clock. I would like you to take up your duties tonight, when you have rested a little from your journey. Tomorrow morning, you must be in my bedchamber by six."

When Phoebe had gone out of the room, Arabella gave a little pirouette of joy. At last! To have her own maid. And London tomorrow! Or nearly tomorrow. There was this tiresome insistence of Caroline's that they spend a night on the road. As though it could not be done in a day if they were to set off really early, and be just a little hard on the horses! Wouldn't it have been worth it? The poor creatures could have rested afterwards, and she knew that Caroline had made the journey in a day before now. But it was on account of Baby Charles, of course. Well, if they were really on their way, she supposed she could put up with anything.

They were off, and the journey was tedious. For all its new coat of paint, the family carriage was old-fashioned and cumbersome, and Richard elected to ride alongside. When she settled down in the musty interior, and felt the hardness of the upholstery and the lurching movement of the springs, Arabella envied him the air, even though it was chill and damp as the sun had not yet gained its strength. She gazed out eagerly at the little familiar villages as they passed through them, looking out for milestones, and admired the colours of autumn and the rich farmlands, with here and there the brown earth exposed by the plough. Phoebe sat opposite, and Arabella remembered gratefully the lightness of the touch of the hairbrush, and the expert way in which she had been assisted with dressing. But oh! why did they have to pause? Why stop to eat? Why spend the night? she could hardly sleep for anticipation when night did come, and they had left their native county behind them.

Caroline travelled in a different spirit. She had all the comfort of her husband's presence as he rode within sight of the carriage window, and the pleasure of his never-failing attentions when they stopped; she had the happiness of seeing her infant son sleeping in Phoebe's arms, or holding him in her own; but her last visit to Welby House had left scars on her mind which made her flinch from re-entering it. There she had learned what jealousy was, and hate, and what dark places can lurk, unsuspected, in one's own soul. She did not show her fears outwardly. She seemed as serene as ever.

Surely Richard, as the miles went spinning by, must have had similar heartburnings at the thought of Welby House, where he had lived a life so different from the present. Surely it must bring back bittersweet memories. But if it did, he did not mention them, any more than Caroline would have voiced her alarms to him. And in the end all was unnecessary.

Arabella, after the long ennui of the journey, was once more agog, as they approached the outskirts of London. It was a magnificently fine day in October; pausing on top of a rise in the ground, they looked downwards over the city. Mist and smoke drifted upwards, obscuring the pattern of the streets and giving the whole a muffled, mysterious witchery. As they gradually descended the slope, the city spires which had pierced the haze so beautifully to catch the gilding sun, rose above them, and were no longer so noticeable as the dirty bustle of the streets, the shouting and the noise, pressed around them. Arabella was silent, unable to speak for excitement. It was bigger than Linchester; oh, much, much, bigger. Just a few streets of this crowded place, just a handful of its churches, would have made Linchester, so far—until this day—the biggest place she had ever seen. Surely there could not be more of it? But there was more, and more, and more. Here and there they passed dignified squares, still gleaming from the hand of the builder; now and then Richard appeared at the window to indicate a new imposing terrace, just rising from an oasis of green fields, but on the whole both sisters would have had to own they were thoroughly lost, and they could not have said which way they had passed, or whether they had retraced their steps.

Just when they thought they were never going to arrive at Welby House, they found themselves travelling down Piccadilly and turning in at Clarges Street, and then they were alighting at the house built by her indulgent father for Richard's first wife.

"Walls to be wrought with stock brick, with a stone cornice . . . the low storey ten-and-a-half feet high and the chambers ten feet clear, the panwood lintels and sleeper wood of good oak, a sufficient usual scantling. The spars of red sawn firwood four inches by five inches, oak sash windows glazed with new castle crown glass with free stone soaks . . . all the doors to the rooms to be framed, and hung where needful with sufficient locks, bolts, joints, hinges, among which locks to be seven brass locks about ten shillings and sixpence the piece . . . the best dining-room to be wainscotted with Pedestall and Dentill Cornice . . . the Vestibule to be stuccoed, the best stairs to be carried up in a neat good manner . . . one chamber to be hung with paper at sixpence a yard and another two chambers to be hung with paper at fourpence a yard. The windows to be furnished with seats and shutters, all the room-tops to be thick lathed, and finished with lime and hair. The best staircase walls to be finished with plain stucco, the floor of the Vestibule to be covered with diamond flagged paving, stone and black marble . . ."

Arabella climbed down from the carriage. She had her feet on a London Street! She looked down at her shoes and tried to realize the wonder of it, and drew in a deep breath. It even smelt different to Linchester. There was excitement in the air, and here, anything would be possible! While she was standing dreaming, Caroline was already entering the Vestibule with its diamond flagged paving, and finding that the house itself seemed so different from that of her previous visit that she remained quite cool, and was able to feel herself mistress of it; and as for Richard, his life with his first wife, led mainly in this house, seemed so far away to him, so hidden and forgotten, that he showed nothing of agitation or sensibility.

They had not known that their tenants had, as well as re-decorating the Saloon, re-coloured the stucco of the Vestibule and the staircase walls. Instead of its previous light shimmer it was dark: deep terracotta—colour of Tuscany—with only the untouched doors and mouldings to relieve the darkness and heaviness.

Arabella had followed behind, and stood silent, while Mrs. Jackson, the housekeeper since the house was built, came forward to greet them, and Lucy, who had been waiting for them with impatience, ran down the stairs to be caught up and kissed as though the family had been apart for more than a few days, and close at her heels came Martha, Henry and Kitty, until the darkness of the Vestibule was alight with their gaiety.

Everything was perfect! She would not have cared if the tenants had painted the interior black, and the exterior too, and done what they wished with the scantling and the spars of red sawn firwood and the seven brass locks at ten and sixpence the piece, as long as the dwelling stood in the bustle of Town! Arabella looked at the closed front door, and imagined Joel opening it to the finest of company. The cosy domesticity of the present scene bored her, and she slid past and ran upstairs, her mind on Masquerades and

Theatres, Love and Lotteries, Dowagers and Dukes . . . she was in a fever to see the Egyptian Saloon.

The dark of evening had drawn in, and as Arabella arrived, sure-footed, at the head of the stairs, the wide landing had barely enough light for her to see what she was doing. She flung open doors, and peeped into rooms, and almost missed the Saloon altogether by thinking she had opened the door on to a gloomy closet. But surely such a doorcase and so finely wrought a door could not open only on a cupboard—she returned, and looked again.

She had been right, and she swung the door wider and let in what light there was, showing gleams of brightness from rich ornaments of gold just detectable in the darkness. She entered with trepidation.

Down in the Vestibule Caroline wondered where her sister was, and, picking up a lamp from one of the tables, followed her upstairs.

"Oh, Caroline!" cried Arabella. "I'm so glad you've come—do you know, I thought this room was a cupboard, and can you blame me with those black walls—" A frieze of Egyptian figures on a black background encircled the room.

"I've heard of the Egyptian style," replied her sister, "but this!" —it was the furnishings of the room, more than the walls, which caught her attention—"The colour is almost garish."

There was pale yellow, blue-green, and everywhere the glimmer of gold; it was the combination with black which gave the garish effect. The furniture was massive, fashioned mainly of mahogany. Sofas, supported by grinning crocodiles, astounded them. Tables, of serpentine and porphyry, were borne up on sphinxes. The chandelier was an assembly of winged lions, and the lamps were upheld by twining serpents. On the mantelpiece, the figure of Horus with his hawk head looked over at his fellow god, Anubis, shaped, with his jackal head, in bronze.

Over in the corner was, what they were to discover in the light of day, a mummy in an elaborate sarcophagus, guarded by the figures of seated priests. The blossoms of the lotus stood everywhere.

Caroline sat down in an armchair, and tried to imagine herself comfortable, with her hands resting on the sungod, Ra, and her head leaning on a bronze cow, symbol of the goddess Hathor.

The room seemed alive. Scorpions in bronze, beetles in gold, and lions in black, appeared under arms and on feet of furniture, so that the dancing light of the lamp made Caroline imagine them to be moving, relieving the massive silences of the room with scuttlings and stirrings.

Arabella's eyes were a-sparkle. What a setting!

"An evening here could never be dull!" she cried. "Ecstasy, yes; the depths of despair, yes; it is a room for violent emotions! Anguish! Glory!"

"It certainly doesn't go with Mr. Watts' flowers," said Caroline prosaically. "He's been and put them everywhere, in all the household pancheons, pitchers, vases and buckets, making the house look as though it were already Christmas, with berries and evergreen leaves to welcome us, because he has to be out of town."

Arabella danced in a narrow circle in the lamplight.

"Good evening, my Lord," she said. "Did you leave the Duchess well? How is the Prince these days, His Highness of Wales?"

Chapter Two

"How d'ye do, Mr. Watts?"

As he woke from sleep Cornelius thought he heard Caroline Welby's gentle countryside voice greeting him. It must have been the vestiges of dream . . . climbing out of bed and going to the wash stand, he poured cold water from the ewer and vigorously splashed it over his face, dressed, and in his usual brisk manner went out of the house and into his garden.

The thought of Caroline was not quite driven away; but the absorbing interest of his flowerbeds took first place in his mind. It seemed to be the only legacy from his father, a yeoman farmer, and the long line of rural ancestors, that to see things growing, well tended, was one of the first pleasures of his life. Not that he ever regretted leaving the farm, as one by one his elder brothers had done, and coming to London to make his fortune; he still remembered the thrill and excitement of it! Young Sam, in the custom of Borough English, had now got the farm, and he deserved it, for he had looked after the old folk in their last years, and been a good son to them. He, Cornelius, loved the bustle of the crowded city, and returned to it after his business trips always more glad than before. Every time he returned to this ancient building, which housed the offices of Waveney and Watts, and his own chambers over them, and the garden—once attached to a medieval Guildhall—which lay behind, he was visited by this joint sensation, of delight, and of fear.

Delight, because of its beauty; fear, because when the lease was up it was almost certain not to be renewed. Property speculators had their eyes upon every piece of open ground in the city, and the fashionable architect, Nash, with his close connection with the Prince of Wales—suspiciously close, some said, when Mrs. Nash was so pretty, and so much younger than himself—would want to build upon it one of his elegant terraces. Or Sloan might snap it up, and erect upon it something expensive and no doubt extremely profitable.

Then this long yew hedge, beside which Caroline had once walked with him, which had grown here since the days of Good Queen Elizabeth (this autumn morning it was festooned with cobwebs so closely set they might have been woven into one length of lace, and so bejewelled with dew that the whole of the court, at a ball, could not have compared—with all their diamonds —to its beauty)—all this would be torn down and done away with. These rose-red bricks, so neatly laid in the path beneath his feet that it wound away before him like a strip of rich embroidery, would be hacked up and thrown on one side or, at best, used as rubble in the foundations of the new.

Well, the new must rise on the ashes of the old; but when it happened, he knew that he could not go on living here, but must move out to one of the new suburban residences—at Tottenham, perhaps—where he could buy garden ground and know that it could never be taken from him.

The gardener appeared round the end of the hedge, and Cornelius Watts nodded cheerfully at him.

"Morning, Robins," he said. "I'm pleased to find all the beds looking so tidy. I was back too late last night from Lord Morecambe's to have a look at them. Have you got the pines moved?"

"We've nearly finished putting the new tan into the fruiting houses—me and the lad'll start moving the plants today, sir, all being well. Then I thought we might get the beds of aromatic plants top-dressed."

"Good, good. Don't forget the cucumber seeds on the twentieth, or we won't have any earlies for Christmas."

Walking on, Mr. Watts began to hum to himself. The immaculate beds pleased him; and he had another cause for rejoicing. Of all his friends—and he had many—the dearest to him were the Welbys; and they would by now have arrived in Town. Should have come the day of his departure, and would by now have quite settled and established themselves . . . this morning he would take a chair and pay them a visit, and perhaps invite them for a dinner, unless they asked him first to join them at their board. Or an evening of tea-drinking might suit them better. Whichever way it was, he felt cheered by their presence, and looked forward to conversation and other social pleasures in their company. But for the moment he had forgotten—they had with them that confounded Arabella—

Robins, behind him, felt gratified and relieved. His loyalty and respect for his master was absolute, but there was no denying that he had a temper when things did not please him; it was short-lived, but stormy while it lasted. He expected other people to be as capable as himself. But when he was pleased there was no one with a brighter smile, and a smile and a few words of praise from him made you feel as proud as Punch.

Mr. Watts' thoughts were still divided. He bent down and put his hand tenderly to the dead stalk of a lily now prostrate on the earth; looking round, he called out to Robins,

"Do you remember this one? How beautiful it was."

Unbidden, the thought came into his mind of a girl he had known long, long before. When he had first come to London, and was still young and wild. Fair, fair as a lily. And those French emigré families were usually so dark. But his mind shied away from this unbidden thought. It was because of this hidden part of his life—so seldom brought to mind—that he had turned to working, slaving all hours of the day and half the night, getting on in the world which valued money above all things . . .

Later, when he was rich and influential, women in plenty had angled after him, the young, the not-so-young, and the positively elderly. But no one else had touched his heart, until he had met Caroline, and she was the wife of a client who was also a friend. The other thoughts faded from his mind, leaving Caroline in possession. To meet a woman who thought of him at once and only

as another human being, to be treated with straightforward sim-
plicity, had knocked him off balance, and Caroline had gained his
allegiance before he was aware of it. As he had grown to know
her, his admiration of her character had increased; but her
youngest sister! Now there was all that he dreaded in a female! He
ruffled his old-fashioned powdered hair in annoyance at the very
thought of her; and this was after only one meeting, and that
some years ago.

Frivolous, idle, and vain; he had read her character instantly;
and of such young misses, intent only on flirting and fashion, he
had long ago learned to beware. He must bear with her presence if
he was to enjoy the companionship he craved, for since his friendship with Caroline, his garden no longer satisfied his every need
and his solitary hearth seemed cheerless, and even lonely . . .

The young lady in question was at that moment lying in her stylish bed, in the centre of a pretty bedroom. She stretched out lux-
uriously, reaching with her toes to the very bottom, and flexed her
arms above her head, enjoying the pale sunshine which entered
the room as Phoebe opened the shutters. The wallpaper—at fourpence the yard—was swagged with tiny roses, held by ribbon; the
satin-wood furniture was inlaid with garlands of husks and honey-
suckle; the draperies were of delicate muslins. She felt gloriously
idle, and indisputably vain. How could she help it, with the prospect of longed-for enjoyment, and the edge of a hatbox reminding
her of the vastly becoming bonnet she had bought the previous
day? The bonnet brought with it the thought of the gown of yellow and white cloud, purchased, and now in the hands of one of
the most sought-after of dressmakers.

Dear Papa! How generous he had been! She hoped the poor
man was in good health and not plagued by his rheumatism.
Why! She could send him some essence of mustard, with two and
ninepence of his own money, it would be so beneficial! Here in
Town it should be possible to obtain the genuine article, which
could be distinguished by its black ink stamp with the name of R.
Johnston inserted on it.

"Dear Papa!" she said aloud, and Phoebe looked up attentively
from her morning duties about the bedroom. "It's all right,

Phoebe, I am only talking to myself; I have a conscience about Papa, you know, and am liable to fling myself into a post-chaise, and rush off to Linchestershire to see him; but it would not please! I am here to take myself off his hands, and find a husband; the London young men must be superior to the dullards of Melton. My wrapper, Phoebe. I will write to him." What fun it is, she thought, as she settled down to write a long and affectionate letter to her father, having sent Phoebe out to buy the mustard. What fun it is, knowing I might meet this husband of mine any day. She was at a table by the window, and the early morning street cries rose to her ears as she put her conscience to rest by writing her letter.

"Sweet child!" thought Charles Hill when he received his little parcel. "Sweet child! How she will enjoy herself! and—" he groaned as an incautious movement sent a twinge of pain through his knee—"how pleased I am that she is not here!"

Mr. Watts left the garden, and went indoors to his office. A tall, slightly stooping young man had just been shown in, and was standing apparently trying to decide whether or not to wear his eyeglass, which he took out and put in several times, while scrutinizing the furniture of the room.

"My Lord!" exclaimed Mr. Watts. "It is an unexpected pleasure to see you here. Why did you not send for me? The fire is smoking, I see. Just a moment, and I will cure it," and he attacked the coals with a poker, until they burned brightly.

"Happened to be in Town, Watts," said the Earl of Epworth. "Just as easy to look you up. Going off today, I hope."

"Have you opened your house for the season?"

"No—took a berth with Aunt Harome. Don't like London, can't stand the place."

"How is the Marchioness? And your mother? With a home like Arden Priory, I can understand your reluctance to leave it."

"Thank you, they are both well."

The Earl seemed to hesitate, and Cornelius Watts, making little movements with his hands among the papers on the big desk and humming under his breath, waited for him to continue.

"Did you know my uncle, Watts? Father's youngest brother,

was in the army for a short time . . . lived in Piccadilly . . . deuced rake, didn't get on with him too well myself, not my sort at all. Good enough, though. Always get these types in a family."

"I knew him by sight," replied Watts cautiously. "I take it you mean the Honourable Henry."

"Died last month, had you heard?"

"I did hear, yes."

"You weren't his lawyer, of course. I'm the executor. Simple enough job, really," said the Earl, who, in spite of his gentle and hesitant manner, was quite intelligent and capable when he had to be. "Dished out the bequests. No trouble, you know. Could have asked Bruntons to do it, but decided not to. The old chap's died and I don't like the young one; never did."

The Duchess of Doncaster, the Earl's grandmother, had taken up Mr. Watts when he was an up-and-coming young man, and by degrees the affairs of her two daughters, Julia, Marchioness of Harome, who was a widow and childless, and Laura, who had married the Earl of Epworth and had this one son, had come into his hands. He heard the disparaging remark about the rival concern of Bruntons without a change of expression, but stopped humming, and looked even more attentive and interested.

"Fact is," went on the Earl, "one of these bequests is proving a bit difficult, and I wondered if you'd help me with it, although you didn't draw up the will."

"Anything I can do, of course," said Mr. Watts.

It was some time before the Earl, warming his long hands at the fire, said anything further.

"Perhaps you'd better read it," he said at last and, pulling a folded parchment out of his pocket, passed it to Cornelius, then stood leaning on the chimney-piece and whistling. It did not take long to read through the legal formalities and come to the nub of the matter. The Earl had been marking off the bequests as he dealt with them, and there was just one left. Mr. Watts felt that, if he had had a hand in drawing it up, he would somehow have persuaded the testator to word it differently.

"I have a grateful recollection," the item read, "of a girl who was of great comfort to me, and leave her fifty Pounds. She was kind to an old man and lives in Madame Eglantine's brothel. Her name is Mirabelle."

Cornelius felt as though all the blood had left his face for his heart, and found that he was gripping the edge of the table. Mirabelle. Only half an hour before, in the garden, a thought from the past had troubled him. Mirabelle. If a ghost had entered the room, he could not have felt more shocked. There could of course be no connection.

"It is a thing, isn't it?" said the Earl, "leaving money to a harlot. It is a thing. I even asked a girl in the street—a street-walker, you know," in case Mr. Watts had not grasped his meaning—"if she knew Madame Eglantine; but she didn't and—well, I don't go in for that sort of woman meself—" his thin face was pink.

"You want me to find her for you," Mr. Watts' tone was dry, matter-of-fact.

"Yes. That's it exactly. There's such thousands of them! And you'd send me a bill, of course."

"It might take some time. Bruntons should have got better directions. Surnames, addresses."

"They shouldn't have accepted the bequest at all!" the Earl was indignant. "No right to accept such a bequest. He should have given it to her while he was still alive, not drag it into his will."

There was a pause. Then, "I'll do my best. But it won't be easy; it might take some time."

"Good fellow!" the Earl was relieved. "I'll be going, then. I want to get back to Arden. You'll be coming yourself before too long, I daresay."

"Yes, yes. There will be business for your mother. Please give her my respects, and to your aunt too of course. Your servant, my Lord. I'll do my best."

"Well," said Arabella after breakfast, "we have settled down. When do we begin to call on our acquaintance? Who do we expect to come and see us?"

Her voice was bright, but there was a slightly nervous note in it. Caroline looked over at her and wondered how much young Wilberfoss coming to London and finding a bride had really affected

Arabella. She certainly seemed very determined to outdo him. Otherwise why the worry? Husbands happened when they happened, thought Caroline. Aloud, she said,

"We can begin at once, and the Town is full of your acquaintance, is it not, Richard?"

"Admiral Harper lives at Chelsea, and you will like his family, Arabella. They are pleasant, lively young people."

"There will be other Naval officers," reminded Caroline.

"But Family?" persisted Arabella. "Fashionable connections?"

"The Marchioness of Harome is a connection—her husband was my mother's eldest brother—and I know she will be longing to meet you both."

"And you, Caroline? Who do you look forward to meeting?"

"Well . . . there's Mr. Watts . . . I'm surprised you did not mention him, Richard."

"Arabella asked for fashionable connections, dear, and you know he cares little for fashion. If she had asked after men of influence—or people who care so much for their fellow men that they are willing to work to help the unfortunate—then I would have mentioned him. But he is like part of the family. Arabella knows we will see much of him. You haven't met his partner, Waveney, have you, Arabella? He has a charming wife, and a young family."

"I can beat you all," cried Arabella gaily, "for I have a dear school friend in Town, who is wild to see me, and belongs to the first rank of fashion, I assure you."

Caroline was amused at her sister's little air of self-importance.

"And who did you meet at Miss Merchant's who has become so vastly fashionable?"

"You have heard me speak of Jane—Lady Russett's daughter. The Russetts are here, and spending the winter."

"They have never honoured me with their notice, although their estate is in Linchestershire."

"I was staying with them a whole month, last year, you remember, sister."

"When I was brought to bed of Charles? I remember you were somewhere with friends—I had not realized you kept such grand company, Bell."

"They're not so grand really. Nothing like the Carlton House set. But at their home in London, I understand, they entertain scientists, poets, earls, musicians, politicians, and bishops, like a salon in Paris, but better, of course."

"Of course," commented Caroline drily. "You have worried me so much that I doubt if I will dare to speak to them if they walk in through the door."

Richard, who was forever wanting to be in the fresh air, now announced that he was off to call informally on the Harpers.

"Are you coming, Caroline? Or shall I take Lucy?"

"We still have shopping and dresses to think of—Lucy will be so happy if you take her, dear—"

The children were missing their country occupations; Caroline was arranging for them to have the advantage of the best masters, but until the lessons started, they had little to do except drive Betty distracted.

Arabella and Caroline had already been to the warehouses for their ball dresses and new morning and afternoon gowns; but there were such delicious matters to settle as gloves, and stockings, and shoes, before they were ready to startle London by bursting upon Society. They had thought of shawls, and talked of ribbons, and when they set off together on this fine cold morning, they were very happy.

They walked between shops and emporia with William in attendance to carry the parcels, and were almost finished—as their last task they were arranging to join a circulating library—when Caroline saw Arabella, who had strayed to the door, blush, nod, and appear to acknowledge someone in the street outside. As soon as she could, she hurried to the door to join her sister, and was just in time to see two officers, Dragoons, walking away down the street. Arabella knew them, then; it had that appearance. Caroline was suspicious instantly. How could she have made their acquaintance? Naval officers Caroline felt she could vouch for; their behaviour was so disciplined by regulations that even on shore, one could trust them. But the Army! Unknown territory, and, she thought, dangerous. Although she was sure of the greeting, Arabella said nothing, so Caroline made no reference to it. She felt it hardly likely that, of all the young men in London, they would meet those two again. But in this she was mistaken.

On their return they found the visiting cards of Mr. Watts—which did not surprise them—and of Lord and Lady Russett, which did; Caroline sent a note round to invite Mr. Watts to join their family dinner, and looked forward with trepidation to the fact that the Russetts would certainly call again, and that she ought to go and leave her card at their door.

Richard and Lucy arrived back, happy but tired, from their visit to Admiral Harper.

"Do you remember me mentioning my friend, Captain Francis Newcombe, of the sloop *Beagle*?" burst out Richard as soon as he was within the room. "He has captured a French privateer of fourteen guns and forty-nine men, *Le Hazard!*"

Caroline looked interested, and Arabella, her quick imagination reflected in the vivid expressions of her face, exclaimed,

"What a dashing name, *Le Hazard!*" almost feeling herself on such a ship, swinging through waves and billows under a windy sky.

"She has hazarded, and has lost," said Richard, "and Captain Newcombe is the gainer."

Arabella was disappointed at the thought that the ship with the dull name, *Beagle*, should triumph over the romantic *Le Hazard*, and took herself off to the window.

Caroline listened placidly to Richard's naval talk, until it was interrupted by Arabella, exclaiming over the number of red coats she saw.

"Aye, the town is full of soldiers," responded Richard. "I daresay they will be sent out to help the war in Portugal. If they are still here by spring, I will be surprised."

"How frightful!" Arabella's eyes opened in consternation. "All those handsome young fellows! I hope they are not sent to Portugal. They might be killed, and the streets would be prodigious dull without them."

When they were a small party—and tonight Mr. Watts was their only dinner guest—Lucy had been joining them; but she was so tired that she was packed off to nursery supper and bed with the other children, and they were no sooner out of sight than Mr. Watts arrived.

Richard was still so full of military matters that the general gossip through the meal centred on the war; it was not until they were all sitting over their coffee that Mr. Watts had the opportunity of confiding the progress of his garden to Caroline's ears. This pleasure he had looked forward to so much became the more important the longer it was put off. After the profoundly disturbing event of the morning, it was a relief to think of his flowerbeds. What was the fate of *Le Hazard* to that of his pineapples? Later, in the night, the ghost which had entered his office that morning would prevent him from sleeping; but now, when he saw his chance, he began:

"We are beginning to bring the succession pines into the hothouses. The pineapples this year have been exceptionally fine, so we are continuing the same management in the coming twelve months."

"Oh," said Caroline, "now at Curteys . . ."

"Do you think, Caroline," broke in Arabella thoughtfully, "that I should order my Pilgrim hat and cloak in velvet or in Georgian cloth?"

Caroline turned to her.

"Well, Georgian cloth would be . . ."

"I have been propagating double flowers," continued Mr. Watts as though Arabella had not spoken, "which as you know I have a weakness for."

His hostess turned her attention to him.

"I don't know that I share your taste there . . ."

"Gypsy hats are all the crack, Caroline. Didn't you notice how many we saw this morning? Now if I were to retrim mine, with something particularly pretty in the ribbon way . . ."

Caroline swivelled on her seat towards her sister.

"Yes, that would be . . ."

"Double wallflowers, double feverfew, double scarlet lychnis, double sweet williams, double rockets, double rose campion, double daisies, double chamomile . . ."

"You certainly have a range of such . . ." Caroline began to reply.

"I think I agree with you, Caroline; Georgian cloth for the Pilgrim hat and cloak; of course, it is mainly carriage costume."

"It would be more serviceable," thought her sister.

"Yes, I must own the double flowers have become something of a preoccupation; they require more attention than the single, but I find them rewarding; many of them are curiosities."

"Curiosities are less in my line than the simple charms of commoner plants."

"Did you notice that straw bonnet today, Caroline? It was in the milliner's in . . ."

"No, I can't say that I . . ."

"Are your medlars ready?" it was Mr. Watts' firm voice—"No, I suppose they will not be; I still have an abundance of mulberries, if you have a use for them."

"They are not ready, and I will be glad of the mulberries."

"It was trimmed with bands and tufts of folded sarsnet . . ."

Richard had been listening with amusement, but decided it was time to intervene.

"Arabella, did you not say you wanted to start a piece of embroidery for me?"

His sister-in-law was at once all attention.

"So I do, Richard. I must have an elegant piece of work for when visitors call. It is so very vulgar to be caught darning one's stockings, or working on clothes for the poor. A cover, or screen, or whatever you fancy, will be the very thing. I cannot compete with Caroline when it comes to delicate work on muslin, so content myself with the more sturdy articles."

"Did you not suggest a Naval theme? Shall I help you to draw it? I have been thinking the matter over, you see, and deciding whether I prefer a sextant in place of honour, or a picture of the globe; and am at your service to plan out on paper any manner of knots, and coils of rope, to suit you."

"We will plan out the pattern between us, dear brother!" cried Arabella, with playful happiness. She retired to a table, and she and Richard were soon deep in discussion.

The next morning Cornelius Watts began his search for Mirabelle. He could have sent out his clerk, or employed one of the street urchins of both sexes, who swarmed the pavements. But he had passed a night without rest; in spite of the comfort of seeing Caroline, in spite of the irritation of seeing Arabella, the female presence which disturbed his sleep was neither of these, but one whose very existence he thought he had forgotten.

So he went out himself and began his search, going down alleys he knew of and seeking out information from people whose appearance presented a sharp contrast to the Earl of Epworth and his relations.

In his snuff-coloured coat and plain thread stockings, dark green breeches and wide black buckled shoes, he had a plain, slightly old-fashioned appearance. It was designed not to attract attention. The bully boys of the town ignored him, where a Corinthian walking down the street would have drawn all eyes, and been a target for pickpockets and every other kind of dishonesty. If anyone did take a fancy to trying for Mr. Watts' pocket handkerchief, a glance at the set of his jaw, the alertness of his walk, and the breadth of his shoulders, would have persuaded them to look for easier prey; he could walk through almost any assembly, any crowd, or any quiet alley or rubbish-strewn entry, and be hardly noticed by the inhabitants.

Yet, as he paused at the junction of two narrow lanes, a child, coming up and taking his hand, and looking up confidingly into his face, asked him for a piece of bread. He looked down at the pinched little face.

"Where is your mother?" he asked, and the voice, which could be harsh, was gentle. The child pointed to a woman, holding a baby, sitting on a doorstep, and Mr. Watts went over to her.

"Is this your child? Have you no food?"

She looked up hopelessly.

"No, Sir, we haven't." She seemed too exhausted, too indifferent, to beg.

"I won't give you money," he said, "but if you come with me I'll buy you something to eat." He took the little family to the next road, where a stall sold thick slices of bread and butter, and pies, and stood waiting while they ate. He did not want thanks; but he did ask, knowing it hopeless because she was not the kind of woman who would know, if she had ever heard of Mirabelle.

As she shook her head, he realized that he had asked because any one of teeming crowds, in many streets, could have been Mirabelle . . .

Caroline did not really expect Lady Russett to call. She was herself so unpretentious that she almost feared contact with the giddy upper circles of Society. She was sure that, in spite of the card, in spite of Arabella's assurances, they would not call again; so when they did, she was all astonishment. Appearing as William opened the door of the Egyptian Saloon, framed in the doorway with the backdrop of the terracotta walls behind her, her ladyship paused, striking a seemingly artless pose. It could not have been more effective. She was a woman of ideal height, and in the prime of life, with commanding grey eyes, dark hair carefully curled in tendrils round her face, and a clinging severe gown of deep gold. As she moved forward into the saloon the Egyptian furnishings were for once put into their right relationship—Thomas Hope himself could not have created a better juxtaposition. Her turban was of the same deep gold as her gown, her ornaments of plain dull gold, her slippers white.

Caroline, feeling at once fussily overdressed, cheered herself by the inward remark that really, under that gown, Lady Russett had very little on; waspishness can be a tonic, to even the best of women.

Crowding in behind Lady Russett were Lord Russett—tall and distinguished—their elder daughter, Miss Farley, and the younger one, Jane. Lady Russett, apologizing for the unconventional time of their visit—they were on their way to a grand dinner—kept Caroline so occupied that she hardly had time to glance at the girls. She came to the conclusion that Emma was a handsome girl, with her father's build, but spoiled by a hard expression like her mother's. Jane was of a similar figure, simply dressed in white, with a mass of soft brown curls, and pink cheeks; she seemed tongue-tied and awkward, and hung back. But then Arabella stepped up to embrace her, and Caroline saw the warm expression and sweet smile that her sister had celebrated.

"You will want to become a subscriber at the Royal Institution, will you not?" asked Lady Russett. "The Marchioness of Stafford,

Countess Spencer, and the Countess of Bessborough hold subscription books."

"Oh," said Caroline in surprise, "I don't think I've heard of it."

"Not heard of the Royal Institution? I assure you, my dear Mrs. Welby, that Albemarle Street is jammed with the carriages of all the best families when a lecture is to be heard, particularly when Mr. Humphry Davy is lecturing."

"Is it suitable for young ladies?"

"Yes! Both mine are there frequently, you may be sure. Unmarried daughters can be introduced, at a subscription of only one extra guinea, at any time."

"We will have to see about it," said Caroline weakly. The three young ladies in the room were all talking together, and she could not gauge from the backs of their heads how they felt about lectures.

"For the lower classes, we have started Sunday lectures after church," went on Lady Russett, "and this coming Sunday there is one at St. Botolph's. Do come! It is important for the poor to see that we support such ventures. They ought to have the chance to spend the Sabbath evening in an uplifting manner."

"What would they do otherwise?" enquired Caroline innocently. "Of course, at home, they play football on the green after service."

"How shocking!" cried Lady Russett. "That is the kind of thing which must be stopped." Her hearers, who thought the village games rather amusing, and particularly Richard, who was not above joining in for a few minutes, all felt guilty. It was soon apparent to Caroline that Lady Russett was above frivolous pursuits, and that the visit was being made very much with a purpose in mind.

"You will, I am sure," said Lady Russett, "be chaperoning Miss Hill to all those so delightful routs and riots, and evening squeezes, that they are so fond of at their age; and Almacks—where I can assure your admission—and the Royal Drawing-room. Alas! I will not be able to do the same for Miss Jane Farley. I have such a very full programme; apart from the lectures, there are Scientific Demonstrations to attend. My husband likes to have me with him on his book-buying expeditions, and then he is in so many Societies! and of course, I like to go to their meetings, too."

Lord Russett glanced up at that point. He had occupied most of the visit in talking to Richard, but Caroline realized that he was fully aware of the conversation between his wife and herself. He stopped his own flow of eloquence, and gave Caroline a beaming smile when she took up the obvious hints and said that if she might have the pleasure of escorting Jane as well as Arabella to such parties as they were invited to, and it would certainly be an advantage to have the entrée to Almacks, it would not be the least trouble in the world.

Lady Russett responded with obvious relief, that the fish for which she had condescended to angle had allowed itself to be caught, and the sight of Jane's shy smile, and Arabella's delight in the prospect of her friend's company were so gratifying that Caroline forgave Lady Russett her manoeuvring, and accepted an invitation to a dinner at her house.

"I shall only be giving one party, later in the winter; one must make an effort, however distasteful such events must be to one's sensibilities. A select dinner party is so much more agreeable, don't you think, Mrs. Welby? On Mondays we have eight or ten notables to dinner; and Thursdays are devoted to evening company without regard to numbers; but we only give tea and fruits. You must join us often—that is, when you are not taking out the girls—such a relief that Emma does not share Jane's immature tastes! She finds as much pleasure in the society of genius as we do, is that not so, my love?" Miss Farley agreed that it was.

Jane begged for permission to return on the following morning, to talk about clothes and fashions, and it was graciously given.

"Is she not the dearest creature, Carrie?" cried Arabella, almost before the door had closed behind the visitors.

"I know you think so, and I am looking forward to knowing her better, for your sake, and then I will be able to tell you if I agree with you," was Caroline's moderate response.

"Lord Russett must be very clever," remarked Richard, "for his talk is too difficult for me. He has some scheme to enable men to fly, which I think impossible; and he is working on a design for a pump to be used in mines; I think I have a better idea for it, but he would not listen."

"We had such adventures at school!" said Arabella. "Did I tell you about the time Jane dressed up as a boy, and quite deceived Miss Rose? Or the oak tree we climbed, last year, when I was at Littlethorpe Park?"

"No, you didn't tell me," replied Caroline, wishing she didn't know now. Really, the things Arabella got up to . . .

The following morning, while Cornelius Watts set out on his solitary quest in the streets, and Caroline and Arabella were wondering what time Jane would arrive, Richard was occupied in drawing out, on large sheets of paper, as well as he could with one arm and no one to help him, an adaptation of a ship's pump for use in mines; and he became so absorbed that Caroline had to shake his shoulder, and make him eat and change before setting off to visit Admiral Harper. At last he was ready to go, but refused to leave without his roll of drawings, which Caroline tucked under his arm, and then he set off at a quick pace, obviously still carrying on a debate with himself about gallons per hour.

When Jane arrived Arabella whisked her up to her bedroom. They were dying, she informed Caroline, to dress each other's hair *à la Grecque*, to see if it suited them, and give Phoebe an idea how it should be done. Phoebe was so clever! a paragon among maidservants! and Arabella wanted to try on Jane's fur cloak, to see how it suited her, and Jane to try the effect of Arabella's beaver bonnet before the dressing glass.

Caroline, after spending some time with the children, sat down to her embroidery in the morning room. She was making a border for an afternoon gown, although it had occurred to her that one with the border painted on, like the dress Miss Farley had been wearing the previous day, would be less time-consuming, and just as elegant. Lady Russett might affect to despise the world of fashion; but her costume, and that of her daughters, betrayed a master hand, and were no doubt the latest rage . . .

"Have you read this?" asked Jane, bending over the advertisements in the newspaper. "Hubert's Roseate Powder, for removing superfluous hairs on face, neck and arms. Do you think I ought to use some, Bell?"

Arabella peered into the delicate face of her friend, and examined her roseleaf complexion.

"I don't think so," she replied. "I don't suppose it means eyebrows or eyelashes, does it? They are still worn, I believe."

Jane pulled at the scarcely perceptible downlike hairs on her arms.

"Do you think I ought to take these off?" she asked worriedly.

"No, I don't . . . I don't think either of us need use that—but look, here's something that might be useful—Amboyna Tooth Powder—for cleansing and beautifying the teeth—I don't think yours need beautifying, Jane, but everyone's need cleaning occasionally. Should we try some? Two shillings and sixpence the box. Phoebe, you can get some for us, next time you are out on an errand. You can easily go round by St. Paul's churchyard."

"I think for my complexion I'll just go on using Gowlands," concluded Jane after some thought.

"You can't do better," replied her friend. Then, after a pause—"Do you know who I saw the other day? The two dragoons who rescued us from that thunder shower."

"No!"

"I did," Arabella smiled saucily, "and they saw me, and bowed and smirked, most flatteringly."

"How exciting! I wonder if we'll see them again—they were rather forward, though, weren't they, Bell?—not, of course, that it matters to me whether or not we see them. Oh, Arabella! Do ask Phoebe to go, if we've finished with our hair. There is so much I have to tell you. It's so long since we met. Over a year. You'll never guess what has happened."

"Phoebe," said Arabella, "you may leave us. Will you take Pug with you? I think he wants to go into the garden."

No sooner had Pug and Phoebe gone, than Jane, dropping her head into her hands, gave way to misery.

"What!" cried her friend, surprised at this change of mood. "Dear Jane! We have been apart for a year, and now we are together again, instead of happiness, does it only give rise to tears? Come, Jane, what is the matter?"

"I was quite happy," replied Jane weakly, "and so pleased to have you in London, Bell, you can't think; until you mentioned the Dragoons, and it reminded me of the time you spent with us, and how idyllic it was—do you remember the Spencers? You must do."

"I never think of Littlethorpe Park without remembering them. Your home has such elegance, Jane, is it not strange that we were always happiest at the Rectory? Oh—you must not think I mean that I was not happy at the Park," and Arabella's face grew soft with concern, as she sat down near Jane and put her hand on her shoulder.

"We were happiest at the Rectory, were we not?" said Jane through her tears.

"You always seemed most at ease there," Arabella was anxious to say the right thing; "the simple pleasures of a large and healthy family are restful," after restraint and formality, she would have gone on to say. The visit to Littlethorpe Park had been a trial—one had to be so careful always to say and do the right thing! Not to sing, or romp, or slide down the banisters, or hide with a book if one did not feel like company. But down at the Rectory it had been so different.

"How right, how perceptive you are, Arabella! Lady Russett finds me a daughter so little to her taste that I am intimidated, I must confess. Emma outshone me in the schoolroom, and she does so still. She is happy in the world my mother and father inhabit, as I can never be . . ." Arabella nodded sympathetically. "I am bored by lectures, prefer a country dance to my mother's tunes, and a game of tag with the young ones to the conversation of my mother's guests."

"But this is not matter for tears!" This was wasting a morning of lighthearted joy. How often they had longed to be in London together! "Why, when you are married, quite soon—don't shake your head at me, you know you intend to—once married, you need never hear a sonata again. And can play tag, if you want to, in your own garden. Do have a shrubbery and we can all play hide and seek in it."

"Do you think I can stand up against my mother?"

"No, I do not . . . nor do I think you should, dear Jane . . ." Arabella, who could not remember her own mother, thought of her dear, fond Papa. "Has she not your best interests at heart? You cannot accuse her of anything except a certain indifference—

a preferring of Miss Farley to yourself; and the best of mothers must have preferences among her children. You are dissimilar in your tastes, that is all. When you meet someone you can happily marry, your mother will not oppose you."

Arabella drew these opinions from a conviction she had that, of his children, Charles Hill preferred Caroline; and she had never minded. As long as she could twist him round her little finger, she did not care that he scolded her with being a flighty witch.

"But she has opposed me!" cried Jane, indignation drying her tears. "She has forbidden the match! She had brought me here to Town to be miserable. You think she cares for me? What is this caring if it demands the sacrifice of all my future happiness? What does she care for me when she is happy to shuffle off the responsibility on to your sister, it is so boring for her?"

Arabella looked at her, and could think of nothing to say, except, "Who is it?"

"Robert Spencer."

"Oh!" Arabella got up, and walked up and down the room. This was serious indeed! For a few moments she faced the fact that the sweets of love would overcome the claims of friendship, and—for she knew at once that the relationship was serious—that Jane would value Robert's companionship above her own. She felt pangs of jealousy and envy, but was too goodhearted to encourage them.

"Well!" she exclaimed gaily. "So you have stolen a march on me! I suppose it was obvious that he was fond of you, even a year ago. You have known each other all your lives."

"All our lives, and now to be so cruelly parted! Just when we had discovered our love for one another."

"You have been much apart, though, Jane. All the years you and I were at school."

"Three years," struck in Jane.

"And all the years he was at Oxford."

"Four years, but some of it was at the same time, Bell."

"All the seasons which you and your family have spent in London——"

"Have only made our affection sweeter, when we were together, and made us realize that it has flowered into Love."

"Did he approach your parents?"

"Yes—and—oh! Bell! They were so unkind! Said he must never speak to me again, and sent for his father, as though Mr. Spencer were at fault! He loves me like a daughter, and Mrs. Spencer has always had a fondness for me. I have fed the hens with her, and baked cakes, as though I were part of the family. There is not so much disparity between us. He is the son of a gentleman, well educated, and only in need of a preferment in Holy Orders to allow us a life much like that of the Rectory, and I ask for nothing more."

"La! I do not believe in marrying for money. But, my dear, there is little comfort in marrying without any." On Arabella's inward eye had flashed a picture of the curate's wife at Curteys Percy, who was also a gentleman's daughter, and who, weighed down with the cares of eight children on a small stipend, presented a sad picture compared to Jane, who sat looking charming in all the bloom of youth and the freshest of muslins.

"Why, Miss Hill, I did not think you were so worldly!"

"Perhaps I am——" she laughed self-consciously—"no, do not think me so. But it seems one must look for fortune in marriage— Wilberfoss showed me the way one is supposed to think! And do not forget how vastly experienced I am. I have been giving Mrs. Hunt her instructions these five years. Jane, I do not believe you ever ordered a leg of lamb. I would fear for your happiness as the mother of a large family on a small income."

"Here is seriousness! Here where I expected sympathy!" and Jane began to cry in earnest, and Arabella, putting her arms round her, wished she had held her tongue. She tried to retrieve the situation.

"You know I like Robert immensely—how could anyone not like him?" Jane sniffed and nodded in agreement. "I think some of that abominable common sense so characteristic of my sisters has rubbed off on to me, like rouge on to a handkerchief. It is so romantic that you are being persecuted for love! Come, I will do nothing but encourage you. Anything but have the bonds of friendship broken. Count on me, dear Jane. Fly to Gretna Green, and I will cover for you! I will ride on the top of the coach with a pistol, and shoot any who come in pursuit!"

Jane laughed through her tears, dried her eyes, and put her handkerchief away.

"How ridiculous you are, Bell! First you are telling me that I would not make a poor man's wife—though I don't see why not—then you are suggesting that I run off to Scotland—which would not be in our best interests at all. I have not had the chance to finish my story. I have promised to give him up."

"Give him up! and you have just had me encouraging you!"

"For the time being; for the time being, Miss Hill! and he has promised to give me up for the time being; and I am brought to London to see if I can be distracted and fall in love with somebody else; and Robert has a curacy in Cornwall. But of course we have no intention of giving each other up, and if I do not marry him I will marry no one, as Mama will find out. She will like me left on her hands less than she will like the marriage in a year or two. Robert is to look for preferment."

"Well—a secret love is a very comforting thing to have."

"And with you in the secret, I can talk about him to my heart's content."

"Oh, yes," said Arabella, bored already. "But I do hope you are going to try to enjoy life, just a little."

"I intend to—if only to confound Mama—I will dance, and flirt, so that she thinks I have forgotten him. But if she takes me to any more scientific demonstrations, I shall yawn."

This threat of rebellion was great indeed from gentle Jane. Now that she had shared her secret, and her friend had abandoned sense for sensibility, both were happy. They talked of Balls, and Officers, and Flirtations; "For I intend to flirt a great deal," Jane remarked; "Robert knows I will be true to him, so there is no danger; and once we are married, you know, one cannot do so."

It was that same morning that Cornelius Watts, trudging round the streets, and checking at the twenty-ninth house of ill-fame, found someone who had heard of Madame Eglantine.

Chapter Three

The next day found Cornelius standing in a side street outside a house of medium size. When the door was answered he sent in a note, written on a small folded piece of paper, announcing that he wished to see the lady of the house on business; and in a few minutes he was shown into an over-furnished back room.

"Madame Eglantine?" he asked.

The occupant of the room was already dressed for the day, in a massive gown of blue silk, patterned with gold. On her head nodded an overpowering headdress of dyed ostrich feathers, and her features, creased by age into a series of grotesque folds, were rubbed with white and with carmine in a way which appeared very obvious by the light of day. Her eyes, sunk into the pouches of flesh, looked at him as expressively as two small pieces of flint.

"I am Madame Eglantine," she said. "You say you know of something to the advantage of one of my young friends who share this house with me."

He ignored the circumlocution.

"If you have a girl called Mirabelle." If it cost him an effort to say that name, it could not be seen by an observer. His face was as implacable as Madame's own.

"I always have a Mirabelle. I always have a Cloe, and a Phyllida, an Aurora and a Cynthia, and usually a Daphne."

There was nothing for it but to explain.

"Did you have a client, the Honourable Henry Dunnett?"

"A friend used to call sometimes of that name."

"Was he a—visitor—to Mirabelle?"

She hesitated, and then said, "Yes."

"Can I see her? He left her a bequest in his will."

To his surprise, Madame Eglantine paused, closing her lips. He would not have thought her anything but positive, but she glanced everywhere but at him before replying, and then it was as though the words were dragged from her.

"The Mirabelle who was a friend of his has left me, these two months."

He knew that she was saying this unwillingly. In such a case he would rather have expected her to produce the current Mirabelle, and try to fob him off with her; he had been prepared for such an attempt at deception. Would have expected her, in that case, to go on to fleece the girl once the bequest had been handed over.

He became aware, in the silence of the room, that she was waiting for him to speak, and that there was something almost of fear in her stillness.

"Can you tell me more about her? Her real name, if it is not Mirabelle? Her address?"

"She is one of the damned!" spat Madame Eglantine. "You are foolish if you seek her out."

"I must seek her out," he replied mildly. "I have undertaken to find her."

"I can give her a message," said the woman. "She still calls here sometimes."

"Have you the note I sent in?" he asked, and when she handed it to him, he wrote on it rapidly. "Here is my name and address. If you can tell her to come to see me?"

He smiled politely and turned to go. Madame Eglantine remained motionless in the centre of the room until the servant had shown him out, then she unfolded the paper, and read his message. She shuddered, and started after him, reaching the street door in time to watch him walking firmly away.

"So that is Cornelius Watts!" she said to herself. "After so long, to come here. Oh, if he had come sixteen years ago!" She had almost cried out after him, but she did not. She turned back into the house, and tucked the piece of paper behind the mantel clock.

"Strange!" she said. "To come here and ask for Mirabelle." Her face changed, and the look of fear returned to it.

"Mirabelle!" she said.

At the corner of the street, Mr. Watts had paused to look back. "One of the damned, she called her," he thought. "But are they not all? What hope is there for them?"

The Russett's dinner party was all that Arabella had hoped, all that Caroline had feared, and all that Richard had expected. Their home was near Welby House, of similar size and style; but the company assembled was very different to any that had so far graced the Egyptian Saloon.

Arabella at once began to become radiant, in the way she had when exhilarated, as they were introduced, and this had an instant effect on at least one of those present.

"This is one of our young Poets, Nathaniel Eeles," gushed Lady Russett, depositing a thin, dark young man by Arabella's side. He looked suitably modest, and tossed back his head, to shake a heavy lock of hair from his forehead.

"I am all trepidation, Sir!"—she gazed up at him—"having never met a poet before. What can I say to one who has converse with the muse?"

"Say anything, fair lady, for your voice is music," he bent over her hand and kissed it. For once she was speechless. Linchestershire beaux did not kiss hands.

"I am not yet widely known," he admitted, "being still unpublished. Like our respected young genius, Humphry Davy, I circulate my poems only among friends."

"Humphry Davy? Is he not at the Royal Institution?"

"He is."

"But I thought he was interested in chemistry."

"Among the lectures given at the Royal Institution—from Drawing to Mechanical Inventions—Humphry Davy's on Chemistry are the most popular. He is not here tonight, but you will meet him."

"And he is a poet too, like yourself?"

"A very good one. His friends, Robert Southey and Samuel Taylor Coleridge—" Nathaniel glanced at her to make sure she was suitably impressed—"think highly of his work. It was on account of their friendship that Mr. Coleridge agreed to give a course of lectures earlier this year on The Distinguished English Poets. What a feast to put before the Philistines of London! Food for the Gods!"

"You would be there, of course, Mr. Eeles, taking in this Manna?"

"It would have been an incomparable treat—" his tone was lugubrious—"but they were never given. Mr. Coleridge was too unwell to carry out the project." He sounded so dejected that Arabella's look was all sympathy; it must have been very expressive, for suddenly Mr. Eeles went down on his knees, and said in a carrying whisper,

"Miss Hill! Will you do me the honour to accept my hand in marriage?"

"Mr. Eeles!" she cried. "Do get up. Someone will see you. Do you usually propose to young ladies you have only just met?"

"I have never before met my twin soul," explained Mr. Eeles in a tragic tone.

"Please. Get up."

He got up, and leaned towards her.

"I have startled you. But I thought that as we were twin souls, you must have felt instantly as I did. I was too precipitate. I will wait. But I beg you, marry me."

She fanned herself vigorously, and smiled at him, without replying.

Mr. Eeles, without more words, stood beside her, leaning on the wall with his chin sunk into his chest, and, crossing his arms, appeared to wrap himself in silence. She thought this was probably the natural habit of poets, and began to talk more generally to other people near by. Jane was much occupied with her duties as daughter of the house, but she came over for a few minutes, and it was soon time to go in to dinner. Mr. Eeles had not spoken again. No one appeared to have noticed his dramatic collapse to his knees, and she had taken little further notice of him, but it was intriguing—who can receive such a proposal and forget it? She wondered if he often behaved so.

After dinner he again stood beside her, but said so little that when he was struck by inspiration and went out, she could not remember how many minutes it had been since she last noticed him. He did not reappear until the evening was ending, and the Welbys stood talking on the stairs, in a little knot of people waiting for their carriage. He was at her elbow, with a sheet of paper in his hand.

"This is for you," he said in a low tone, giving it to her. "We will meet again, and I will ask you again, until we are one, to marry me." He gazed into her eyes with great intensity, and was gone.

"Upon my word," said Richard.

"Who is that young man, Arabella?" asked Caroline. "The one all in black. I saw him standing next to you, earlier, and he must have dropped something—he was kneeling on the floor."

She was confused.

"He is a poet, Mr. Nathaniel Eeles—didn't Lady Russett introduce him to you? He is one of her protégés." She undid the sheet of paper, and found a few lines of verse.

> *"My heart is a spear of gladness*
> *Piercing the night of fear*
> *Because you have banished sadness*
> *With your presence here."*

"Well, it's better than I could write," said Richard.

"I don't think poetry is a very reliable way of making a living." Caroline sounded dubious. At that moment the carriage was announced, and they left for home.

"Did you enjoy it?" Arabella meant the evening.

"Tolerably; I did so wish I could hear Sir Joseph Banks talk about plants. Is it so very wonderful that they have found a metal called sodium in soda? I have seen soda dissolved for doing the washing many a time, but I've never noticed any metal in it. I don't find that sort of thing very interesting."

"I would love to see the galvanic battery they used, and know how it was done; it was very expensive, and is a powerful one—

designed by Volta—and they discovered a metal called potassium in potash, dear, when they split it and divided the oxygen from it."

"Yes, my love, as I said, it is no doubt very wonderful."

Arabella was absorbed by the thought of her poem. Mr. Eeles was no doubt an oddity; but she could not help feeling flattered at such an instant conquest. If only she could feel sure that he was not the same with every new face that caught his fancy . . .

The following morning there was another sheet of paper, brought to Arabella as she was sitting having her hair brushed. She read,

> "*TO MY GLOIRE DE DIJON*
> *If the shape of a rose should give me joy*
> *Its velvet smoothness my senses decoy,*
> *Soft against my skin the tender petal*
> *Will teach my heart, less fiery a metal*
> *Can with the strength of beauty live and grow.*
> *If this is madness, I am mad, I know,*
> *Let me in all my life not saner grow.*"

"I think that's rather neat," Arabella laid the verse down on the dressing table.

"Excuse me asking, Ma'am, but that isn't from Mr. Nathaniel Eeles, is it?" asked Phoebe as she wielded the hairbrush.

"It is." Arabella's tone had an undercurrent of sharpness. "What do you know of him?"

"Oh, nothing, Ma'am. But he used to visit at the house where I had a place before, and I recognized his hand, Ma'am. It is a very unusual and striking hand."

"So it is," her voice had softened; "I really hadn't noticed, but you're right, Phoebe. You are observant. The capitals are certainly very fine, and the lines even; striking is just the word to describe it. Do you know much about Mr. Eeles?"

"Nothing to his discredit, Miss Hill. He is poor, but I believe all poets are. He washes his own shirts in the river."

"Oh!" It was something of a revelation. Arabella turned the sheet of paper over in her hand, and felt that her pleasure in the poem had somehow been sullied. He would certainly be anxious to marry, and the smallness of her fortune would not deter one who had so little . . . the flattery of Mr. Eeles' proposal was not quite as acceptable as it had been before . . .

The day of their first great Ball had arrived, and in comparison, the dinner at the Russetts' was very small beer. It was to be at the Marchioness of Harome's, the famous mansion built by Lord Linchester and with a portico added to the design of Lord Burlington in 1760. It did not contain a Double Cube Room; but this deficiency was more than made up for by the Oval Ballroom, famous throughout London, which occupied the centre of the magnificent pile, making the surrounding corridors and anterooms odd and inconvenient shapes.

They were reliably informed that all London would be there. There was, of course, a great deal of exaggeration in this information. The larger part of the population, from bankers to costermongers, maids to milliners, had not been invited to attend . . . but . . . those who mattered to the world of high society, and a sprinkling of the upper nobility, were to be present, with as many other people as the Marchioness regarded either as friends or as ornaments to her ballroom. It was enough. Arabella was afire with excitement.

She had made her début, thanks largely to the recommendations of Lady Russett, who had spoken of her to all her friends. Everywhere that Caroline had escorted Jane and Arabella they had been objects of interest and attraction—Jane for her shy sweetness and Arabella for her elegance and quick liveliness.

Charles Hill had said, "If a young man suits Arabella, I have not much doubt of him suiting me. He will get three thousand with her and a third of what I leave when I die." "Don't talk of dying, Father," had been Caroline's quick reply. But in London a young woman's fortune was important, and the eligible young men who were out for more, did not pay serious court. It was not clear that—apart from Mr. Eeles—any suitor was emerging. But here was the Ball, with its endless possibilities.

Caroline's gown was a rich rose colour, with long sleeves, a back without a seam, and an antique stomacher cut to the front of the bodice. It was becoming; but she was overshadowed by Arabella in coloured net over white satin, which gave a silvery rainbow effect of great delicacy and beauty.

Mr. Watts arrived to share their carriage and on the way they stopped to pick up Jane, and the chattering of the excited girls filled the vehicle.

The streets of London were already dark, but very far from being empty. Other carriages and barouches rumbled along, among the lumbering drays and carts making late deliveries and the lurching of busy hackneys with their fares. They peered out of the carriage windows, and Jane wondered if the other travellers, too, were bound for the Marchioness of Harome's . . . link boys were escorting fine ladies and gentlemen, their torches flaming in the damp night air like fireflies on a summer evening. The light, flickering as it was blown hither and thither, lit up here a Pilgrim cloak and hood, with the lady so concealed balancing along on pattens through the coated streets; there it showed a gentleman with his cloak swinging wide, so that the girls caught a glimpse of immaculately tailored legs, and a splash of white where the subtle light picked out the cravat at his neck. "Look, look!" cried Arabella, but at what or whom she could not have said. It seemed that all London was on the move and it was everything she wanted to look at. The streets were stirring with life where her well-known country lanes would at this time be deserted, with only the solitary carriage of a visiting family, or the trudge of a labourer going home from the alehouse. Even in Linchester most houses would be shut up for the night, so that merry-makers felt alien to the good folk tucked up in their beds. London was different. It was an anthill which did not rest, by day or by night; the subdued all-pervading movement thrilled her. If she caught a glimpse of a ragged beggar slinking off down a side alley, or a cripple waiting for alms, it only heightened the effect of luxury of the other wayfarers, those on their way to pleasure, or to vice.

As they arrived, climbed down the carriage steps, and passed into the shelter of the portico, the night, with its mingling of darkness and flame, was forgotten in the brilliance of the illumination of innumerable lamps and candles. Other people were pouring in like moths drawn to the light.

"How bright it is!"

"Dazzling!"

As they moved towards the staircase Caroline, who had been making mental calculations of the cost of the candles and oil, had to stop trying, for the stairs, and then the ballroom itself, were seen to be swimming in even more brilliant illumination. There was a crush of people. The women in diaphanous dresses, revealing the outline of their limbs, were radiant in the displayed beauty of arms and breasts, often so barely covered that Caroline was blushing for them; the men wore the more subdued accents of colour, except where the scarlet of the military shone out, or the silks and satins of those men who still peacocked in the manner of the *Ancien Règime* glowed richly.

For a moment, the newcomers hung on the edges of the gaiety; but their entrance had not been unnoticed. Jane and Arabella were greeted by the Marchioness as soon as she turned from Caroline, and they made their curtsies gracefully, then waited as she welcomed Richard and Cornelius. It was with a faint feeling of surprise that Arabella saw the real friendship with which the Marchioness obviously regarded the lawyer, and she eyed him speculatively, for the first time realizing the respect in which he was held.

Now they were over the first shock of entering the ballroom, they began to pick out here and there friendly faces turned towards them with smiles, and Richard was greeted at once by some Naval officers who were present with their wives, and from across the room Admiral Harper semaphored to them cheerfully.

Hardly had they moved away from the entrance than the opening strains of a cotillion brought people on to the space in the centre. Jane was at once in request by a young unmarried Naval officer, but Arabella stood unasked, until Caroline spoke to Mr. Watts.

"You have been unbendingly quiet, Mr. Watts, the whole way, and added nothing to the sparkle of our party. Come, I cannot have you failing to find pleasure in a Ball as brilliant as this; you must dance."

"Then you must honour me with your hand, Madam," he replied with alacrity.

"No! I have promised Richard that my first dance will be with him, or no one. Please me by dancing with Arabella."

"What! Have I to dance with that termagant?" he exclaimed. But Caroline was determined, looking at him with sweet persistence until, as she gave her own hand to Richard, and began to move towards the dance floor, he capitulated with a little shrug of the shoulders and approached Arabella. She, glowing with excitement, had been watching the gathering dancers with her foot tapping, but gave him her hand with some slight reluctance. A cotillion with the worthy, but oh! so boringly respectable Mr. Watts, did not strike her as the most delightful of propositions, not when she could see red coats, and dashing men of fashion . . . but she was favourably surprised. He was not quite in his dotage; he was as healthy as a steel spring, with a neat foot and a lightness in the dance which matched her own. She became exhilarated with the music and the movement, and, forgetting to look round the room for officers, gave herself up to enjoyment. She laughed and sparkled up at Mr. Watts, as she shimmered in her delicate gown through the figures of the dance until at the end they both relinquished their partners with reluctance. Cornelius was the more reluctant of the two. He was stirred by Arabella; her closeness and the intimacy of the dance had revealed that she had an attraction for him which he had not suspected. His quietness during the journey to the Ball had been caused by the emotional exhaustion of the search he had been engaged in. It seemed he was now nearly at the end of it; but old passions had been woken and remembered, and he had, it seemed, become vulnerable, as though he were a youth again.

Caroline, when she saw the sprinkling of dashing red coats in the ballroom, had felt an uneasiness which she did not wish to define. But as she danced happily but gravely with Richard, she forgot her vague fears, and the sight of Mr. Watts and Arabella, flushed and bright as they ended their dance, gratified her. She was soothed too soon. Youth is drawn to youth; and between handsome officers and a vivacious girl, one dance with an older man is a very flimsy barrier . . .

They went on dancing with one another and with their naval friends until half the evening was over. Arabella declared there was no excitement in the world to compare with a Ball, and Jane agreed with her.

Mr. Watts had met some old friends who invited him to join them at cards in another room, and he had consented. Everything seemed to have changed for him. Life, which had been so settled, so secure, was suddenly an experience turned on its head. Now, to feel attracted, where he had least expected it, at a time when the whole basis of his existence seemed to be shifting like sand, was something he needed to think about, to mull over. Such a feeling could have incalculable consequences. To get out of the ballroom and play cards was a salvation. With three-quarters of his mind he could try to reassess his situation, and his emotions.

Caroline was growing tired, and was glad to hear that refreshments were being served in the anteroom; Richard insisted that she rest and indulge in ices and orgeat, and she was not reluctant. Both girls were dancing.

"They are safe enough," said Richard. "They will come and find us when the dance is over. You worry too much, wife. No harm can come to them here. If we wait till the dance is over, everyone will be crowding in for a rest, and we will have to wait. Come now, and we may be sure of a seat, and perhaps a chicken leg."

They secured their chicken legs, and in the ballroom there was a pause between dances . . .

There were two particular officers who were attracting Arabella's attention. She thought she recognized them, although they had not been near enough for her to be positive; but she knew, in the mysterious way in which these things are known to young people, that it was inevitable that during the course of the evening they would meet. Sure enough, she saw him—the taller, thinner one—looking at her intently, speaking to his friend, and moving towards the part of the room where Arabella had been joined near the wall by Jane.

"Don't look now," she whispered urgently, "but—you remember what I said about seeing the Dragoons who helped us in the thunder shower?"

"Yes, what about them?"

Arabella had no time to answer. The officers had approached within earshot. In another few seconds the tall, thin one spoke,

"I have been able to find no one," he said, "who is able to introduce us to two young ladies of such elegance; but perhaps we may dispense with a formal introduction, for we have, if memory serves me rightly, met before, and been introduced by circumstance, in the water meadows of Linchester."

Jane blushed, and Arabella smiled, and Captain Wilmott and Captain Bodley considered themselves introduced.

It was the work of a moment for the officers to discover that the ladies were not engaged for the next dance; they had been intending to join Richard and Caroline in seeking refreshments.

"Ah," cried Captain Bodley, "first let us dance; then, if you will bear with us so far, I will find seats, Captain Wilmott will find refreshments, and we will all enjoy them together."

No idea could have been more pleasing; and when Caroline returned to the ballroom it was to see her two charges under the escort of the attentive officers, who were carrying plates of dainties, and making themselves generally useful. She distrusted them instinctively. Why, when a naval uniform incited such confidence? She could not explain it, but spoke of it to Richard.

"We can see them, my dear, and while they are within view there is no cause for alarm. Young ladies are bound to enjoy the company of officers; they always do. And while we are hearing, with such anticipation, of General Sir John Moore's march to join up with the reinforcements waiting off the coast of the Peninsula —which will, we hope, together assist the gallant people of Spain to drive out the tyrant from their soil—while all this is happening, my dear, we must all feel the warmest interest in His Majesty's Army. I understand, of course, that you have a preference for the Navy," he added, smiling down at her, "and I wouldn't wish you to change your tastes. I will allow you to talk to those two young officers, as is your sister; in fact you have a duty to do so; but mind, you only dance with me, or Admiral Harper, or Captain Adams, or one of their parties; oh, or Watts, of course. But I am too anxious to keep your love to let you dance with any Army officers whatsoever."

Caroline informed him that he talked a good deal of nonsense, and borrowed a little of Arabella's pertness to announce that she would dance with every officer in sight, if she chose. But she was more relieved by the Marchioness than by Richard when that lady remarked how pleased she was to see young people meeting eligible partners, and did not Mrs. Welby think Captains Wilmott and Bodley very excellent young men? This Caroline felt she had to reply to in the affirmative, so that when Arabella, noticing at last her eldest sister's return to the ballroom, conducted Jane and their escorts over to her, she felt already committed to approval.

"It was irregular, Mrs. Welby, not to be properly introduced," apologized Arabella, "but we had already met, informally, of course."

Captain Wilmott broke in. "May we have your pardon, Ma'am? Our only excuse is our prior meeting, and the fact that we could find no one free to perform the office etiquette demands."

"You remember me telling you of the thunder shower, sister, which came on so suddenly, when Jane and I were out walking in the water meadows near Littlethorpe Park; and the gallantry of the two officers who insisted on coming to our rescue and lending us their cloaks, and indeed, if it had not been for that protection, we would have been wet through, and no doubt caught our deaths, you know," and Arabella wound up this heavily edited version of the incident in the casual tone of one who had never been ill in her life, and had often been wet through without catching her death, or anything else.

"You must feel grateful to those who saved your sister's life," whispered Richard. So Caroline gave in. She was formally introduced, and must submit to the acquaintance. After all the Marchioness had spoken well of them, and she could find out more of their backgrounds in the morning.

For the rest of the night Arabella, dancing with Captain Wilmott, was in a dream of delight. She knew exactly what type she admired in a man, and she had always found tall, slim men, with neat, dark heads, immensely attractive. When they combined these features with an easy manner and amiability, she was in a fair way to being very interested indeed, and when the Captain's brown eyes met hers, and lit with unmistakable pleasure, she felt that before she dropped hers, he must have read the answering response.

Jane, even in a ballroom, could not forget her childhood sweetheart; but no young creature can hold out against the excitement of a well-dressed, happy crowd and the rhythm of the dance. If she did not have the same interest in Captain Bodley that she could see Arabella felt in his friend, she at least found him an entertaining companion, and her natural softness of manner led him to think that she felt much more. Artlessly, she gave him a good deal of information about their daily habits, so that he felt quite satisfied that she meant to attract him, without her having any such intention.

It was two in the morning before they left; many of the crowd showed every sign of staying until dawn, but families with young ladies in their party were not staying so late. The dragoons parted from them with compliments and expressed hopes of meeting again, and Captain Wilmott hinted that he might call at Welby House. He gave Arabella a look which assured her that he would be reappearing in her life, by hook or by crook. She did not put any great dependence on it, although she hoped very much that they would meet again. London was a large place, and officers notoriously fickle . . . Jane, on the other hand, had received a pressure of his hand on her arm and a few low-spoken words from Captain Bodley, which made her certain they would meet again. She was in an innocent flutter which, together with the extreme tiredness which manifested itself when they were seated in the carriage, kept her from speaking. It was a silent and uneventful drive, compared to the noisy anticipation with which they had driven through these streets a few hours before.

Thankfully they stopped at Jane's door, and Richard escorted her to the entrance. Thankfully they resumed their journey and the streets, at their most silent in all the twenty-four hours, at this dead hour sounded with their passing. Thankfully they reached their own home, and bade good night to Mr. Watts, who had his horse and groom waiting for him. Thankfully they went to bed, putting off all discussion of the Ball until the next morning.

"How dull it is," said Arabella, "the morning after a Ball!"

Caroline agreed with her. They had risen late, and were sitting in the window of Caroline's bedroom before starting the business of the day, but neither felt like anything so much as returning to bed, and reliving the scenes and experiences of the night before.

Mrs. Jackson, the housekeeper, had been given instructions for the day; Baby Charles was taking the air in Betty's arms; the older children were in the company of their dancing master, and the sound of his fiddle and the thump of their feet could be heard faintly through the ceiling.

"Where's Richard?" Arabella paused in her survey of the figs and medlars of the flat garden at the back of the house, where old Pug had been setting off a cat and was now looking under the bushes in the hope of fresh enemies to conquer. But she had hardly spoken when her brother-in-law entered the room, looking far more alert than either of the ladies of his family. He was closely followed by Phoebe who had a letter for Arabella, which she handed over without a word.

"Is that from Jane, Bell?" asked Caroline. "Really, you two are quite amusing. No doubt you will be seeing her later in the day. Does she say when?"

Arabella, who, after a quick peep, had slipped the letter into her pocket, coloured and hesitated, but before she could speak, Richard said,

"Caroline, would you mind if I left you for a couple of days?"— Arabella had quietly left the room—"In order to bear Admiral Harper company? We have heard there is to be a boxing match. You know how long it is since I had the opportunity to see such a thing—not since I was last living in London, and not often then. I know you do not care for the sport . . ."

Caroline looked up at him in surprise.

"Have I ever urged you to give up any of your pleasures? Though I did not know you followed the prizefighters, Richard; you have not mentioned it before."

"I have not told you yet who is to be fighting. Cribb! The great Cribb! Even you must have heard of him."

"I have heard of him," said Caroline blankly. The thought of Richard and the Admiral going off on such a jaunt did not appeal to her; yet she could think of no reason to urge against the plan except her desire to keep Richard at her side. She read herself a little sermon on selfishness; and conjured up a bright smile.

"You will enjoy it, Richard; how Dick will wish he could be with you! I have Arabella to keep me company, and have I not managed in your absence before?" But her heart cried out that that had been far different.

"It will only be for one night," he said, "and the Admiral does not care to go unless I accompany him—since his illness in the spring he likes to have someone with him, in case of a recurrence —and his good wife is so set against prizefighting that she will certainly not go. You could not be persuaded to come with us, I suppose, Carrie?"

"No," she said decidedly. "I have no more taste for it than Mrs. Harper, I admit. The sight of two men battering each other with bare fists till the blood flows and one of them is knocked senseless has no charms for me. When Dick and Edward Palmer set to, I can hardly wait to stop them; and if there is a fight outside the alehouse I pretend not to see it, and make all haste home . . ."

Richard looked disappointed, but said no more, except to detail the arrangements he had tentatively made with the Admiral. They had no social engagements for the next few days of such importance that they were an obstacle to the plan; whose carriage was to go, and which inn they were to stay at were the only matters which needed discussion, and with only the pleasure of the two men to be considered, there was no delay.

Once safe in her bedroom, Arabella had read her letter, which was from Captain Wilmott; he had written it as the grey light of dawn touched the rooftops, and he was unable to sleep because of the memory of her bright eyes. Trembling, she scratched out a reply, folded and sealed it, and sat down looking fondly at it when she had written the direction.

"Phoebe!"

"Yes, Miss Hill?"

"It will not be convenient—when Mrs. Welby and I are out driving—to deliver this note. We are not going in the right part of Town at all. I think I will trouble you to take it." She gave Phoebe the note. "There is not the least hurry in the world, but you might as well go now. It does not matter in the slightest if anyone knows," and here she laughed lightly, "but it will be quickest for you to go down the back stairs and out of the area door."

"Much quicker, Miss Hill," answered Phoebe. Her look held reassurance—nay, connivance—and she went at once.

The days of Richard's absence passed pleasantly enough, and Jane spent much of the time with Arabella; the fashions did need so much discussing!

Mrs. Harper was sitting with them in the Egyptian Saloon when they heard the carriage, and in no time the two wandering husbands walked in, smiling and cheerful after their excursion. Within quarter of an hour of their return they were giving a lively account of the fight, Richard on one side of the fire taking the place of Cribb, and the Admiral standing opposite and impersonating the redoubtable Gregson.

Twenty-one rounds of varying success were described vividly; betting had continued—so even had the result appeared to be—up to the sixteenth round; then in the twenty-second round, Gregson had aimed a blow on the left side of Cribb's face, which fell very short; Cribb followed him up, and after closing on him—Mrs. Harper viewed her husband in Richard's grasp with some apprehension—succeeded in throwing Gregson with great force on his back. The Admiral (as Gregson) was tumbled over, very gently, on to the rug and lay on the ground for several minutes; everyone's eyes were fixed on the Admiral, wondering if he was indeed defeated (he was, the Admiral informed them, quite stunned from the fall) and at last Gregson (impersonated by the Admiral) gave in to Cribb (represented by Richard Welby Esquire).

Another battle had been fought, for a purse, between Docherty and a man by the name of Powell, from Lewisham in Kent. This battle had lasted an hour and a half—but the spectators of the imitation of it staged by Richard and the Admiral were glad that their mock battle did not last so long. Mrs. Harper gave a little scream at one point, but, not, Arabella felt, so much from apprehension of accidental damage to her venerable husband, as from the fear that he was about to fall on top of her.

Docherty won, and the sixty-four rounds had gone quite

quickly. At the actual fight, the watching crowd of spectators had found it not a minute too long.

The two friends had returned, happy and tired from the fresh air, to their inn in the evening, to spend their time like all the rest of the crowd, drinking and eating and talking over the fights, going over every blow and feint a dozen times.

"I was surprised, as I walked along the corridor to my bed," said Richard in an aside to Caroline, "to see our maid, Phoebe. I did not have the opportunity to speak to her, but I would swear to her anywhere, that way she has of turning lightly on her heel and I thought I heard a strain of one of her favourite songs—

> *'Happy soul, that free from harms,*
> *Rests within his Shepherd's arms!'*

as I was climbing the stairs."

"That was odd," said Caroline, "Phoebe has been away. She asked permission to visit her aunt, who was dying."

"Not Mrs. Hunt?"

"No, I asked that, of course; it would have been much to all of us if it had been our dear Mrs. Hunt. An aunt on her Mother's side, I believe. But how very odd, that her aunt should live in the very place that the fight was held!"

"Just coincidence, I daresay," said Richard. "And after all I could have been mistaken. It was only half light, and the girl was some way off, on the landing. The whole place was packed with sportsmen staying the night—we had a job to get a bed, and at last had to sleep together, and Lud! the Admiral does snore."

Caroline wondered whether to tax Phoebe with this discovery of her whereabouts; but after all, the girl had not said where her aunt lived, except that it was some way off; and she might well have lived in the place of the fight. Aunts had as much right to live there as anywhere else.

"I'll tell you who else I saw," went on Richard. "Lord Alvaney, and the members of the Four in Hand Club; and the two officers Arabella and Jane met at the Ball—the Dragoons—what were their names——"

"Captains Wilmott and Bodley," answered Caroline. "It seems the world and his wife were at your prizefight."

"The world perhaps, but not his wife," smiled Richard.

The general talk in the Saloon, while this conversation had been carried on, was of the Art of Prizefighting; the harm it does, canvassed by Mrs. Harper, and the good sport it is, a view supported by the Admiral; Arabella, supporting the opinions first of one, and then of the other, added fuel to the flames to such an extent that in the end Caroline had to intervene, or the two respectable old married people would have come to fisticuffs themselves, and a third contest might have taken place upon the hearth rug.

It took some time to restore peace and tranquillity. Several glasses of Bishop—a favourite drink with the Harpers—did something to help; and one of her dainty suppers, in Caroline's best London manner, sealed the peace between them. The Admiral's cheery pink face, and his wife's long yellow one, were restored to their normal amiability, and they went off to their carriage arm in arm, more like young lovers than old married people of forty years' standing.

Phoebe had returned from her journey with a letter to Arabella from Captain Wilmott, who, she explained, she had met by chance on her return journey. Arabella took it without a word, but her hand shook visibly, and at the first opportunity she dismissed the girl and broke open the seal.

Chapter Four

The impact of Phoebe on the Welby household had been a mixed one. That she should make an impact was inevitable. Her duties involved her with everyone, from Caroline down to the kitchen boy; that it was of the kind it was was due to Phoebe herself. No one would have thought it a sudden or startling impact, for she was a quiet-moving girl, graceful and quick. Yet there was that about her which was sudden, for those with eyes to see; and with her quiet footfall, she could produce a consequently quiet kind of startle.

"She is a paragon!" Arabella had exclaimed; but Phoebe often startled her, when summoned, by being inside the room, with no warning of her approach. The door had opened so softly, and her tread was so light, that her mistress would turn and find her there, just when she was about to become irritated at the girl's delay. How long she had been standing there, with that demure expression, Arabella never knew; so she could not scold. If she was not sure if she liked Phoebe or not—that was mere abstract speculation. She worked efficiently, and Caroline wrote to her father and asked him to tell his housekeeper, Mrs. Hunt, how pleased they were with her niece. But there was something . . .

She was not always silent. Often, as Mrs. Hunt had told them, she sang the new Methody hymns as she went about the house, and Richard Welby listened to the fresh young voice with pleasure. To Betty, his wife's maid, that voice brought unpleasant thoughts, and she could not hear it without a grimace of distaste. Had not Mrs. Hunt wanted Caroline to dismiss herself and hire Phoebe in her place? It had not been possible, of course. Betty remembered with pride all the times Caroline had said she was indispensable. Betty had become reconciled to living a maiden, but that, she thought, was something Phoebe would hardly do. Not with those eyelashes . . . and the way she looked at William . . . she was wasting her time there. He had eyes for no one except his whey-faced little Hannah. But there was Joel Tomkins; well, she was welcome to Joel, six feet of muscle and a head full of emptiness . . .

William was deeply distrustful of Phoebe. Why, he did not pause to think. Why did he not believe her innocent expression, and that pure singing voice, blithe as a bird? She professed to be devout—he doubted her; she gave the impression of sweet youth— he thought her sly.

Not so Joel Tomkins. From that first day he had been her slave, and he was so still.

The kitchen boy, if anyone had thought to ask him, could have told them something about Phoebe. He had been sitting one day on the cold flagged floor of the larder, when Mrs. Jackson was having her after-dinner nap, and William and Joel were busy with their upstairs duties, and helping himself to raisins out of the barrel. Phoebe had found him there. She had entered the larder softly, and he had not heard her. He expected a cuff or a hiding, or that she would shout for Mrs. Jackson, but she did none of these things. At first she just stood and looked at him until, not knowing what else to do, and doubly conscious of the large piece of cheese he had started with, he had begun to rub his eyes with his hand, trying to raise a whimper, and looked up into the pretty contours of that face with the heavy-lidded eyes, hoping to find fellow feeling. She bent down towards him, and said in her low, musical voice,

"What can you do to reward me, if I don't tell Mrs. Jackson? I've been watching you for some time; this isn't the first. Last week alone there was a piece of pie and some sugar."

He had given her his sixpence, which he had saved so carefully;

but the next time he was paid, she waylaid him, and with a few remarks about raisins and Mrs. Jackson, she had taken all his wages, and not left him a ha'penny.

Phoebe's duties started early in the day, for Arabella, the country-born, woke early, and having woken, had to rise; and having risen, had the longing to be out in the air, and the general wish to be doing. Since Caroline had begun to chaperone Jane, Arabella had formed the habit of dressing simply and, with William or Phoebe as escort, to please her Ladyship, walking over to the Russett's establishment and bringing Jane back with her in time for breakfast.

On the walk there, Arabella and her attendant rubbed shoulders with the early inhabitants of the streets, women selling cresses from door to door, milkmaids, with their cows behind them, furnishing an instant supply to the jugs brought out to them; the men who ran the street stalls and had spent the night sleeping under them, making their breakfasts and getting ready for their day of selling gloves, cravats, scarves and stockings; they saw bundles of rags tucked into dark corners which were, Arabella knew, waifs without a family to care for them, who must exist somehow in the hectic streets. Usually she took the opportunity to do a little shopping for Caroline, and bundles of cress and other country produce, picked almost before daybreak, found their way in William's or Phoebe's hands to Caroline's kitchen.

Once Jane had joined her, Arabella returned by a different route. She could view the streets calmly, but Jane would have been reduced to tears by the waifs, and frightened at the sight of the old drabs sleeping off the drunkenness of the night in alleyways. Their way back lay through a small park, and was only a little longer than the walk through the streets. Its public walks were well gravelled, and at that time in the morning they were almost the only walkers among the tall trees, which dropped unexpected gouts of water on their heads, and the bushes, which were saturated with rain and dew. Most mornings were fine enough for the girls to enjoy their walk among mists or frosts, and they arrived at the breakfast table bright-eyed and lively, with tales to tell of the wildfowl on the lake, the robin in the park, or the quaint habits of the old park keeper, who spent his time sweeping up the last of the leaves and cursing the stray dogs.

Five days after the Ball at the Marchioness of Harome's, they were not the only inhabitants of the park. No sooner had they turned in at the lower end of it, than they heard the unusual sound in that quiet backwater, of horses' hooves, and the jingling of harness, and saw, sweeping towards them in the mist, two officers of the Dragoon guards, magnificent in their uniforms, brilliant with the sparkling accoutrements of their profession, and most definitely the same two men that they remembered so well from the Ball.

They were approaching—they were drawing their horses to a halt; they were sweeping off their helmets, and bowing in the saddle!

Jane blushed. Arabella gave a flirtatious smile, and a sideways glance from her bright eyes. In less than two minutes greetings had been exchanged, and the two horsemen were on their way, jingling off towards the lower entrance, and the girls and William were alone again. Captain Wilmott's glance had rested on William with a wary expression, and Arabella decided on the instant that she preferred Phoebe as her morning escort. William was too intelligent, and altogether too closely in the confidence of his mistress!

"What a strange chance," cried Jane, "that they should ride in the park just as we were walking through it! How cross the park keeper will be about his gravel! It is quite scuffled up. How very handsome Captain Bodley looked, do you not think so, Bell? How horrid that they might be sent overseas! This wretched war."

William, listening to the girls' chatter as they walked in front of him, felt relieved when he realized that Caroline had apparently met these two officers at the Ball. He did not suppose, therefore, that she would object to this meeting in the park, but he felt uneasy about the encounter. The way Miss Hill had looked up at what's-'is-name, the tall one! and Miss Jane Farley; he had a soft spot for her, she could do no wrong in his eyes; but she had looked so susceptible when she blushed! After a thoughtful walk home, he decided to say nothing to Caroline. If such a meeting occurred again, it might be his duty; but for the present he would hold his tongue.

The incident set his mind running on his own Hannah, and her modest ways, and he determined to wait no longer, but to go to Meeting the next Sunday; it would not please her if she knew he had been so many seventh days without attending.

The following morning William was getting ready to accompany Arabella to Lady Russett's when she stopped him abruptly.

"Thank you, William. I would like Phoebe to go with me in future. Please find her and tell her so."

"So, she's growing in favour, is she!" exclaimed Mrs. Jackson, "and you're put out, William. Well, I'm not surprised, if Miss Hill prefers her to your long face. I don't remember you being so miserable, once over."

That morning there were again the sweeping horses in the park, with their flowing manes and clattering hooves. The following day the officers appeared on foot, and there was a most delicious quarter-hour of dalliance, which Jane seemed to enjoy as much as if there had been no Rector's son in the offing. Captain Wilmott suggested making a formal call at Welby House, and the next day this call took place.

Caroline admitted to being "in" when the officers enquired at the door. She had found out that they were generally well thought of, both in Society and among their brother officers at Stephens Hotel. They appeared, bowed, seated themselves, and accepted the refreshments offered. Conversation on the campaign in Portugal, and the postponement of the next session of Parliament, took up some time. Arabella, bent over her embroidery of a sextant, presented a modest aspect which pleased her sister; she was not so pleased with Jane, who had set aside her work to help with the cups and saucers, and was sending Captain Bodley sidelong glances which Caroline thought rather bold. The visit passed; the proper length of time had been spent; other company was announced, and in the bustle the officers took their leave. Captain Wilmott crossed over to Arabella, and for some seconds they were in quiet conversation; Captain Bodley parted from Jane with a handclasp, and a look which Caroline, had she seen it, would have thought full of undesirable meaning. She did not see it because

Admiral Harper, his wife, son and daughter-in-law, were taking up her full attention, and she barely had sufficient notice for the departing warriors to fulfil her position as their hostess.

Next day was clear and still, and Arabella, in love with all the world, hummed cheerfully as she skipped round puddles left by the rain of the previous night, and looked on all things, including the sleepy Phoebe, with benevolence. She loved the cluttered streets; she loved the bleary washerwomen, trundling their carts from door to door; she felt in her purse for a copper for a dirty little urchin who was usually hanging round a certain doorway, and watched with pleasure as he skipped off to buy a hot pie. She was thinking of nothing as much as red coats, and meaningful glances from sparkling brown eyes. How brown eyes varied! Some, with a bit of hazel in them, could sparkle and flash; others, like William's, were as soft and dark as a pansy and so lugubrious! Faithful and intelligent, of course, but she was better pleased to have Phoebe. She looked round at the girl, unable to remember what colour her eyes were, and was surprised to find them a gooseberry green, before they were rapidly veiled by the white eyelids. So! She had been taking in all the sights of the morning as avidly as her mistress, and that modest downward gaze was just a front!

Although she had half expected them, there were no officers exercising their horses in the little park that morning. Well then, she remarked to Jane, their arrangements were evidently unaltered, and they only had to look forward to the morrow.

They returned, presenting two innocent faces to William and Joel, and, leaving Phoebe downstairs, went up to join the family.

It was towards noon on that same day that Madame Eglantine stood facing a slim, black-clad figure, in the same overfurnished room that Cornelius Watts had seen. Today's visitor stood against the window, and the winter sun was bright. It seemed as though the sun's rays fell on that blackness only to be absorbed into it, and Madame Eglantine longed to tear her away from the window and thrust her out of the house. It was impossible to read the expression on the visitor's face as she stood absorbing the light, for round her the rays dazzled, coming low, almost horizontally, into the room. Madame Eglantine felt that it was of no use trying to hide her own emotions of fear and terror, for that sun on her face showed it all to the pitiless glance resting on her.

"You will go to see him?" she asked. She had given the girl she called Mirabelle Mr. Watts' note.

"I will go," was the answer. "But not yet. The time is not yet."

"But it is a legacy! You fooled that old man. He thought you cared for him, and were innocent, and he wished to take you out of this life and provide for you. If he had guessed that it was you who picked his pocket, he might have done differently."

"But he did not know. He was taken ill, and died, and the money I found in his pocket took me out of your reach, and now it is I who has the power."

Madame Eglantine did not dispute it. She sat down and rested her forearm on a table, to stop it shaking. Indeed, she was shaking all over . . .

The visitor she called Mirabelle walked over to the mantelshelf and put the note back behind the clock.

"Are you not going to claim it then?" Madame sounded surprised. Now that the black figure was near to her, she was still more afraid.

"I shall claim it when I am ready."

"You will not know his address; are you not taking the note?"

"I have memorized it. You know how good my memory is."

There was no reply to this, so Madame made none. She was acquainted with that memory.

"We have other matters to discuss," said her visitor, very softly . . .

For Jane and Arabella, it had been a happy day. They were in a mood of anticipation which made the minor grievances of life unimportant, and mishaps a source of amusement. Their plans for the next day, secret from all except Phoebe, kept them a-bubble. A drive in the park had gratified them; the colour of their ribbons had been admired by a dandy of their circle, and the brilliance of their complexions had been remarked on by the Marchioness of Harome, who had stopped her carriage with the whole object of telling them they looked well. On their return from the drive it

seemed that the day could only be fittingly completed by a dazzling evening.

"Do we dine alone, sister?" asked Arabella.

"Not quite, my dear. Mr. Watts will be with us."

"Oh! Mr. Watts! I do not regard Mr. Watts. If only Mr. Watts
is to be with us, I regard us as without company."

"I wish you would appreciate him, Arbel. I do not know a wiser
or more sensible man than Mr. Watts, more upright and true.
How do you think he has reached his present eminence? Everyone
trusts and respects him."

"I would prefer an agreeable rogue; the conversation would be
more lively."

"You would profit from listening to him with attention, and
not irritating him by pertness."

"He is with us forever, sister. One cannot walk out of the door
without falling into Mr. Watts' carriage, or pass through the vestibule without colliding with his greatcoat; and everything of his is
so very distinctive! Not to be confused with the taste of more ordinary mortals. I do not dislike him, sister. One does not dislike
the air one breathes, or the chair one sits on, and it is in precisely
this fashion that one contacts Mr. Watts, as something so ever
present that it is no longer of interest."

"There are other things in life, Bell, apart from bonnets and
possible husbands."

"Oh! How I wish there were! But how can Mr. Watts and his
news of the great world of wars and politics compare to the black
hat in Barnetts' window? Or his solid and worthy figure to the
charms of a Dragoon guard in the person of Captain Wilmott, or
the poetic elegance of Mr. Nathaniel Eeles?"

"But you do not dislike him, Arabella?"

"No, indeed. I think him all that is amiable, serious and respectable; and in this character, I will continue to tease him,
sister, as much as I can."

Mr. Watts had had a busy week, and was looking forward to a
quiet evening at Welby House. He had been warmly invited to
come early, and he did so, telling Joel Tomkins that he was expected, and making his own way up to the Egyptian Saloon. The
afternoon was dark, but it was too early for lamps and candles; by

the light of the fire Jane and Arabella were working off their high spirits by playing spillikins with Lucy and Martha. Caroline was upstairs, seeing the twins and Baby Charles safely into bed, and Richard was changing his clothes, so the group by the fire were all of the family that were available as company for the moment.

They were so happy and absorbed that they hardly noticed Mr. Watts' entrance, so he took an armchair and settled down to watch them.

Martha had only recently learned the game, so she was not very skilful; Jane was enjoying herself thoroughly, but her tall, Juno-esque figure was not well adapted to the quick darting movements which the game required. Arabella and Lucy were the undoubted champions, both deft and nimble, and the whole laughing group was a delight to the eye.

The watcher, silent except for a "bravo" at a lucky catch or a slight groan of sympathy when the little quills went scattering, found himself noticing the likenesses, and the differences, between them. They were all dressed in white, and the soft firelight showed them to advantage. Martha was the darkest of the four; tall for her eight years, her hair fell in glossy ringlets, and her eyes were deep and soulful; Lucy, at eleven the next in age, bid fair to be a beauty, for her curls were golden and her eyes—oh, so large and innocent—of speedwell blue. Both the children wore simple round gowns, short sleeved and frilled.

Jane was still in her morning dress, as she was due to go home soon and change for dinner, and Arabella, wearing her simplest evening gown—she was not going to waste her best toilettes on her brother-in-law and Mr. Watts—wore a single string of corals and had a homemade head-dress in her hair.

Mr. Watts enjoyed the general effect of light, airy fabrics daintily embroidered, moving round firm young limbs. Tall, gentle Jane was glowing even pinker than usual in the warmth of the fire. What had drawn her and Arabella together, he wondered? They were not so much alike—unlike, really. There was not much doubt that Arabella was the leader of the two, with her sparkling dark eyes, and her nimble trim figure, with its flying ribbons. Perhaps it was not a good idea for Mr. Watts, who had already discovered at the Ball that Arabella had a strong attraction for him, to sit there in the dusk, thinking that one hardly ever got the opportunity to notice the colour of Arabella's eyes; he thought they were dark grey; but they were so constantly busy expressing the interest of the moment, varying with her passing emotions, that he could be mistaken, and that might not be their colour at all.

The sky outside had changed from day to night, and Mr. Watts' attraction to Arabella had deepened considerably before Caroline's entrance stopped the game.

"You are all in the dark!" she exclaimed. "Mr. Watts cannot read, or write if he should so wish. Bell, you should have lit the lamps."

For the first time since he had known her, Mr. Watts was not pleased to see Caroline.

"I have been more than happy in the firelight," he assured her.

The game now broke up, for Lucy and Martha must go to bed, and Jane's carriage was at the door. Lady Russett was giving a grand dinner, to which the Welbys, to their relief, were not invited; Jane would only just be in time, if she went now, to be ready. Fortunately, the Russetts kept late hours. She was loath to go. She hung on Arabella's neck, and demanded a sisterly good night kiss from Lucy and Martha; but at last she could tarry no longer.

After dinner Caroline suggested cards, but neither Arabella nor Cornelius were inclined to play, so she and Richard began by themselves, arguing amicably, and scoring points against each other with the greatest satisfaction.

Arabella sat at the window until the lamplighter had lit the parish lamps, and stayed on until she felt cold; then she closed the shutters, let down the curtains, and joined the group by the fire.

After a week of arguing legal technicalities, Cornelius had not felt like the hurly-burly of London night life. The theatre, or his club, had had no charms for him that day, his own hearth even less. This evening *en famille* soothed him with its comfort and elegance, though he did not care for the Egyptian style, and would be glad when the family from the West Indies sent for their furniture, and it could return to being an English drawing-room. When he first knew her, he used to be abrupt, almost peremptory, with Arabella; but now he spoke gently:

"You and I must amuse each other, I see, Miss Hill," he said. "There is no talking to these old married people; they are too absorbed by their runs and jacks and flushes. What have you been doing of interest today?"

"Why, Mr. Watts, I saw a most delightful hat in Barnetts' window this morning; black, with French lace; I have seen it each day this week, and determine each day that I cannot afford it, only to realize on seeing it again that it is impossible to live without it."

He smiled.

"But you cannot expect us to talk long of hats, or have me express a preference for blond lace over black; the conversation would soon be over. It is not that I am quite without interest in fashion; I think the present mode, without tight lacing, much more becoming—and surely more healthful—than the artificialities of a few years ago. There are some of the dashers of the Haut Ton who go too far, but ladies of your family are not prone to such excesses. With modesty, nothing could be more charming than the current dress. But—my contribution to fashion as a topic is now exhausted."

"Then we must be silent, Sir, for other topics I have none."

"You alarm me, madam. Can you not converse on Art and Music?"

"I cannot."

"What a relief! But you play very pleasantly."

Arabella was pleased. The Russetts' pretensions had tired her of talk about Art and Music as the two chief objects of existence. At the same time she had a true and cultivated taste, and enjoyed fine painting as much as anyone; and her piano, though her playing could not approach the heights of Lady Russett's technical accomplishment, gave her many hours of pleasure. This unforced and sincere compliment, just when she was trying to be provoking, soothed and gratified her. There was a comfortable silence for a few minutes, before Cornelius spoke again.

"What was it, if I may presume to ask, which formed so absorbing a study in the street, as you gazed out of the window?"

She dimpled at him.

"Why, Mr. Watts, you know your Johnson, as well as I; when one is tired of London, one is tired of life; and it must be so, for life of every form and shade is to be found in her streets, from the most brilliant happiness, to the last depth of misery. A London street is a book which I would never tire of reading. And of course, there are the hats! You must not forget what a number and variety of hats one can see in any ten-minute gaze from our window; and as I have already told you, my main interest in life at present is the untiring pursuit of hats."

She gazed at him provocatively, but he, who was bent on getting to know her better, reacted only by asking,

"Do you never imitate your sister, and take an interest in the wider affairs of the world? Are Napoleon and his excesses nothing to you? Do you not seize on the news-sheets as the rest of us do, longing for the latest news from the Peninsula? Do you not spare time to tremble at the horrors of war?"

"I have grown up with war, Mr. Watts. My childhood was spiced with the stories of the guillotine; the fear of invasion was as strong in Hill House as in Piccadilly; but as to the papers, there is nothing in them of interest."

"Nothing of interest!" He was too much taken aback to say more. She pressed home her advantage.

"Why, no; and they themselves admit it. I will prove it to you." She got up, and searched around the room for the latest news-sheet. Richard, who had paused in his card-playing to listen, felt in the chair behind him and produced the paper, handing it to her without a word.

"Here!" she cried with energy, anxious to prove her point. Close to a candle, she searched for, and found, the column she wanted.

" '*Recent foreign newspapers received.*' Now listen to this, Sir. '*The French contains nothing more than an account of Bonaparte having left Ranbouillet.*' Is that of interest, Mr. Watts? But worse is to follow. '*The Gottenburgh Mails and some Hamburgh papers to the second ult.—contents extremely uninteresting.*' " She looked at him triumphantly. "You see, condemned out of their own mouths! '*The Emperor Alexander was expected at Riga on the tenth, from Erfurth.*' Not vital I think. '*Some more Spanish papers to the twenty-sixth ult. have reached town, but the news they bring is not very important.*' Now did I not say that the news-sheets contained nothing of interest?"

She handed him the paper, folded open at the page, with a smug expression on her face.

"One for his nob," said Caroline to Richard.

"Why," said Cornelius, "you have proved me right in every one of my suppositions and hopes. The news is of such interest to you —it is today's issue, I see—that you have, earlier today, not only seized on Mr. Welby's copy, and read it from cover to cover, but you have been so intensely disappointed to find that no real progress has been made, and the impression made on you was such, as to print on your mind the very source of your disappointment, so that you were able instantly to find out the items which had displeased you, and read them out to me with spirit. You are greatly interested in the affairs of the nation, Miss Hill; and I will look forward to many interesting conversations with you on the subject." He crossed his legs, one over the other, cocked his head on one side, and smiled at her. If at that moment a slim black shape, which absorbed the rays of the sun, was threatening his happiness, he was not aware of it. He was happy and stimulated, and Arabella, who, while he was speaking, had half looked as though she were about to give way to an April shower of crossness, began to laugh.

"The game is mine, I think, Caroline," said Richard, "and I hear the supper table."

Chapter Five

Jane and Arabella had found some wool to match the design in the footstool Arabella was embroidering for Richard.

"But I don't want a footstool," he had objected.

"You will want one when you get gout," Arabella had retorted sternly.

"Why not a screen to protect my complexion from the heat of the fire?" he had asked.

"Everyone knows that sailors have no complexions. Sea air is the ruination of them. You should use Gowlands, Richard. I am making you a footstool." And there the matter had ended.

The embroidery had been going well until she ran out of a particular blue, which had proved most elusive in the London shops, and had caused the girls to trail about searching for a fresh supply on several mornings, through places where no one but themselves would have expected to find any. Barnetts' much bedizened black bonnet, for instance, was not in a place where most people would have thought of going for sewing wool but they had passed the article of dress in question several times in their search.

This morning the elusive shade of blue was more amiable. It was found in the very place one might expect to buy it; and in good time the young ladies arrived at the Exhibition of Waxworks.

"You can go, Phoebe," said Arabella, "and pray give Mrs.

Welby the message that I am expecting to go on to Lady Russett's; I don't know what time I may be back."

Phoebe had hardly left her mistress, and was walking along the pavement, when she passed the two officers, Captains Wilmott and Bodley. She paused, and dropped a bob of a curtsey.

"The ladies have arrived, Sir," she said to Captain Wilmott, and stood meekly with downcast eyes.

"Very good! Excellent!" He felt in his pocket and gave her a slim purse, weighty for its size. Captain Bodley made as if to chuck her under the chin, but she side-stepped neatly, and went on her way. The two officers went on to visit the waxworks.

Caroline, when she had seen the girls off that morning, had been told that, apart from shopping, they were wild to see the waxworks, and she had raised no objection. In the most becoming of bonnets, and protected from the frost by their Pilgrim cloaks, they had gone escorted by Phoebe, and when their bright faces had gone from sight Caroline had gone to the Egyptian Saloon for a little quiet thought. She found the gloom very conducive to thinking, and she was worried about her sister.

She knew Arabella's quick mind; knew her preoccupation with the matter of the moment, the way that whatever was uppermost in her thoughts came out, willy nilly, the way her desires and prejudices were open and immediate, so that to have her hide anything was unknown. But now she was not being her own straightforward self. It was true that her surface preoccupation was with the black hat which she could not afford to buy; everyone was heartily sick of hearing of its perfections, and would be pleased when it was either purchased or forgotten, replaced by the next whim. But there was something else in her mind.

Caroline had one day surprised Phoebe descending the back staircase with a note in her hand, addressed, Caroline saw in an instant, in Arabella's handwriting. The girl had at once slipped it into the bosom of her dress, so swiftly that Caroline had not read the direction. She had not challenged the girl, or demanded to see it . . . perhaps it would have been wise . . . an intrigue? No, it would be a note to Jane Farley. Arabella was to be trusted. She knew as well as anyone how careful a young unmarried girl had to be, knew that to write to a young man was quite unthinkable until one was engaged to marry him, and even then it was better not, until after the ceremony . . . it was instant disgrace for an unattached girl to do such a thing—why ever had it come into her head? Arabella would never so forget herself. At one time she would have staked anything on that. Now she had a thread of doubt. What had occasioned it? Only that Arabella was brighter and more vibrantly radiant than even the realization of her dream of a winter in London would warrant, and had a secret preoccupation which she had not divulged to her sister.

Caroline was not long alone, puzzling over Arabella. The door opened quietly, and the five-year-old twins came tiptoeing round it, Henry first, pulling Kitty behind him. They did not appear to notice Caroline; Kitty was reluctant, and it took a good many fierce whispers from Henry to get her as far as the hearth rug; and there she stayed, arguing quietly, while Caroline watched, amused, from the shelter of an exotic screen.

Henry won, and the two of them advanced to the sofa, which was supported by a quartet of crocodiles. Henry went to the right, and Kitty the left, of the two at the front of the piece of furniture, and each placed something on the open maw of the mahogany reptile, and then stood back, watching eagerly, to await results.

After a few breathless minutes Kitty turned to her twin.

"They won't eat while we're here, you know," she said. "They're shy."

"We'll go out, then, and wait a bit." They tiptoed from the room with fearful glances to right and left at the gloomy sphinxes and lamps supported by snakes.

Caroline went over to the sofa and found that each carved crocodile had been fed with a small fish—and she remembered the cry of a street vendor earlier in the day, "Fish! Fresh fish!" It would not be so fresh in a week's time, she thought, if I had not spotted them . . . and, taking out one of the pieces of clean rag she carried for when Baby Charles committed an indiscretion, she removed the fishes and wrapped them up in it, then retreated hastily behind the screen as she heard the children returning.

"They've eaten them!" exclaimed Henry with awe. Both children stood gazing at the crocodiles in astonishment.

"They didn't eat those bits of meat last week," Kitty remarked. In her hiding place, Caroline shuddered. So that had been the smell; and they had blamed it on the Mummy in the corner. Just as well the Russetts had declined their invitation!

"They must like those," said Henry. "We'll have to get them again."

Caroline determined to drop a word in Betty's ear that the twins must not feed the furniture. All thought of Arabella had gone from her head. For the rest of the day she was completely wrapped up in her children and their concerns. When Phoebe came with her carefully worded message—

"Miss Hill said she might stay the night at Lady Russett's, Madam,"—she was so intent on the children that she received the message almost with indifference, just murmuring,

"Oh, that's all right, then. Yes, you may go, Phoebe, thank you."

Arabella entered the hall which housed the waxworks, and lingered slightly at the doorway, trailing her hand on the jamb of the door, and glancing behind her. Then she went on into the building, her head down, her gaze averted. She was hoping, trifling matter that it was, that where her hand had rested, Captain Wilmott's hand might rest . . .

"They are here," said Jane in a low voice.

"They?" returned Arabella, in some surprise, as though she could not think who was meant.

"Captain Wilmott and Captain Bodley have just come in."

"Oh!" and Arabella fiddled with the cuff of her glove.

"Ladies, your servant," said Captain Bodley, making a leg. Captain Wilmott followed him, and sent a meaningful glance towards Arabella.

"So we are not alone in our visit to the waxworks!" said she of the recalcitrant glove, smiling a greeting.

"I am sure that Miss Hill is never alone, unless she wishes it," replied the tall thin Captain, with an air that proclaimed the speech to be meant as gallantry.

"La, Sir!" she flipped him with her glove and turned to follow Jane, who had gone some paces farther into the room.

"And what do you think of the waxworks?" asked Captain Bodley of Jane, in a soft and familiar manner.

"We have hardly begun to inspect them," looking around her. The figures were ranged about the walls, some behind tables, seated so as to appear at meat; some standing up; and others sitting on stools.

"They are very lifelike," pronounced Captain Bodley. "That fellow over there; one would think him about to draw his sword. He has a warlike air."

"Warlike! Yes, that would appeal to you!" responded Jane. "Oh, Sir, you soldiers are so very warlike! So hard and fierce!" and she looked up at him as if in trepidation. "We women are only weak vessels beside you. I was looking at the silks on this modelled lady here, and your mind has rushed forward with celerity to that warrior, who I declare frightens me with his grisly aspect. One would think him new come from some field of slaughter."

"You are not so fearful as your friend," said Captain Wilmott to Arabella. "I am sure that I see in you a firmer spirit; you would see the glory of war, and revel in the spectacle of the victorious conqueror." He implied praise, and she replied,

"You quiz me, Sir!"

"Not I; I merely admire that boldness rare in your sex."

"Boldness, Captain Wilmott?"

"That was the wrong word to use. It implies too much." He cast about him for the right one. "Firmness; that is more my meaning. You have a noble firmness, which would be to your advantage in trouble."

She bowed slightly in reply; today she was far less talkative than Jane. Firmness! She felt little of it towards him. She moved forward, and gazed earnestly at the next group of models.

"They are very sallow, are they not?" remarked Jane. "I wonder what they are made of."

"I did hear," Captain Bodley answered her, "that beeswax is a large part of the composition, though no doubt there are other ingredients."

"Well, that accounts for it," thought Jane. "Beeswax is very yellow, really."

They stood and gazed mutely at the figures nearest to them.

Somehow this simulated skin, these imitated eyes and faked noses, gave the girls an eerie feeling. How could something look so like life, yet have no life? It was the same difficulty of confusing the image with the reality, the shadow with the substance, that the twins experienced with the crocodiles. Here a lovely young girl had been modelled, and stood in a slender imitation of youth; there a courtier matched this lady, and a musician bent over his fiddle to play a minuet, but no music could come from the instrument by the agency of those waxen hands.

They moved on to where several eminent statesmen sat in a group apparently discussing the affairs of the nation. Jane whispered to Arabella, and giggled; one at least of the party often graced the board at the Russetts' more distinguished dinners, and now Jane took her vengeance for many boring speeches she had heard from his lips by pulling a most ferocious face at him. Captain Bodley, hovering amorously near her, caught a sideways glance at it, and was most perturbed until she turned to him, smiling, and explained her action. At once he saw it as the most tremendously smart joke and, going up to a modelled General, he waggled his fingers in his direction. This jarred on Captain Wilmott, who went to his brother officer and remonstrated with him, pointing out that to behave so in their situation—officers of the King in the time of a hazardous war—to behave so was tantamount to treason. Captain Bodley laughed, and shrugged his shoulders, and for a few moments it looked as though the waxworks expedition might end in pistols for two; Bodley could not be made to see the seriousness of his offence; but at last, being an easygoing fellow, and loath to fall out with his friend over so slight a matter, he gave in and made the waxen General reparation by a most handsome salute in his direction.

They somehow drifted, chatting, round the waxworks for far longer than they realized. The sky was already losing its brightness as they emerged into the street again.

"It would be a pity," said Captain Wilmott, "to break up our party so soon. When friends so congenial are met it is always too early to part . . . May we offer you ladies some refreshment before you go? I had in mind one of the excellent goose and game pies of Mrs. Ringrose at the Rose and Crown. They are famous.

Even the French Emigrés were comforted for the loss of their chefs when they tasted Mrs. Ringrose's pies. She sends them all over the country, you know."

There was no doubt that the ladies were hungry, and particularly Jane, who had a hearty appetite. If there was one delicacy which appealed to Arabella more than anything else on a cold winter's day, it was goose and game pie; she had never tasted one of Mrs. Ringrose's, but Captain Wilmott was right about their fame. She had heard of them.

"Well . . ."

"Shall we?" asked Jane hopefully.

"Very well . . . We will accept your invitation, Sirs."

Captain Bodley had already set about hiring a hackney, and in a couple of minutes, before any minds could be changed, first Jane and then Arabella was handed into the vehicle. It was dark, and rather smelly, and the girls were in danger of being bumped about; and if the officers—in that enforced intimacy—tried to protect them by putting their arms round their waists, it was a very understandable action, and rather a pleasant one.

It was farther than Arabella had expected to the Rose and Crown. In spite of the delicious confusion of Captain Wilmott's attentions, she grew the tiniest bit anxious. Although she had sent a message to Caroline, it struck her that this might act two ways. Jane, she knew, had told Lady Russett that she intended to go home with Arabella to Welby House, so if they were delayed beyond their wishes—and this journey was certainly taking some time—no one would be alarmed; no one would come to search for them. No doubt she was being anxious for nothing, but as she felt her companion's breath warm on her cheek, she wondered.

"We're right out in the country!" exclaimed Jane. Arabella, with the Captain's hand on hers as she climbed down from the hackney, had not had sensation to spare. Now she looked round her. They had come to a hamlet among green fields. It was surprising how quickly on this side of the city one could leave behind the streets, although the deep throaty roar of London was still audible, a hum in the distance.

The Inn itself was a trim, plain building, and inside crowded with people, mainly of the middling sort. The officers made a way through, and found a corner, where they could all be ensconced together round a table. With leisure to look about, Arabella and Jane were not too displeased with what they saw. Two showily dressed girls could have been actresses, but they had dined in the company of actresses, and even of demi-reps, before in the larger entertainments. There was a certain cachet about some of them, and they could not be disregarded. Most of the customers were good, solid citizens, and would probably have been less acceptable to Lady Russett than the showy girls.

The goose and game pies came up to every expectation. As the meal progressed, and the wine circulated, the two men became more free with their attentions; they broke into song once or twice, but as very noisy singing was going on in the next room, and Captain Bodley had a very pleasant light tenor voice, it was not objectionable; they drank a toast to Arabella's bright eyes, and Jane's rosy lips, and Arabella wondered if she ought to protest at this freedom; but Captain Wilmott pressed his lips to her hand, lingeringly, and she forgot all such ideas. Their corner was cosy, and retired, so that they were not in the eye of the company, and they were enjoying themselves enormously.

After the goose and game pies there was the most tremendous discussion about what to have to follow. Custards, they understood, were available; and baked Apple Johns; and when the two men got up to go over and order, Arabella's sleeping instincts awoke. With Captain Wilmott's thigh pressed to hers no thought had been possible, except for the sweetness of the sensation; she had become almost drowsy with languor. Now a cool waft of air brought her to herself; she looked across at Jane, flushed, laughing at nothing, with her mouth lolling open, and with a shiver of apprehension, decided that her friend was a little drunk. But they had drunk nothing but a light wine, and not a great deal of that! She picked up Jane's glass, and sniffed it.

"Have some, Bell, have some," said Jane. She certainly sounded drunk. But the glass! that had a smell which was certainly not the wine Arabella had drunk. It was a heavy, sweetish smell. Laudanum? Arabella put it down hastily. Had Jane been intentionally given some noxious substance? And they were miles from home! Arabella thought they had better ask to be taken home, without delay; they would not wait for the custards or creams, or whatever the captains were ordering. Jane must be got back to her home. Arabella got up and struggled her way through the crowd towards the two men. The good-natured drinkers in the Inn impeded her progress so that she was near the officers for seconds before she could catch their attention, wriggling towards them, through the people. She had ample time to hear what they were saying to Mrs. Ringrose, before they could know she was there.

"Two bedrooms, Mrs. Ringrose," said Captain Bodley.

"And good big beds," added Wilmott. "Big enough to romp around in. I'm not one of your quiet sleepers, Ma'am."

"Just for the one night?" asked Mrs. Ringrose. "Or will you and your ladies be stopping longer?"

Arabella stayed for nothing more. She struggled her way back again to Jane, who leaned slackly against the back of her seat, with her bonnet off and her cloak askew.

"Jane," whispered Arabella, leaning across to her friend and almost hissing in her ear, "be ill!"

Had Mr. Watts been there he would have discovered one of the things which endeared Jane to Arabella, and had done so since their first meeting at Miss Merchant's Academy. At the shortest notice she could feign illness so convincingly that it would deceive an apothecary. How useful this talent had been for enlivening the more dreary wastes of Education! How excellent for escaping the tedium of sermons! It was now some time since circumstances had rendered the operation of Jane's talents desirable, but she did not hesitate to follow Arabella's command. She had found in the past that to follow Arabella's lead made life more exciting. Her facility had not decreased, in spite of lack of practice; she began to produce the slow beginnings of what was to be a very orchestration of symptoms. Arabella had feared that in her friend's fuddled condition she might not respond; her quick brain had been searching for alternative plans, even as she leaned across to Jane; but as she saw the response, she relaxed, and was even able to turn to the officers with feigned pleasure, when they returned to the table in the corner, and pretend to take an interest in what sweets they had ordered.

It was not long before the two young men became perturbed at the growing indisposition of their companion, and Arabella, with every appearance of taking charge in a desperate situation, got up from her corner and went in search of Mrs. Ringrose.

"Madam," she said, "my friend is taken ill. I fear I must take her to visit your House of Convenience. Can you direct me? With that relief she may feel a little better."

"It's across the yard," said Mrs. Ringrose doubtfully, "and at this time of year the ground is inches deep in mud. Ladies usually use a Pot in the back chamber. I hope you're not going to blame my pies, mind? We never have any trouble with them. Sent all over the country, you know."

"I hope to send one to my father. No, have no fear for the reputation of your pies. Give me a little brandy and show us the way to your back room."

Holding the brandy in one hand and supporting her groaning friend with the other as well as she could, Arabella declined the proffered help of Captain Bodley, who looked both worried and chagrined, and with a brave smile assured the Captains that she was sure half an hour alone would soon restore Jane to her normal self. They tottered through the crowd, who did their best to give way, to the doorway Mrs. Ringrose showed them.

Once inside, Jane kept up her barrage of cries and groans while Arabella flew to the window and looked out.

"How fortunate we're still on the ground floor," she panted, wrestling with the window.

At last she managed to open it, and lean out. There was only a very little drop to the ground outside, but by the fitful light of the rising moon she could see that the earth below was indeed all mire and mud.

"Why, Bell?" whispered Jane, in between groans.

"They were planning to seduce us," explained her friend, and in a few sentences said what she thought had been planned for their entertainment. Jane's head seemed to have cleared remarkably, and she took this in silence.

"What now?" she asked.

"We're going," replied Arabella, and swung her legs out of the window.

To those who climb trees for pleasure, this venture was easy. A few seconds took them to the ground in safety, a few more and they were at the entrance to the inn yard from the lane, looking to right and left. To the right past the side of the Inn, lay the high road down which they had travelled earlier.

"Have you any money?" hissed Arabella. "It will cost us several pence a mile on the stage, if we can find one."

"Lud! I haven't as much as that," replied Jane, feeling the weight of her reticule in a worried way.

"We'll have to manage without money, then, for I find I have nothing left in my purse but a few farthings. I don't think we can go that way." She indicated the road. "They will go there at once, as soon as they find we are missing. What's down here?"

What was down there was the Thames, slipping past in all its strength and power, even in this more upstream section of its flow.

"We can't swim in this weather, Bell."

"We can row," said Arabella, falling over the first of a line of boats pulled up on to the bank, and secured to a group of posts. In summer they were hired out to pleasure seekers wishing to venture on the river; but in winter they sank into the river bank unheeded until the first of the townsfolk felt the stirrings of spring, when they were hastily painted and furbished to serve the trade. Upstream was the more serviceable craft of the ferryman; but Arabella could not see so far in the darkness. She settled on a boat and set to turning it over and pushing its keel into the water. Jane helped, and between them they succeeded, jumping in quickly as soon as it was afloat. Arabella had been soaked to mid-calf in the process, and the craft was not river-worthy enough to stop Jane's feet going the same way, and her delicate shoes, already muddy, being soaked by the water that seeped in through the planks. Arabella had pushed an oar into her hand, from a pile that were just inside the door of a shed on the water's edge, and taken another for herself. She pushed firmly against the muddy bank, and they swung out into the middle of the water and began a silken progress downstream.

For a while the two sat without either speaking or rowing. They looked backwards to the dim lights of the little hamlet, and as they receded found it difficult to make out the brighter lights of the Inn. They had heard no hue and cry; so far they had probably not been missed, and when they were, it was most unlikely that anyone would look to the river.

"I'm sorry, Jane," said Arabella. "I'm a sad romp, and, I fear, a flirt. I enjoyed every moment of Captain Wilmott's attentions; that we should come to such a pass did not occur to me. We might have lost our maidenhood, and then who would have married us? We would have been disgraced, and cast out from decent society. Our families would prefer that we drown," she finished lugubriously.

"I do hope we don't," answered Jane, peering down at her feet. "Don't you think we ought to bail this out, Bell?"

"What with?" Jane just sighed in reply. At least the water swishing in the bottom was getting no deeper.

"Do you really think they meant to seduce us? It seemed a very respectable Inn to me."

"Oh, yes . . . quite respectable . . . but what I heard made me sure their object was our downfall. And your glass, Jane! It had something—it smelled of something—perhaps gin, or something more potent—"

"I did drop some of the mixture the apothecary gave me for my headache, into the wine," volunteered Jane, who appeared, now Arabella had leisure to notice it, much more sober than she had seemed at the Inn. For a while they sat and in the gloom watched the water as the boat drove through the gentle swish of ripples. They were being carried along swiftly enough to make rowing seem, for the moment at least, unnecessary. Thank goodness they had been forced to take notice of Caroline and wear their warm Pilgrim cloaks, though their bonnets were left behind at the Inn. They shivered even in the substantial fabric wrapped round them. The banks melted into the water in the darkness, and could not be distinguished; only now and then, when the moon came from behind the clouds and lit a group of trees, or a riverside villa, did they realize that they were still on the river and not upon some unending ocean, where there were no landmarks, and nothing but the stars and clouds overhead, the heaving water around. The majesty of the night and the deep tranquillity of the universe above them, the endless swell of the water beneath, like the deep breaths of a mother who carries her children ever onward, made words seem petty and meaningless. Soon the whole scene' at the crowded Inn, with its shouting and songs, seemed as irrelevant as a card game seems to a worshipper in some vast cathedral.

At last Arabella and Jane began to row and, bent in time, listened, now their ears were attuned, to the sound of the water as it flowed from the prow of the boat to the stern, one wavelet after another. They heard the dip of their oars, and the spatter of drops when they lifted them clear of the surface; their hearing seemed so keen that they could detect as they passed the movement of a vole in the river bank, and thought they could tell where an otter slipped into the water. A cry on the bank told them a vixen was hunting, and the nearer plop of a frog and small secret sounds told them that the night was alive around them.

Their hands, unprotected, were soon rigid with cold, clenched to the oars as though they would never undo again. The Pilgrim cloaks fell back and exposed their forearms to the cold. Round the middle and over the shoulders, they kept warm by muscular effort; but as time wore on and night deepened, the ache in their shoulders strengthened and became worthy of the name of pain. Their feet were soon so cold as to be insensible, and damp and pain crept upwards to their knees. Jane was regretting the warmth and light of the Inn, and wondering how many miles they had to go.

At last they came once more among buildings, and the banks seemed to close in now they were defined by the villas and crescents of the outlying city. Rain began to fall, at first thinly, then as the moon was hidden by vague, formless clouds, with increasing persistence, so that the slowly rising bilge was swelled by splashing rain, and the protective cloaks became sodden and useless.

Jane began to shiver; at last she was no longer able to control it, and shook helplessly. Arabella felt the tremors through the foot which was resting against hers, and took both oars. She began to guide them towards the left-hand bank of the river, forcing her arms to rise and fall in spite of her weariness and pain. She drew in closer and closer to the houses, and did not ask Jane to help.

"I'm sorry," whispered Jane in her turn. "I had the headache yesterday, but thought it had gone. Can you manage without me, Bell?"

"Of course," said Arabella curtly.

She was looking for a place to land. At last, as the river seemed to come alive around them with late travellers of the city being ferried from shore to shore, or pressing upstream towards their homes, she saw a flight of steps which she fancied had a hospitable look, and decided to try to reach them before she had to tackle any of the Thames' bridges. One oar and then the other dipped skilfully into the water, swinging the boat towards the bank; the dimly seen flight of steps came nearer, and nearer. At the head of them could be seen a house with a light in its window, and beyond that the black bulk of a bridge.

"Here," whispered Arabella. She slowed the little craft to a stop and held it steady with an oar.

Chapter Six

"Look, there's a handrail. Can you catch hold of it, Jane? Mind! You'll tip us over . . . right . . . can you get the painter? Just hold her a minute till I get out . . ."

It almost tipped; but not quite. Her foot, insensible of the blow, hit against the step; she felt forward and placed it firmly on the stone. Although the other foot almost flew from under her, she caught hold of the shaking Jane and stood safe. Then it was the work of the frozen fingers to tie the boat up.

"You know what we've done," said Jane in a low voice. "We've trapped ourselves. There's no way round this house. It enters straight on to the steps. To get up into the Town, the only way is through it."

She was right. The little flight of steps led to the door, and only to the door. On either side the bank fell away. The foundations of the house went down vertically, it seemed, into the Thames itself.

"Then we too must go through the house."

"They might be thieves or robbers."

"What have we to lose?"

"Our reputations," replied Jane sharply. "Our clothes. Our lives."

"It is such a kindly light. Such a friendly set of steps. I cannot believe the worst of the inhabitants. I am going to knock. If they seem threatening, and we are quick, we can get down into the boat again and away . . . but pray we do not have to."

It was not possible to take more than a sideways glance into the lighted room although it had neither curtains nor shutters because of the angle of the stairs; so Arabella beat on the solid door with her knuckles, and at last it opened. An old man stood there in a passage, for the door did not open, as the girls had thought, into the lighted room; he was holding a lantern; white wisps of hair framed his face, haloing it in the lanternlight.

"Who is it?" He spoke almost fearfully. "Is that you, Jack?"

"I beg your pardon, good sir," said Jane, who had taken heart at his looks; "my friend and I are benighted upon the river. May we come through your house and up on to the road, so that we can walk home?" Her voice trembled with cold and fatigue. The old man's eyes had grown used to the dark, and seen them.

"Come in," he said. "We refuse shelter to no Christian."

They followed him into a bare room, simply furnished with a table and a few chairs; a Bible lay open on the table, and an old woman sat with her hands folded in her lap, looking at them with a face of that extreme beauty which the very old sometimes possess when their souls are filled with tranquillity.

"Who is it, Isaac? Young women? They can be up to no good, on the river at this time of a winter's night." She looked them up and down. "They cannot be ladies, although their dress is modest —no gentlewoman would be out so late upon the river."

"We are better than we appear, good people," said Arabella, with a trace of arrogance in her voice. "We have been foolish, but not wicked; and only want to get home again to our families."

"What families?" enquired the old man. His bright blue eyes were fixed upon them. His face was broad, with wide cheekbones, so that it was almost wider than it was long, and bronzed with the weather. He had a wide, square forehead and his neck was almost as wide as his head, so that it was obvious how strong and muscular he was, built like a clinkerbuilt boat.

"The Welby family at Welby House, and Lord and Lady Russett."

"It seems to me," said the old man to his wife, "that we have had one, recently come among us, an attender, who is in service to a family named Welby."

"William Pigeon," agreed the old woman.

"William!" cried Arabella. "Now I see! You are of the people called Quakers, and you have met our William—he is acting as butler, and is everything that a family needs in a sturdy manservant."

"We have not formed an opinion," said the old woman cautiously. "First impressions can be very wrong ones. He seems an upright young man, and is hoping to marry a Friend from the Linchester Meeting."

"Hannah Sharpe!" cried Arabella. "Our dairymaid?"

"But what sort of family is he serving," said the old man to his wife, "when the ladies of the family row about the river alone when dark has fallen?"

"We did not have that intention," pleaded Jane, who feared that far from being a recommendation that they knew William, they were more likely to prove his undoing with their flighty ways. No doubt reports could pass from one Meeting to another.

"He would not approve of our foolishness," remarked Arabella, "and would no doubt have prevented it had he been on hand to do so." (For he'd certainly go tittle-tattling to Caroline, she thought, if he had known we were misbehaving. And meanwhile, good people, this is getting us nowhere, and we are cold and wet, and Jane is shivering and not at all well, in earnest this time.)

It seemed that William's name was to be a passport to help, after all; for the old woman got up and set a pan of milk to warm on the fire, and took bread and broke it into two basins; then, when the milk was on the verge of boiling, which it soon was, for the fire was clear and bright, she poured the hot liquid over the bread and set the basins before the two girls. They had sat themselves down, at her husband's request, on two stools and, taking up the horn spoons, they ate the bread and milk with enjoyment. They had spent a great while getting very cold and wet since they had eaten Mrs. Ringrose's pies, and Jane almost stopped shivering when the warm food was inside her.

At last the old man put a great wide-brimmed hat on his head, took a stout stick in his hand, and prepared to escort them on their way.

"Wait," he said, when they were all standing, ready to go, "what about your boat?"

"Oh, it isn't our boat," said Arabella airily. "It belongs to the Rose and Crown, we suppose. We took it to get down the river."

"Took it?" Both the Quakers gazed at her as though she had pronounced blasphemy. "You took what was not yours?"

"And we have taken her in, and given her bread!" moaned the old woman, sinking down on her chair.

"Do you gentlefolk not realize," said the old man, "what it is to steal? For a theft such as this, a poor starving man would be deported, if he escaped hanging. And you stand there on our hearth so cheerfully and tell us that the boat that swings on its rope at the bottom of our water stair is stolen."

"We'll send William, tomorrow, to take it back, and pay Mrs. Ringrose for our use of it," offered Arabella, but the old man's face clouded at her words. They had been unfortunate, she realized at once. As well as damning William by showing him as serving in a family which could not control its daughters who ran wild in consequence, she was now making him connive at a theft.

The old man straightened his shoulders.

"We will not bring anyone else into this," he said. "I know the river as my hand, and I am known to Mrs. Ringrose of the Rose and Crown, even as far upstream as it is. She knows that she can trust the word of Isaac Sutherland. I will ask her to send you a reckoning for the use of her boat. No doubt she will charge you far more than is warranted, for the way in which you took it."

"Goodbye to my black hat," muttered Arabella rebelliously.

"Goodbye, Mistress Sutherland," said Jane politely. "We are most grateful for your kindness." She smiled sweetly at the old woman, Arabella echoed her thanks with as good a grace as she could and they went out after Isaac Sutherland and picked their way by the flickering light of his lantern up to the level of the high road, and turned towards town. The winter dusk had thickened completely into night long since, and even the moon was hidden by the rain clouds, but the road was still busy with chairs, hackneys, and a few late travellers on horseback.

Arabella told the old Quaker that they would cheerfully go alone, it was not very far, and they hesitated to trouble him further; but he looked so scathingly at her in the lanternlight, that she desisted; and indeed, they were glad to have his protection. The dark alleys leading off to either side of the road looked only too likely to be the hiding places of footpads, and the foolish adventure needed no compounding.

"You haven't found her, then?" The Earl's long hand was tapping on the arm of his chair. Mr. Watts was at Arden Priory.

"It can't be much longer before she gets in touch. A legacy has a powerful effect on the mind of the ordinary class of folk."

"At least you found Madame Eglantine." The Earl sighed. "I suppose that's something."

Cornelius Watts stiffened, but did not reply. The name of Mirabelle was with him day and night, disturbing his peace; and he could still hear Madame Eglantine, saying, "She is one of the damned!"

"I'll be coming to Town in a week or two. If she hasn't appeared by then, I'll go and see Madame Eglantine myself. Not that I don't thank you, Watts," he added hastily. "I just want to be rid of the business."

There was nothing to say to dispel the Earl of Epworth's gloom; nothing to do, but take leave, and ride back to London. It was very early in the morning, and, wherever possible using the bridleways inaccessible to coaches, and being a first-class horseman, Cornelius made good time on the journey, and realized as he reached the outskirts of London that he was an hour earlier than he had expected. He was tired, but on the spur of the moment, to try to settle his restlessness he decided to make a detour, and at the time that Arabella and Jane were climbing out of the window of the Inn, he was riding into a quiet street which he had first entered twenty years before.

He dismounted, tied up his horse, tapped at the door of a cottage, and then waited.

It was in one of those villages which, once considered quite far out of London, had by the middle of the eighteenth century become embedded in it, yet kept their rural air. There was still a

duckpond at the end of the street, and the withered stalks of hol-
lyhocks tapped against the windows of the cottage. Cornelius
could not help remembering how he had felt, those twenty years
before. How exciting it had seemed that his feet were walking a
London street! Although neither of them knew it, his thoughts at
that time had been very much those of Arabella not many weeks
ago, when she too found London to be her promised land. Now
Cornelius looked down at his feet, humorously. There was still no
place on earth that he would rather be. But not everyone shared
his feelings.

An old woman, with white hair showing under her cap, opened
the door at last, and peered out at him.

"Nanny Green," he said.

"Cornelius Watts! I'd know thee anywhere; you still stand
straddle-legged, like a cock crowing on a dunghill . . . come in."

He went into the dim firelight, and she waved him to a joint
stool by the hearth.

"You haven't gone back to your valley, yet, then, Nanny? I
thought I might not find you here."

"No." She sat silently opposite him, then said dreamily, "I shall
never see it again. Never see Gaunt Moss frowning, like, against
the sky, or the river running down between the stones and rocks,
with water cold and sweet. I will not taste that water again until I
taste it in Paradise."

"Is it for lack of the cost of the journey? I'd make you a gift of
it."

"No!"—now the negative was contemptuous. "I'm not too
proud to take it, don't think that. But the parish here will have to
keep me, if I need it, and I've no settlement up there—they could
send me back."

"Your own people!"

"There won't be any now that remembers young Annie."

For a while the old woman gazed into the fire, and the tired
Mr. Watts was content to be silent.

"You didn't come, after so many years, to ask how I did," she
said at last. "You're looking well. You've done well for yourself,
anyone can see that." She took the collar of his coat between her
fingers and felt the cloth. "That's a hardwearing bit of stuff. I'll

bet I know the moor those sheep heafed to . . . in the daylight at one time I could have told you the man who wove it . . ." The clothes Arabella had spoken of so slightingly were carefully appraised by the old woman. "Those are good stockings, I couldn't have knit better myself. You choose well, Cornelius. Have you chosen a wife yet? Maybe you've a crowd of little uns."

"No wife," he answered. "No children."

Both their minds were back in the time many years before. Nanny Green sighed.

"Aye," she spoke slowly. "It was a bad business."

"Did you ever hear of them? After they went to France, did you ever get a message? Did Mirabelle write?"

"I'm glad you've come, Cornelius. I couldn't have died happy without seeing you, and confessing that I did you a wrong. I lied to you, Cornelius."

He looked at the transparently honest face of the old woman, and found himself unable to say anything. She got up and searched about, producing a brown bottle from a cupboard, a saucepan, and a jug of water.

"You'll take a toddy with an old friend?"

He nodded, and Mrs. Green set to make it. It was not until they were both supplied with a steaming toddy that she said anything further, and then it was not to the point.

"You remember first coming here, Cornelius? Just a lad you were, seventeen or thereabouts. A noisy, cheerful, racketing lad. The old Chevalier and his daughter were already my lodgers when I took you in, and you all got friendly in no time."

"He was kind to a rough young man," said Cornelius, "until he saw that I had fallen in love with Mirabelle."

"A sweet, gentle girl she was."

"There aren't many girls like that. I've only met one since— Miss Jane Farley; she has something of Mirabelle's sweetness."

"But the Chevalier didn't think you were good enough for his daughter, did he? Isn't that the truth?"

"It's true enough. That's why I left you, and went to live in; I thought that if I worked hard and got on, he might change his mind; but the next time I came back to see her, they had gone, and you told me they had gone back to France. The Chevalier thought it was safe, and they went."

"That's what I told you, and I beg your pardon for it; but it was not the truth."

He looked at her face in the dim firelight.

"I can't believe that you would tell a lie, Nanny, not if your life depended on it."

"I'm ashamed of it. Here, in the time of my old age, you hear me, Cornelius. It's the only time in my life I told a lie, and I was tempted—the Chevalier gave me money to tell you that, and I was in great need of it. If I had thought it would make any difference to thee—then not Satan himself would have tempted me. But he was determined you were never to have Mirabelle, and so it didn't make any difference, I thought."

"I don't understand this," said Cornelius, "because they did go to France. I worked hard, and began to make money, and when you told me they had gone to France, I waited a bit longer— another year or two, maybe three—and then wrote to him, and begged permission to marry Mirabelle—but he replied that she was dead."

"Your letter reached him then, the Chevalier?"

"Oh, yes. I sent a messenger, very trustworthy, and paid him well; he found the Chevalier. Living alone, I heard; poor, but still haughty; he wrote back to me, and I still have the letter I was brought from him, saying that Mirabelle was dead."

"Maybe she was, by that time. But when I told you they had gone back to France, it was because she was being courted by some rich man, with a handle to his name, and the Chevalier didn't want you hanging about, even if you were making a fortune. They left this house and got lodgings somewhere else."

He stared thoughtfully into the fire.

"It couldn't have made any difference," he spoke slowly. "As you say, Nanny, he would never have let me marry her, so it made no difference. Perhaps it was for the best. Thinking she was in France, I got on and made money. Then when I heard she was dead, work had started to mean much to me for its own sake, and I thought no more of marrying. Until lately, that is. Lately, I have wondered . . ."

"This Miss Jane thee mentioned?"

"No. Now I'm older, sweetness is no longer enough. I want someone I can talk to, share with . . . I spend what time I can trying to make things better in this city . . . my partner and I started a training school for girls, like the Royal Institutions' training for young men, but in a very small way. And there are other things I have a hand in. I would want a wife to support me with her concern for others, and not live only for herself. A lively girl, with a generous heart."

When Cornelius left Nanny Green, it was much later than he had intended. They had sat on in the firelight, chatting of other days. Glancing round the room, Cornelius could almost see again Mirabelle, with her golden head gleaming in the soft light, coming into the room from the stairs, walking to the table to lay something down, smiling gently at him. It was a sweet sadness, looking back to the days of his first love, his first youth. His heart which, perhaps, in all these years of work and striving, had forgotten some of its tenderness, except to plants, animals, and the young lost ones of the city, was waking again to the warmth of deep and tender love . . .

At last he said farewell to the old woman.

"See thee does not leave it so long before coming again," she admonished him, but even as he promised, they both of them knew that it would almost certainly be their last meeting.

He rode, deep in some sort of wordless meditation, back into the main route. The night was dark and wet, and the day's long journeyings were making themselves felt in aching muscles, and tired mind. Wayfarers on foot were few on such a night as this. There were other horsemen, and the jingle of hackneys, the rumble of carriages, were all around him. At the side of the road he noticed, idly, a group walking along with a lantern.

They were trudging on in silence. It was still raining, and since the girls were already sodden, from that point of view it made no difference; but all the difference in the world to their spirits. The horseman clip-clopped up behind them, and to him there was something familiar in the gait of at least one of the party. The warmth in his heart was chilled. Some escapade! Some madcap prank! He drew up beside Isaac Sutherland, and spoke in a voice cold with disapproval.

"Surely I do not see Miss Hill?" were the words that astonished them.

Arabella swung her head up to a defiant angle.

"It is!" Cornelius exclaimed, looking first at Arabella and then, with keen suspicion, at the old Quaker, who stood four-square, holding the lantern so that it shone up at the stranger. "Who is this?"

"I might ask who you are, friend, who accosts a young gentlewoman in the public way. I am Isaac Sutherland, of the people called Quakers."

"I give you good morrow, sir. I am Cornelius Watts, of the City; an old friend of Miss Hill's family, and known to the parents of Miss Farley. May I ask how it comes about that you are taking these ladies at this hour of the night to . . ." He was addressing himself completely to Isaac, and ignoring the girls.

"Oh! Mr. Watts!" cried Arabella. "This good man and his wife gave us shelter, and he is taking us home. Could you—could you—could you hire us a hackney, for Jane is so tired and wet, and so am I, and we haven't any money?" Untrue, for they had at least twopence; but not enough to be of use.

He agreed, though his manner was frosty. But he hired a passing hackney which luckily had a reasonably fresh horse, instructed the driver, and thanked Isaac Sutherland; and with the thanks of both girls, and their assurance that they would be quite safe in Mr. Watts' care, the Quaker turned and hurried back to his own house. Mr. Watts rode behind the vehicle, and came up beside it as they arrived at Arabella's home.

"Come and stay the night, Jane," urged Arabella, but Jane refused in a whisper.

"Another time," she said. "But now I want to get home. Please, Bell," and the tired note in her voice was enough for Arabella. With a kiss she got out and found Mr. Watts' arm waiting for her.

"Please don't tell my sister," she begged him. "We've learned our lesson, it's been miserable. Let me go in the kitchen way and up to my room."

It was against his judgement, but he gave in, and she slipped down the stairs to the basement, and swung open the door to the scullery. Going past the kitchen door, she called softly, "Phoebe!" and the girl came out and attended her upstairs, without showing any surprise.

Mr. Watts went on to Jane's house, and took her to the door. Her parents were out, so he handed her over to her maidservant. He had thought of scolding her, in a fatherly way, for this evening of apparent indiscretion, automatically blaming it on Arabella; but in the lamplight of the entrance he could see what a state she was in, and he had not the heart to scold, but gave her hand a friendly squeeze, and found himself saying that he would say absolutely nothing.

Phoebe helped Arabella off with her wet things, and into a loose gown of the Turkish style. In front of the mirror, she began to take out hairpins and lay them one by one on the dressing-table, before brushing out her mistress's hair.

"You need not mention this, Phoebe," remarked Arabella, "to anyone."

Phoebe did not answer; but her eyes moved round, until in the mirror she could be seen to be looking rather intently at a neckhandkerchief figured with Ayrshire flowering, which Arabella had but lately bought. At last Bell came to a conclusion. She reached out and picked up the kerchief, and handed it to Phoebe. Phoebe took it, and tucked it into her pocket.

"Oh, thank you, Madam," she said. "Of course I would not think of speaking of your affairs. It was not necessary to make me a gift."

"I don't suppose you, as a Methody, could wear it anyway," said Arabella. "Aren't you against adornments?"

"Well—modest white things are acceptable," her maid answered. "And I am not as convinced as I was of the rightness of my beliefs. Joel Tomkins is a worshipper at the Parish Church, you see, Madam."

"Oh . . . sets the wind in that quarter . . ." Arabella said no more. She did not know whether she despised herself more for offering the kerchief, or Phoebe for taking it. Uppermost in her mind was the longing for rest and oblivion. She hoped Phoebe had given the bed a good airing with the warming pan.

Arabella got up in the morning none the worse for her soaking, her spirits as bright as usual, and went in her accustomed way to call for Jane. But when she arrived at the Russetts' house, the butler told her that Jane was indisposed; and, having asked to see her, Arabella went up to Jane's bedchamber to find her still in bed, and looking flushed and feverish. It was obviously best not to stay; Arabella gave her friend a gentle kiss and left her to rest.

The next day Jane was too delirious to recognize her; she tossed about, calling out for Robert, and Arabella left her feeling very worried indeed, more chastened and ashamed than she had been at that moment when Mr. Watts had intercepted them as they struggled towards home. The blame was all hers! Her spirits were down, way down, and she was miserable and depressed. She blamed herself for the whole Waxworks scheme—though she was no more to blame than Jane, and much less than the Officers; she blamed herself for the agreement to eat goose and game pies, though Jane had wished to go at least as much as she; she blamed herself for the sudden exit from the Inn via the window, and the soaking they got on the river. There at least she was justified, for if she had told Mrs. Ringrose of her fears, that good-hearted woman would have seen that they got safely home, without the dramatic flight; but even in this unhappy moment, that course of action never occurred to Arabella. She made herself judge and jury, and condemned herself, without seeing how she could have behaved otherwise. She decided that one should never go adventuring without at least a guinea in one's pocket. If Jane should die! How should she bear it? So many people, apparently in the pink of health, were carried off on less provocation. Alone in her room, she wept, then making an effort, went down into the morning room, and stood looking out into the garden, and trying to put her new opinions into words. After being motionless for some time, she remarked,

"Flirtation is an excessively bad thing."

"Oh, excessively," agreed Caroline, looking at her in surprise.

"It arises from health, youth and high spirits; but it can have dire consequences."

"Indeed it can," agreed her sister.

"Seduction, illness, even death, can arise from it," announced Arabella solemnly.

"Whatever gives rise to these moral reflections?"

"I have been observing the world, sister; I am resolved in future to safeguard my reputation from any imputation of lightness."

"Well, if you mean you are going to be more restrained and less like a jack-in-the-box, it will be a relief to me."

"The Cyprians one sees in their carriages seem to do well out of lightness, in fact immorality," remarked Richard, who had been sitting lazily on one side of the fireplace.

"Richard!" remonstrated his wife.

"The drabs in the streets come off badly," replied Arabella. She realized that she had sounded sententious, even to the point of absurdity; but she had suddenly seen how thin the dividing line was, over which she might step so lightheartedly. She could settle to nothing, missing Jane; and—it was hard to admit it—but her heart had been touched by Captain Wilmott, brief and frivolous though the association had been; she could not now exist without thinking of him. Unbidden thoughts; a recollection of the glance of a bright hazel eye, a shadow reminding her of his shape, bringing unwanted some outline of his movement to her mind. Richard sometimes had a turn of phrase not dissimilar to Captain Wilmott's; earlier in her walk through the streets she had glimpsed a red coat, and thought of him. How their evening at Almacks, the previous week, had been spoilt for her because he was not there!

"There are but six red coats in the room," she had declared pettishly to Lady Russett, who had opened her eyes in the staring way she had and had exclaimed,

"I hope you do not run after officers, Miss Hill; that would be vulgar, and bad tone; and out of place in a friend of my daughter's." Arabella had heard the rebuke meekly without giving a pert reply. For it had been too near true. She had felt that as they walked round the waxworks, she would have run after Captain Wilmott to the ends of the earth if he had asked her. And then to be so suddenly disillusioned—to have so quick a conviction that by love they were to be betrayed. Had she—was it possible that she had been mistaken? Had he all the time been honourable, and the deceit a figment of her active imagination? Was dear Jane the victim of a mistake? It had been a mistake over the wine glass; the smell was Jane's medicine. It was the beginning of the longest week Arabella had ever known.

Jane did not recognize her own mother; she cried out all the time for Robert Spencer, and spoke deliriously of trees, and rowing, and water, and the old Rectory at Littlethorpe; so that Lady Russett was concerned enough to put by one evening party, and sit for a whole hour at the bedside of her younger daughter.

Caroline did not want Arabella to break her engagements; she did not think long evenings at home, spent in worrying the lives out of herself and Richard, would help Jane's recovery. So the evening card parties were attended, and the dinners eaten; and if anyone remarked on Miss Hill's lack of spirits, they were met by eyes so large and tragic that they thought they had trespassed on some hidden tragedy, and retreated with murmurs of sympathy.

The news of the day met with scant attention from Arabella. The brief rumour that there was an imminent possibility of peace was soon countered by the news that the French people had accepted conscription, making it less likely that Napoleon would cease to wage war when he could have unlimited armies. Parliament was prorogued to the eighth of December, but Arabella was blankly indifferent. She heard of news of captures at sea, which so excited Richard, and, through him, Caroline, with as little interest as she used to hear of stock and harvest from her father. She had been forbidden to visit Jane for fear of infection, and one day dragged by after another. A very little interest—a very little—was aroused by the fighting in Spain; the long roll-call of troops which were to serve with Sir John Moore were listened to—they were leaving Lisbon; the Eighteenth Light Dragoons; the First Battalion of the Second, the Third, the Fourth, the Fifth, the Sixth—the Second Battalion of the Forty-third—the Third Light Dragoons—the First Battalion of the Fourth Company of Foot—she lost count as the list marched on. All this backed up by still more troops left in Lisbon! Surely the French would not have a chance. The Spanish people themselves did not side with their oppressors.

They were only waiting to rise and throw every Frenchman off their soil. Then there was the array of ships on the Tagus; the *Hibernia*; the *Audacious*; the *Ganges*; the *Plantagenet*; the *Resolution*; the *Nymph*; the *Lively*; the *Comus*; the *Undaunted*; the *Myrtle*; the *Nautilus* . . . Richard read out their names and made them sound like a roll-call against the tyrant.

Nor was life in England only exciting by means of these vicarious adventures. Parliament had been prorogued again, this time to the sixteenth of January; a Charity Ball had, it was announced, been opened by a Minuet, followed by a Strathspey; Indelible Marking Ink, for marking linen, had been put on the market at the immensely reasonable price of 4/- a packet; and the Lottery, rendering a multitude of adventurers happy (far happier than by the prospect of battles in Spain), by the chance of winning a fortune at home. Halves, eighths, even sixteenths, of a ticket could be purchased, and everyone knew someone who had heard of someone who had won a lottery, and become rich for ever with this one stroke of fortune.

Everywhere, Spanish fashions in costume prevailed in honour of our Spanish allies. Although usually considered too commanding for the streets, they came into their own in the evenings, when substantial British matrons appeared in their dressmakers' idea of the dress worn in Spain. Caroline did not think the style suited her; so she bought instead a scarlet mantle embroidered with black velvet in the Tuscan manner, with a full collar; but she could interest her sister in nothing.

A week had passed in this unsatisfactory manner when Arabella, out shopping with Phoebe, decided to ignore her sister's prohibition, and again visit Jane. She was allowed up into the bedchamber, dark with drawn curtains, and bent over the bed. Jane appeared to know her, but was too weak to speak. On her way out after a very few minutes Jane's maid intercepted her and asked for a word. They went into the antechamber.

"I'm so glad you've come, Miss Hill," said the woman. "I don't know what to do for the best. Here's Miss Jane been crying and calling out for Mr. Robert, as if her heart would break; and here he is in Town, and wanting to see her, and there's nothing I can do about it."

"In Town? Mr. Spencer in Town? How do you know?"

"He sent Miss Jane a note. Oh, it was very wrong of me, Miss, but I didn't know what to do; I guessed it was from him, and—I didn't want to give it to Her Ladyship—she's so down on them, and he's as good a young man as ever was; I opened it, and it seems he's in London for a few days. Oh, the sight of him would do my mistress more good than all the Apothecaries."

"It would," said Arabella thoughtfully. "You haven't let Miss Farley see this note?"

"She was delirious, Miss, until this morning. I daren't worry her. If she knew he was near and she couldn't see him it would make her worse. But Mr. Spencer ought to know how things are. They have engaged themselves to each other, even if Lady Russett doesn't agree."

"May I see it?"

The note was produced.

"So! He's putting up there—it's not far away. Look, do you think we can arrange for him to come in and see Jane?"

"In her bedchamber, Miss?"

"It doesn't matter when anyone's as ill as Jane is. Don't you think it would do her good to see him?"

"It would be like a tonic. It would make her want to live."

"Then we'll try. But Lady Russett mustn't know. Can you be secret? Then I'll bring him." Arabella thought, and remembered how Jane had once, at school, dressed up as a boy, "and quite deceived Miss Rose." Her resolutions about good and circumspect behaviour were entirely forgotten. "I'll bring him in disguise, dressed as my maid. And I'll stay in the room all the time, so there can be no impropriety! I'll bring him today if I can, or if not, in the morning. No more now; I'll go and see Mr. Spencer."

She made all the haste she could, and on the way catechized Phoebe.

"You're taller than me, Phoebe. How tall? Does that cloak have a decent hem? Let me see—a good two inches. And it has a hood, that's better still. Thank goodness, I've got my chatelaine, it has a very useful pair of scissors. Useful for cutting the stitches of hems, Phoebe dear. You are going to stay in the Inn in your petticoat until I come back for you. Don't be silly, girl. I'm not asking you to be in public. I imagine Mr. Spencer will have a private room you can stay in. I'm going to have a different maid, that's all. No, you've done nothing to displease me. Do be quiet. Here we are."

Robert Spencer was in, and Arabella and Phoebe were shown up to his sitting-room directly. He was delighted to see Arabella, knowing from Jane's letters that she was in the secret.

"For we consider ourselves affianced, so it is quite proper for her to write to me," he said.

"Lady Russett would not share your opinion."

"Do you think I would risk harming Jane's reputation? We will marry, I assure you, Miss Hill; so the correspondence is not improper. Has she sent you to me with a note?"

"Jane is ill, Mr. Spencer; very ill; until this morning her life was despaired of, and she may even now succumb."

"No!" As she looked at his face, Arabella's heart melted with sympathy.

"I'm sorry to bear such bad news. Her maid has your letter, but thought it wise not to let Jane see it."

"If only I could see her! I leave for Cornwall again tomorrow. Oh, if there was some way to see her, if only for a moment! But Lady Russett would never allow it."

"I think such a meeting would do nothing but good." She hesitated, then plucked up courage to make her outrageous suggestion. "Would you go to see her disguised as my maid?"

The young man turned to face her and his cheeks flamed. She, on the other hand, had had time to get used to the idea; it had lost its enormity; her eyes were level, steady, determined.

"Yes, yes, I know you are a clergyman; but you have not been one very long, so perhaps the dye is not yet very deep. It is only a matter of months since you were a university student. Be bold! Faint heart never won fair lady."

It did not take long to overcome his scruples. She pulled Phoebe's gown over his head (it would not fasten behind), her cap over his ears, and topped it all with the cloak and hood.

"You make a very passable maiden," announced Arabella with satisfaction, "though I don't think I would hire you, you have such a villainous countenance . . . you have toothache, and must put this tippet round your vast chin, sir . . . Phoebe, you will be safe here, we will not be long. Sir, please do carry this basket."

They were nearly caught, as they went up the stairs. Lady Russett, newly out of bed—it was barely midday—and very sleepy still, was passing along the upstairs corridor and caught sight of them.

"Miss Hill! What are you doing?" she called. "Who is that woman with you?"—fortunately Robert had his back to her, and was poised with his foot raised to take the next stair to the floor above—"Your maid, is it? Why not leave her in the Servants' Hall?"

"I am going to see Jane, but only for a minute, Ma'am, and my maid is carrying the basket—a few trifling gifts," replied Arabella with an air of helpless innocence.

Lady Russett approved highly of young ladies who were totally unable to carry baskets, and had always thought Arabella far too plebian in this respect; so she gave a slight nod, and went on her way. Robert and Arabella breathed freely. The maid guarded the door, and Arabella gazed with great studiousness out of the window; and Jane and her sweetheart spent a few minutes together. One look at Jane's face, dimly visible in the dark room, calmed Arabella's conscience; it was transfigured with joy. If Jane were to die—the possibility still existed—she would die happy.

The return journey was hair-raising until the front door was closed behind them, then their worries were over. Arabella could not help noticing how quiet Robert was; she caught the gleam of tears in his eyes; but he pressed her hand gratefully when they parted, as Arabella set off with a re-clad Phoebe to go home again.

Jane had indeed been very ill; the congestion on her lungs had put her life in danger. But from that day she began to recover quickly; an hour after Robert had left her she was announcing a desire for beef tea, and the next day she sat in bed propped up with pillows, and the curtains open, so that when Arabella went to visit—a letter to Caroline from Lady Russett had brought the news of the improvement, and Arabella flew as though her slippers had wings—the whole household had stopped feeling anxious about her.

Arabella on her hurried visit the previous day had hardly had time to notice the alteration in Jane. Now, with the daylight falling on her face, one good look wiped all the joy from Arabella's expression, and she went up to the bedside very soberly. Jane reached out a hand and touched her.

"Was it a dream yesterday? I have you to thank, Bell."

"No dream, but a secret," and Arabella tried to smile.

"How are you?"

"It is I who should be asking, how are you?"

"So much better, since yesterday . . . and now that you're here. Lord, how tedious it is to be ill!"

"I've brought my work," said Arabella, sitting down and getting out her wools, not looking at the thin white face on the pillow, until she could control her emotion, "so that they could not accuse me of exciting you. I will sit here, and not talk if it tires you."

Jane smiled wordlessly; speaking did tire her, and she was content with the presence of her friend.

Before leaving, Arabella thought she ought to pay her respects to Lady Russett. Never a favourite, she did not expect more than a few cold words, and she entered the drawing-room hesitantly, but was greeted with an outstretched hand and a warm smile.

"Do come here, my dear Miss Hill. You've been to see Miss Jane Farley? I'm so pleased. You found her much better than yesterday? Yes, I'm delighted to say, she's on the mend. My dear, may I introduce a cousin of ours? A distant cousin, newly arrived in town . . . Mr. Augustus Nadis . . . I'm sure your sister and Mr. Welby would be most interested to meet him. I am giving a little dinner party in his honour—do you know if your family would be able to attend—should we say on Thursday? Excellent— I'll write a note to Mrs. Welby now . . ."

At first sight—and she was one who believed you could judge on first sight—Arabella was impressed with her new acquaintance. He was tall like his cousin, Lord Russett; commanding in presence; and dressed in the height of fashion. How was it that such a desirable parti was of so little interest to Lady Russett? For Arabella knew her Ladyship's ways. He was to be fobbed off with the Welbys, and not treated to the society of the men of genius.

She looked up at him in expectation of some pleasantry.

"May I ask you, Miss Hill," he began in a worried voice, "if you happen to have seen Beau Brummell this morning?"

"No," Arabella sounded surprised. "Should I have done? Is there something special—some reason?"

"If you had seen him, walking along Piccadilly, you know, not acknowledging anybody—you might have noticed how he was dressed, and what he had done with his starcher."

"What he had done with it?"

"How he had folded it, you know. One cannot be too careful in these matters. It can mean the difference between admiration and ridicule."

"I'm sure it can." She was intrigued by this preoccupation, when she had expected him to make some remark about the weather. "Have you come far, Mr. Nadis? From what part of the country?"

"I live in the county of Derbyshire."

"What happiness! You will know the beauties of the Peak. My sister will be so interested to meet you. She has talked lately of a longing to see the precipitous rocks, the forbidding mountains, the tumbling streams, the ancient seats of great families, which are to be found in Derbyshire. We have bought a book of prints of the area, and talk of one day mounting a summer expedition to Matlock."

Her new acquaintance looked at her gloomily.

"Your sister may enjoy such scenes, Miss Hill. If she undertakes such an expedition, the hospitality of my house is at her command. But I dislike country life, and wish my rocks and mountains to be upon the stage at Drury Lane."

Arabella considered his remark, but before she had thought of an appropriate answer, Lady Russett was holding out the note she had been writing, and Arabella took it as a signal that she was to leave. Life, she felt, was not all black. Jane was improving; the escapade yesterday had, after all, been the greatest fun; and this Russett cousin was rather amusing, even if his coat was not red. For a few minutes she had been able to forget that one she had trusted had planned to betray her.

When the Welbys and Arabella made their entrance the following week into Lady Russett's drawing-room the company was already assembled. Mr. Nadis, on catching sight of Arabella, came forward with flattering speed to be introduced to Richard and Caroline, and seemed anxious to join their group. Caroline, who had been told by her sister that he came from Derbyshire, was pleased to talk to him. Summer expeditions were all the rage, and after successfully bringing the family to London, she was thinking that in a year or two it would be educational for the children to make a trip to some other part of the country. At first they talked of Matlock and its beauties, then of the wild grandeur of Castleton, with its frowning castle; the beauty of the Blue John stone, mined near by; the rugged pass, leading up into the fastnesses of the mountains. In spirit they were far from London, and Mr. Nadis spoke with ease and intelligence. Richard and Caroline liked him. It was to be thought of as settled that in a year or two, when the weather and the time seemed right, the expedition should take place, and Augustus Nadis' house should be their headquarters.

"Even if I am not there," he added, "you must treat it as your own."

Caroline wondered rather that they were accepted so quickly as close friends; but she came to the conclusion that he was of a sociable temperament, and would always be asking people, as long as they were willing to visit him; for he said, almost pathetically,

"There is no one to talk to in Derbyshire; my tenants do not know the difference between Hessian boots and the Hussar sort." His woeful expression made them smile. He was eager to be liked and talked to.

"He is a fine-looking man," said Caroline when he had left them. "Perhaps a little hasty; but amiable, I think."

"And with seven thousand a year," added Richard.

"Oh!" Arabella looked round for Augustus Nadis with increased interest, and turned back with flaming cheeks.

"Arabella," said Caroline, "isn't that Captain Wilmott? I don't believe we have seen him for two weeks. There is no sign of his friend, Captain Bodley."

How could he! thought Arabella. How could he show his face here!

Before she had time to feel the first tumult of emotion, he had joined them. At the farther end of the room Lady Russett had agreed to play, and her guests gradually dropped their voices, or stopped talking, to hear her. She was reckoned the best amateur pianist in London. At that moment, however, Arabella could pay no attention to music.

What would Jane think of this? was her first clear thought. If she knew that Captain Wilmott was under her mother's roof! At least Captain Bodley had had the sensibility not to come!

Captain Wilmott had made his way over to them carrying three glasses of wine. Arabella could think of no way of refusing hers, and she was really glad to have something to hold, and play with. She sipped at it as the first brilliant dashes of sound filled the room. Between people's heads, she could see Lady Russett's pale face and bony nose, her glittering eyes; at that moment nothing in the world mattered to Lady Russett except the torrent of sound, and Arabella admired her skill, and revelled in the vigour and dash of the music, as well as she could when close to one who filled her with conflicting emotions. Under the cover of the sound, he spoke to her in a low tone.

"You left our company very abruptly, Miss Hill. Did we do anything to offend you?"

She could not in all honesty say that he had done anything to offend.

"I doubted your intentions, sir," she answered, with a little spirit.

"How could you?" he seemed genuinely surprised and hurt, and turned those hazel eyes upon her with reproach. She quailed under his glance. Her eyes dropped.

"It seemed to me that you intended our downfall—" she had said it, thankful for Lady Russett's burst of sound, which made her words inaudible to anyone but himself.

"You have misunderstood me!" he said in a low, passionate whisper. "You must give me a chance to explain. Your generosity will not deny that. Such a gross mistake must be put right."

She wavered. His tone was urgent, she thought, with sincerity. If she had misunderstood—and she had certainly been mistaken about Jane's glass—then she had wronged him grievously.

He saw her hesitation.

"In the name of justice, you must allow me another meeting!"

he said, very quietly. They stood still, in close proximity. But in
the quiet following the music, while Miss Farley was being persuaded to play, others, Caroline and Richard, returned their attention to Captain Wilmott.

"Where is Captain Bodley?" asked Caroline. "Do we not have
the pleasure of his company this evening?"

"He has embarked, Madam, for the Peninsula," was the answer,
and he gave Arabella an expressive look, as though he was saying,
and to us, the heroes of the hour, you denied your company, and
escaped from us as though we were monsters! Arabella thought
she read all this in his look. A few minutes more and, with that elegance she admired in him, he had taken his leave and was moving away to the other side of the room.

"I don't wonder you admire him, Arabel," remarked Richard.
"A good officer, I would say; not a bad man to be next to in a
fight."

"You think so?" she was pleased, in spite of herself. He had denied any intention of wronging them—could she believe him?
Even if she did—and for some time she had been doubting, wondering if she had jumped too hastily to conclusions, risking Jane's
life, and William's reputation, and her own happiness—for she
was sure she could have been happy with Captain Wilmott whatever his income. What was his income? She had never heard, and
it was not without importance. Love could be worn out by poverty. Captain Wilmott's feeling for her did not seem the kind to
stand through many rubs of fortune. Perhaps she wronged him.
Perhaps she had been mistaken at the Inn.

"We must have Captain Wilmott back again," observed Richard, "for he has taken all your liveliness with him, Sister." His
eyes held more shrewdness than she liked. In a moment she was
all sparkle.

"Why, how can you say so, Brother Welby? Miss Farley is
about to play; I was just waiting reverently for her first notes, and
thinking how much Mr. Watts would have enjoyed the music."

"Do not tell me your thoughts were with Watts, for I will not
believe it, unless you are thinking of some scheme to tease him.
Lady Russett would never invite him—I am surprised she unbent
so far as to ask Captain Wilmott—so he must lose the pleasure of

hearing the music. I daresay you are right, now I think of it. He loves music above most things. But a City man would be unacceptable to Lady Russett." Richard paused, then went on, "Watts was talking to me of you the other day, when he was just leaving; we were standing in the vestibule, and could hear you singing upstairs, and Phoebe singing in the kitchen, and the children singing as they played Nuts in May on the top landing, so I had a regular nest of singing birds. 'Do you not find it very tiring,' Watts said to me, 'having your sister-in-law Miss Hill in the house?' Which I thought ungallant of him, so to serve him right I have repeated it."

Richard was smiling, and hoping to provoke her, she decided; so, as the opening notes of Miss Farley's piece met their ears, Arabella answered,

"And what did you reply, dear brother?"

"Well—I told him you were a volatile, stirring piece of stuff, and that it was a great trial, having you."

Richard had chosen his moment well. At any other time she would have forgotten herself sufficiently to revert to childhood, and tweak his hair, or batter him with her embroidery wool; but at present she was helpless, so, apart from an indignant look, she took his remarks in silence, and only moved away in a dignified manner to the other side of Caroline, and intended to ignore him for the rest of the evening.

She knew that Mr. Watts had cooled towards her since that moment when she had looked up in response to his voice, and seen him towering above her on horseback, chill and disapproving, as she and Jane and Isaac Sutherland trudged along in the mud. His original bad opinion must, she knew, have been confirmed; and, somehow, she was sorry. But she soon forgot him, and Richard's chaffing. Every moment she was looking for Captain Wilmott, but dreaded seeing him. When she did see him, she hoped that he would keep away; and when, as if in obedience to her wish, he avoided speaking to them again, she perversely wished that he had.

At last the evening drew to a close. Augustus Nadis, who had returned to them, had invited Caroline and Arabella to drive with him in Hyde Park on the following day, and they had agreed.

Captain Wilmott did not come over to wish them goodbye, but only bowed his farewell as they prepared to leave. Richard and Caroline waited for her while Arabella slipped upstairs for a quick goodbye to Jane, who was sitting up by her fire, wrapped in a shawl.

"Oh, I have heard the music," she replied in answer to Arabella's enquiry. "Believe me, I have been quite happy sitting up here. I almost think Mother would have postponed it, if I had wished her to; but I did not wish it. Cousin Augustus has been looking forward to coming to London; it would have been cruel to postpone his entry into Society. It is his first visit, you know, Bell. Until his father died earlier this year, he was confined to the estate. He will be like a bird set free from a cage. He is a good fellow. Tell me how you like him, later—come and see me tomorrow."

Chapter Seven

At the correct hour next morning Mr. Augustus Nadis appeared at the door of Welby House in the most elegant of tilburies, the most ridiculous of greatcoats and the most tremendous of neckcloths, which made it impossible for him to bend his head far enough to see his boots. Arabella felt that she was truly living. Surely this was what she had come to London for—elegance, high fashion! She sensed a fellow spirit in Augustus and felt lighthearted for the first time since the day of the Waxworks.

Caroline could not help liking the big, amiable man from Derbyshire. She listened to the faint Northern accent in his voice with pleasure, and enjoyed the occasional country saying he let slip. He brought to mind their simple, generous country neighbours in Linchestershire, and for a while the longing to be back at Curteys Court was almost overwhelming. But she put it on one side. Just a little longer, for Bell's sake. She was so happy . . . looking across at her sister as they got under way, Caroline wondered why she had doubted her. At this moment she was all transparent pleasure. If she could form an alliance with Mr. Nadis, there would be none of the uneasiness caused by Captain Wilmott. Caroline thought Augustus might be well matched with her sister.

Mr. Nadis had lost as little time as possible after inheriting his estate, before he set about fulfilling his life-long ambition. He wanted to join the vortex of High Society which centred on Piccadilly, Carlton House, and Mayfair. He wanted to be one of the beaux and dandies of the Haut Ton; to attend all the fashionable establishments, to join the right clubs, to patronize the right tailors and hatters and bootmakers. This large form concealed a spirit to whom the set of a neckcloth was of more importance than his moorland sheep, and the approbation of the highest circle of the Upper Ten Thousand was heaven, their censure, hell. He was timid; too unsure, in this first venture, to plunge in at the deep end; he might have lost all. By staying with his cousins he knew that he could be guided by their taste until he had developed his own, although he could feel his own capabilities surging inside him, and after less than a fortnight he was already beginning to criticize the polish on Lord Russett's boots, and wonder if he could bribe Joel Tomkins to leave Richard's service, as the Welby boots were always so impeccably kept.

His faith in himself had good foundation, for the dandies they passed took second looks at his greatcoat, and in their glances at his neckcloth he felt there was a certain admiration.

To be driving in an equipage which drew all eyes was a delightful experience for Arabella. Hyde Park on foot was interesting, but when Richard took them driving in the Welby carriage she blushed for shame, in spite of William's paintwork. Beside the other vehicles they looked countrified indeed, and the fact that neither Richard nor Caroline minded, and merely enjoyed being out on a fine day, made it worse. Now she had nothing to blush for, and in response to Augustus' pleasantries she showed herself so gay and animated, and glanced at him with such charm, that he began to consider whether she might not make a very smart hostess, and a suitable match for himself.

The Fashionable Impures were out in force in the Park, mixing with the cream of Society, and Augustus was delighted to see the carriage of Mary Ann Clarke, which he pointed out to Arabella. Her attention was absorbed by the various barouches, tilburies, and landaus; here was one lined with quilted sky-blue satin, there another with rich gilding catching the sun. The horses, such as only England could breed, stepped high and arched their necks, and gleamed from head to flank with the attentions lavished on them.

And the next morning Arabella bought the black bonnet from Barnetts'.

"I thought you couldn't afford it," remonstrated Caroline.

"No more I can," Arabella responded carelessly.

"Oh, Bell!" was Jane's only response, when Arabella took it over to show her, and lifted it out of its hatbox.

"It gives me another hatbox, too, which is always gratifying," said her friend.

"Let me see you wearing it," begged Jane, who was up, and sitting near the window.

Arabella put it on, and came over to her, parading shamelessly.

"Is it not the prettiest thing? Is it not becoming?"

"Indeed it is."

For a whole day, nay, for a week, the black bonnet came up to all the hopes entertained of it. Heads turned in the Park as she wore it, driving with Augustus; Mr. Watts lifted his eyebrows at it and smiled, when they met on the stairs.

"Still a student of headgear, I see, Miss Hill," he remarked.

She returned his smile. Although it is difficult to forgive those who detect us in wrong doing, she had nobly forgiven Mr. Watts for having seen them, wet and dishevelled, walking home from their escapade. She had forgiven him for looking after them and so putting them under an obligation, and she had forgiven him for knowing best and not saying so. From these heights of magnanimity she could find his smile, and the way he set his head on one side when he talked to her, attractive, even in one so near the grave as almost forty, and possessing nothing at all that was in the fashion.

Augustus—after so brief an acquaintance, she was already calling him that in her mind—Augustus had shown no interest in Mr. Watts; so she supposed that if she married the squire, she would hardly see the lawyer again; as she thought this, she felt a little cold, as though that future would be a less rosy place. But, as Mr. Nadis said, how could one wish to know a fellow, who, having decided in his schooldays that he liked grey waistcoats, could still be wearing grey waistcoats of the same shade and cut so many years later? The thing was quite impossible, of course . . .

Arabella had seen Captain Wilmott once more, since that evening at the Russetts'. But, at the time, she had been escorted by Augustus Nadis, and the Captain had merely bowed, and taken a side path. She had not even told Jane of the note she had received from him. In it he had spoken of his love for her, and again begged her to see him privately so that he could explain away her doubts. He had suggested a rendezvous in the Park as evening fell. Phoebe had brought the note, and stood waiting as Arabella read it. There was no word, of course, of marriage . . . Arabella hesitated.

"You would be with me, of course, Phoebe," she remarked. "There would be justice in hearing what he had to say. It would only be fair. But—" She re-read the note, slowly, then walked over to her bedroom fire, and dropped it in, standing and watching it burn. When the last of it was gone she turned to Phoebe.

"There is no answer," she said. "I will not see him."

Jane had taken the news very calmly, when told that Captain Bodley had gone to Spain. He had obviously meant very little to her.

"Poor fellow!" she had said. "I hope he distinguishes himself, without being killed, and comes back safe. Did I tell you, Bell, that dear Robert has preached before the Bishop! And was commended by him."

There were no more early morning walks to fetch Jane. Lady Russett, who had never really approved of ladies being seen so early in the day, blamed the exposure to the morning frosts for Jane's illness; and as they did not want to disillusion her, they met later in the day. Jane was brought over to Welby House by carriage, with full panoply of footmen.

The black bonnet, which had started by satisfying so completely, soon ceased to please. First Arabella removed the bunch of feathers, and put it on in a different position; an infinite improvement, she decided. Then the quilled ribbon, formerly such a popular part of the tout ensemble, was declared to be quite out, and must be discarded immediately. Without the ribbon, the feathers looked lost and uncertain; so they were presented to

Caroline, who was pleased because they went so well with her Tuscan cloak, and so she stitched them into the hat she wore with it. The French lace—so very expensive, and so very bewitching round Arabella's face, could no longer be borne, so off it came; and little by little, the bonnet which had so filled her mind and so fulfilled her hopes was reduced to rather a plain little piece of flattery, though nothing could quite rob it of its neat and becoming line. If Arabella could have seen the expression on Cornelius Watts' face as he paused on the stairs and watched her on one of her first wearings of the bonnet, perhaps she would have treated it more tenderly.

"What possessed you?" asked Caroline sadly.

"Well . . ." Arabella considered. "I must admit that I enjoyed taking it to pieces, more than I enjoyed wearing it, once the first thrill of it was over . . . I suppose, I must be meddling; and the consequences . . ." she twirled the remaining hat on her finger . . . "the consequences can be disastrous . . . better hats than hearts, dear sister! Better spoil a thousand hats, than risk heartbreak with my wildness . . ."

The Earl of Epworth had made what he hoped would be his last visit to Town for some time. His uncle's affairs could now be regarded as settled; the house was disposed of, the effects dispersed, the very last of the bequests made.

With Cornelius Watts, he had gone to the house of Madame Eglantine. He had insisted on going in alone, and Watts had had to return to his office, with nothing to do but fidget about and wonder what was happening, with nothing to salve his itch for action.

The Earl returned, seemingly as anxious to tell Cornelius of his progress as the lawyer was to hear it.

"There was a message," he announced, "but it was only left yesterday. I have an appointment to meet Mirabelle and give her the money, when she has proved her identity."

"I'll come with you," said Cornelius instantly.

"No, you won't," the Earl slapped him on the shoulder and laughed. "I'm not in leading reins." He had very little to say after the interview, and Cornelius could not make out what kind of impression Mirabelle had made on the Earl. His remarks were vague in the extreme. For him, all contact with Mirabelle was over.

As the days of December moved on towards Christmas, the early promise of the relationship between Arabella and Augustus Nadis seemed as though it was likely to be fulfilled. They met, in one way or another, almost as often as Arabella and Jane Farley; when Arabella, with or without her sister and brother-in-law, was not dining or drinking tea with the Russetts, Augustus was eating or drinking with the Welbys. He danced with a certain stately elegance, which Arabella assured him could become all the crack, and he walked, and played cards with them, or took out Jane and Arabella together, as often as he could.

The geese arrived from Curteys; the puddings were in readiness, the mincemeat was prepared in the kitchen; all over the basement of the house the servants could not move for sacks of nuts or barrels of apples, and were bumping their heads on hams hung from the ceiling. The housekeeper put the boxes of figs and dates and Carlsbad plums in her own room, and the sack of raisins in the narrow space near the cupboard bed where the knife boy slept; he was in superstitious awe of them and did not touch one.

"Wife," said Richard one morning as he struggled to put on his boots, "you seem pleased with this young cousin of the Russetts; do you think he is the right man for Arabella?"

"Why don't you get Joel to help you, Richard—here, I'll pull—there you are—why, don't you like him?"

"Oh, liking—I like him well enough. But did you know he tried to bribe Joel to leave my service?" asked Richard. Caroline laughed.

"So that's the cause of this sudden doubt; well, he is a good valet, Richard. You've always said so. And these dandies will stoop to anything in their pursuit of perfection. I think he has placed himself in the front rank remarkably quickly. Only yesterday I heard that he is regarded as the coming thing. He sets up on his own in chambers this week, I believe. He has outgrown the Russetts already. The constant appeal to the intellect distracts him from the real purpose of London life, he told me so himself, only the other day."

"I wonder he does not desert us too. You and I make no attempt to be fashionable."

"No doubt he will, in time. But I am sure that Arabella is the attraction, and if she agrees to marry him, they can desert us together, and we can retreat in comfort to the country."

"But surely a marriage is a matter for mutual respect, and affection?"

"I have no reason to feel that he does not have respect and affection for Arabella," Caroline pointed out.

"A man who tries to steal another man's valet is capable of anything," replied Richard, gloomily.

"We know his family background, we know that he has a good income, and an estate; as he himself would no doubt put it, he is of the Upper Ten Thousand; I have no reason to think ill of him, and he seems very struck with Bell, and she to like his company. Do point it out, Richard, if I have any reason to be uneasy. It is true that she no longer has the brilliance I noticed in her a few weeks ago, but that had something unlike Bell about it, and made me worry about her. She seems happy enough now; yes, Richard, if she accepts him, I will be pleased. She will be well settled, and should be happy."

Richard said no more.

"Well, Arabella," said Caroline later in the day, prompted by Richard's remarks, "what am I to think of Mr. Nadis? Am I to regard him as a future brother-in-law?"

"You may regard him how you will, sister," replied Arabella. "But I will tell you, that if he offers, I mean to have him."

There was something Caroline did not quite like in the tone of the words. She hesitated, then went on,

"I pray you, do not marry only on worldly considerations. To mate with a man one did not love and respect, would be misery indeed."

"I have seen the result of such unions, Carrie. But one's heart may misguide one, as much as one's head. I am arrogant enough to hope that I may avoid the trap of thinking too much of my husband, as well as that of thinking too little. The world is not well lost for love, if one has no vocation for the shifts and con-

/ances of poverty. When I have allowed my susceptibilities to
influence my judgement, I would have fallen into the most hid-
eous errors, and regretted it mightily, when the first flush of love
had faded, and youth had flown . . . may I not make a rational
choice, and believe that on a foundation of liking and mutual interests sufficient love may follow? When I am in the company of
Mr. Nadis, I am cheerful and happy; his doings interest and
amuse me; my heart does not flutter, but neither am I reduced to
misery and despair. We would rub along very nicely together. But
until he is kind enough to offer, you know, I can do nothing."

It appeared to all their acquaintance, that Mr. Nadis would
offer, as soon as he felt himself sufficiently established in London.
There was a comfortable inevitability about it. The Russetts appeared pleased; and if Jane did not enthuse, she did not say anything against her cousin, to Arabella. Richard made no more mention of his misgivings; Caroline was all amiability, and Arabella all
sparkling complaisance.

But Captain Wilmott had not been forgotten.

Arabella had declared that her heart did not flutter when she
met Augustus Nadis, but to pass Captain Wilmott in some
crowded Assembly . . . to catch sight of him at an Exhibition, or
be greeted by him in the Park . . . this was the stuff of which
those imprudent marriages, which she had so denigrated to Caroline, are made. She was still not sure if she had misjudged him; his
indignant denials, his note, had only partly satisfied her. There
were times, in the privacy of her bedchamber, when thoughts of
the joys of surrendering to love were uppermost in her mind;
when she felt that, had she once again been in Mrs. Ringrose's establishment, she might pretend not to have heard that fatal order
for two bedrooms. Her imagination took her through the night
which might have followed, had her upbringing not led her so
very promptly through the Inn window and down the river. But
when she allowed herself the luxury of thinking these thoughts—
alone with her pillow—she was always brought up short by the
memory of Jane. It might have turned out well enough for herself
—might, if it had not ended in disgrace, have ended in a marriage
of sorts. But what of Jane's sweet and simple romance with her
childhood playmate? That would have been ruined forever. Again

and again Arabella came to the same conclusion. She could not regret that retreat. Should she have met him, as he wished, in the Park? That would have been, potentially, even more damning. Without a companion, with only Phoebe, who could too easily be sent off to a distance? No . . .

All might, then, have gone well. A fashionable marriage between Augustus and Arabella might have linked the Welby and the Farley families, and given London another circle, illumined by elegance and wit, to compete with the giddy inner circles of fashion revolving round His Highness, the Prince of Wales. But that was before the episode of Phoebe . . .

Phoebe had, Arabella felt, been getting rather uppish. It was not that she was pert except, perhaps by not being so. There was a way she had of casting down her eyes, of veiling those gooseberry green orbs with her sweeping lashes, which would have been thought modest in any other young woman. Why was it that in Phoebe this retiring gesture—so submissive—seemed sometimes to Arabella almost insolent? She felt like snapping, "Look at me, Phoebe, when I am speaking to you!" But she did not say it. It was not her habit to speak sharply, and there was no fault to find with Phoebe. Mrs. Jackson would have understood how Arabella felt. She could not have said how it was that, when the girl had been particularly provoking, wanting this and wanting that, and she had turned to speak abruptly to her, Phoebe had dropped her eyes and whisked out of the kitchen, leaving Mrs. Jackson with an indefinable sense of having been given her comeuppance, without a word having been spoken.

The girl was always neatly, but not expensively, dressed, and when she wore pretty caps and scarves, and dainty cuffs which must have cost more than one would expect her to spend, it was always, "Oh, Miss Hill gave it to me," which made Betty feel Caroline's cast-offs very meagre in comparison. She was well paid and must, Joel thought, be saving.

Arabella could not have said how it was that she went on giving Phoebe such things. Would it have seemed too very dreadful if Caroline and Richard had known of the episode of the waxworks and the river? Phoebe never mentioned it, never hinted that she might gossip. But now and then her stream of everyday remarks would falter, her attention seem to stray; and Arabella, noticing those eyes fixed on some article—some garnish to feminine attire —would find herself, almost against her will, offering it to the girl, and Phoebe would take it.

Arabella stopped employing her on errands. There was no more likelihood of Caroline meeting her on the stairs, carrying a letter, for Arabella sent her with none. She gave her no little commissions at the shops. Yet Phoebe always seemed, to her fellow servants, to be busy; there was always some little journey for her to make, some business for her to be about. Her neat ankle was a familiar sight in the street, as she tripped off on some errand or other.

When Joel told Phoebe about Augustus Nadis' offer, if Joel left Richard Welby's service and went to his, she reviled him for not taking the chance. He looked at her with the expression of a hurt spaniel in his eyes; did she not realize that to accept the offer would have taken him away from her? Aloud he explained that his loyalty to Richard prevented it. She gave him a look of complete contempt. "Money!" was the only word he got in answer, but he felt like a whipped cur, and had the feeling that he had let her down. There was a tone in her voice which he had never heard before, but it cut. He had prided himself on his influence with her; she had gone with him to services in the Parish church, and lifted her thrush-like voice in the ancient familiar hymns and responses, and deserted the Methodist congregation. He had almost seen his wedding approaching, and wondered if there was a little room at Curteys, or a house on the estate which could be theirs in a few years, when the children started to come. And now she was angry, and let him feel it. He was never to realize that in that one word she had expressed the whole mainspring of her being and her philosophy of life.

The happy, ordered busyness of a household preparing for Christmas was absorbing them all. Secrets were the order of the day. The servants were looking forward to it as much as the family, wondering what their Christmas Boxes would be, and preparing surprises for one another, as gaily as the family upstairs.

Arabella had called Phoebe, but the girl was apparently not within earshot. She had rung, and not received any reply. She had gone to the top of the stairs, looked about, and finally gone down into the kitchen; but no Phoebe.

"Where is she?" asked Arabella in haste. "I need her. Mr. Nadis is calling for me in half an hour, and I am nowhere near ready."

"She must have gone out somewhere," answered Mrs. Jackson.

"But I haven't sent her out."

"Perhaps Mrs. Welby did."

Mrs. Welby hadn't; but she suggested asking Betty, and, the baby of the family being in his mother's care, and the others busy with lessons in the schoolroom, Betty came in to help in Phoebe's place.

Time went by, and still no Phoebe. Arabella returned from her drive—they had been looking from the outside at some houses, and unspoken between them had been the idea that one of the houses, which were to let, might serve as a home for them on their marriage—and found her still missing.

Darkness fell, and she had not returned. The Welbys were going to a play at Drury Lane; but Arabella had to manage with only Betty's help once more for her evening toilette, which ruffled her. As yet there was no concern in the household; it was felt that Phoebe would have some good reason for her absence which, even though she had not made it known, would be a good one. Richard reminded everyone of the time he and the Admiral had gone to watch the Prizefight, and seen Phoebe unexpectedly at the Inn; and when he got home, he found that she had been on a visit to an old Aunt who was dying. No doubt something similar had happened again and Phoebe had sent a message by some unreliable person who had not delivered it.

"She cannot have so many mortally ill relatives," said Arabella. "Surely one is entitled to expect a limited number of dying aunts and messages undelivered, in one's servants."

But as the following day, and the one after it, brought still no returning Phoebe, even Richard began to think that they ought to raise a hue and cry, and ask the Charlies to keep a look out for a young girl in trouble.

"There are so many girls adrift in London," said Arabella, "she will hardly be noticed among thousands."

Joel and William, and the other footmen and boys of the

household, scoured the neighbouring streets, looking into back gardens and down alleyways, thinking she might have been overtaken with some illness; Joel was nearly beside himself with fear and worry. Nowhere did they hear of her whereabouts, or meet anyone who had seen her.

It was on the third day that Joel received a note.

He came into the morning-room, where Caroline was teaching Martha needlework, knocking and then entering hesitantly. Looking up, Caroline could see at once that something was the matter. His handsome face was perplexed, the brows drawn together, lines about the mouth. His shoulders had an unaccustomed sag.

"What is it, Joel?"

"I can't understand it, Madam. There's a note here, as if it had come from Phoebe."

"Well, that's good! What has been happening to her?"

"But how can it be from Phoebe, Ma'am, if Phoebe's dead, or ill somewhere?"

"Joel! If she writes, she must be alive and reasonably well. What does she say?"

"I can't really understand it, Madam."

"May I see?"

She took the note, and examined it. The hand, small, sloping, and precise, was definitely Phoebe's. It was addressed to Joel, and consisted only of a few lines.

"Oh! No!" exclaimed Caroline.

"What is it, Madam? What does it say? What has become of my Phoebe?"

Joel could hardly keep back his tears. These days of being uncertain if Phoebe was alive or dead had been such a strain that it was obvious he was nearly breaking down altogether. It was also obvious that, although he could read simple print, Phoebe's handwriting was beyond him. Caroline was as gentle as she could be.

"Phoebe has left our service, Joel. She asks you to tell us that she has found a position that she thinks is a better one. The wages . . ." Caroline hesitated, "are very high, and she will have a great many becoming dresses to wear. She hopes you will not think ill of her for leaving without saying goodbye, but she will see you before long, and would like to think that if a position for yourself arises in the household, you will follow her. Meanwhile she wishes you well, and will write again. Joel, this is a private letter, just for you. Don't you think you ought to keep it very safe, and not let anyone else see it? Not William, not anybody? Let it just be your very own. You would like to have something of Phoebe's to keep for your own, wouldn't you? And this is her handwriting, written specially for you."

Caroline was speaking to the tall, well-built man as though he were a child, but at that moment he seemed incapable of thinking or acting other than as a child. He nodded in answer to her speech and took back the letter, gazing at it and turning it over and over in his hands.

"Her handwriting—and she wrote it just for me. I will keep it safe, and not show anybody, and when I can go to her, she will let me know—" He repeated Caroline's words like a litany, and finally turned, pushing the letter into the pocket of his jacket, and left the room.

Poor Joel! thought Caroline. But she must not sit here indulging in reflection; it was essential to tell Arabella what had happened. Sending Martha up to the nursery, she went to find her sister.

Arabella was rather crossly sorting out her lace, and deciding what was to be washed, and putting on one side those pieces in need of mending. She already had a petticoat, which she had ripped unheeding in a game with the children, awaiting her attentions, and she was every moment wishing Phoebe back again to take over these tasks.

"Joel has heard from Phoebe," began Caroline, closing the door behind her.

"Heard from her? You mean she is not back?"

"No, nor will be. Prepare yourself for a shock, my dear. Phoebe has been set up in an establishment."

"What do you mean, sister? You don't mean . . ."

"Yes—she has gone to live with some profligate; she has been established as the mistress of a house in Bruton Street."

There did not seem to be anything to say, in that first minute, in reply to this intelligence.

After a pause, Arabella said, "But how did she meet him? Has the girl no shame? Where does she think this will lead?"

"To riches, probably."

"There is no one to mend my laces! And I cannot bear to have Betty do my hair, she pulls as much as she ever did."

Caroline thought her sister quite bewitching when she pouted, and the slight childish pettishness was charming.

"You can hire a lady's maid quickly enough. But what am I to write to Father? What about poor Mrs. Hunt?"

Arabella began to giggle.

"Oh, dear, she always thought Phoebe so perfect . . . but so did I, so demure . . . who is the man who has somehow met our Phoebe, and wishes to racket with the fashionable and display his immorality to the world, as all the others do? The Fashionable Impures! Will she join them? Upon my word, I believe Phoebe capable of anything, now I think of it. See how she has improved the shining hour, and us not in Town three months . . . who is the man?"

"The letter did not say. But we will hear soon enough. Such matters are the very life of Town conversation," said Caroline a trifle wearily; if it were not for the society of plain, good folk like the Admiral and his family she would have been sick of London long before.

"I wonder who it can be," repeated Arabella, much struck.

"Now mind, child! I have told Joel not to show the letter to anyone, and I have veiled the truth from him, although I believe he is so infatuated that she could persuade him black was white."

"I believe Phoebe could persuade anyone that black was white."

And there, for the time, the matter rested. Mrs. Jackson being applied to, she advertised, and then interviewed the applicants, for the post of lady's maid, and submitted a short list to Arabella, who chose out of them a pleasant-faced girl called Margery, who gave excellent references and could come at once, her previous mistress having died a fortnight before. In no time she had taken up her duties, and settled into the household as though she had never lived anywhere else; and Arabella found that she had had much experience with laces, had a soothing hand on the hairbrush, and was willing to learn the latest modes. There was no doubt of the mistress and maid suiting very well.

Phoebe was not heard of for some time.

When he knew of the event—for Caroline's ideas of secrecy did not extend to her husband, or to their friend—Mr. Watts looked grave.

"Surely," he said, "modesty and caution are large parts of the charm of young girls; it saddens me to see them throw away their good name."

Arabella, who had become lately very conscious of her own lack of caution, jumped to the conclusion that he too was thinking of it, and attacked as the best form of defence.

"Why," she cried, "is setting up a mistress considered dashing in a young man, but to be one is reprehensible in a woman?"

"I think as badly of the man who departs from right living and sound principles and debauches an innocent girl, as I do of the girl who glories in her shame."

"Then I know why you do not take part in the Routs and Evening Squeezes, Mr. Watts; you could not do so without rubbing shoulders with the Demi-reps and Cyprians."

"I went to the Marchioness of Harome's Ball, if you remember; we were all dancing together on that occasion."

"The Marchioness is more particular over her guests than many hostesses, and such an expedition is a rarity for you."

"Not only for that reason, Miss Hill; though the spectacle of degraded lives, drunken and debauched, has no charm for me. The surface glitter, the ermine furs and carriages lined in blue satin, saddens instead of pleasing, when I know what it hides. Besides, City men are not welcome in such circles. Our money is hard earned, not won by gaming."

The way of the world could not be altered; so by mutual consent, they changed the subject, and began to talk for all they were worth of the war, which was dramatic enough to supply any number of conversations. There was the disastrous battle in Spain; Sir John Moore's retreat to Salamanca; his orders to Baird to fall back on Corunna; the troops who had been ordered out to the Peninsula now included the First, Third and Fourth Dragoon Guards. Arabella could not help wondering how long Captain

Wilmott would be able to stay in England, and how Captain Bodley was faring.

Mr. Watts was scathing at the expense of the Swiss.

"A Confederate Government to be organized!" he exclaimed. "All the different cantons to have the same form of Government! What nonsense. It will never work."

"But I believe it will," contradicted Arabella hotly. "Not all rule for the people turns out badly."

"How long did France have Liberty, Equality, Fraternity, before tyranny, overthrown in the aristocracy, reared its head among the leaders of the people? And how soon was it before these equal *sans-colottes* were begging Napoleon to be Emperor?"

She had no reply for the moment; but would have the last word, and reiterated her belief that the Swiss might succeed in their idea of a happy confederation.

Caroline did not think it the role of a young lady to argue with an older, and experienced, man. She did not realize that both Arabella and Cornelius now read the newspapers on the look out for subjects of discussion, and that during a lecture Arabella would be storing up points in her mind to talk over with him, while he was constantly thinking of matters to discuss with her.

Caroline was grateful that Arabella did not behave with such spirit with Augustus Nadis. With him she was delectable, and never indulged in raillery. Instead she coquetted with a combination of innocence and awareness which was very piquant . . . if only Mr. Watts could see her then, she was sure he would not be able to help admitting that she had a power to delight.

Augustus felt this power to the full. His pleasure in Arabella's society was so open that all who knew them were counting the days to a betrothal. Driving in the Park on a clear day about the middle of December, with a slight frost in the air—enough to enliven but not to freeze those who were warmly wrapped in furs and broadcloth—both were at a peak of happiness. Augustus' tilbury was gleaming to match the shining coats of his horses; his chin was held so high by his starcher that his vision was limited to the horizontal plane; the capes on his greatcoat were multitudinous, his hat at a rakish angle. Behind him, his tiger was dressed in the smartest livery, in Augustus' opinion, in the whole of Lon-

don; and beside him Arabella's cheeks were glowing under a velvet
Russian bonnet, trimmed with curled floss. She was warm in her
matching velvet pelisse, fastened in front with clasps of cut steel
from the throat to the feet. Grass-green was a colour that suited
her exceedingly, and he had noticed as she climbed into the vehicle her shoes, in a darker green, with embroidered toes . . .

All around them other turnouts were driving along slowly.
Augustus could not allow any to be considered superior to his
own, but he and Arabella derived a great deal of pleasure from
discussing the differences—the grey team of horses versus the
black of the Marchioness of Harome's, the bays of Lady Heworth
versus the chestnuts of Lord Hallam, the gay whisks, the stately
carriages, the flippant tilburies, the gracious barouche-landaus . . .

They waved to their acquaintance in an elegant and not a vulgar manner, and bent their heads to acknowledge the greetings of
others. To see and be seen, that was the order of the day.

"That's a very pretty landaulette," remarked Arabella. "It has a
grace of line more than the common; the horses are unusual too;
it is not often one sees a lady driving such a well-matched team of
blacks; do you know her, Mr. Nadis? Is that officer with her?"

The officer, as the other equipage drew near, was seen to be
Captain Wilmott. Arabella started as she realized who it was, and
her cheeks paled. She buried her hands deeper in her muff and
clenched them together. This was the first time she had seen him
in attendance upon any lady except herself. Who was it?

"I don't know her," replied Augustus. "But I heard he had set
up a mistress, very expensively as they say; a house furnished in
the latest style; nothing is too good for her. The talk is that he has
made her a settlement in case he has to go to Portugal."

The two teams of horses were drawing closer together and Arabella, speechless, was devouring all the details. She had not replied
to Augustus. She saw the purple pelisse, trimmed with chink-
chelly fur; the gold clasps, outdoing her own cut steel; the velvet
bonnet with the full tiara front, and ends pendant on the left
side, after the Hungarian fashion, trimmed with a short lace veil;
she saw the delicate pallor of the cheeks, the modest expression;
she saw Phoebe . . .

Captain Wilmott had bowed, and smiled. They had passed. The traitor was behind her.

Augustus could not help noticing that his companion had lost her animation. She seemed languid instead of lively, weary instead of interested. He passed strictures on the greatcoat of Lord Hallam without receiving the grace of a reply, and his witty sarcasm at the expense of the Duke of York and Mary Ann Clarke seemed hardly to be heard by his companion. At last she almost whispered a request to be taken home; and, with exasperation, for it was not yet the stylish hour for leaving the Park, he agreed, and turned the horses' heads. His annoyance made the drive back to Welby House a silent one, but Arabella scarcely noticed; she wanted nothing so much as to be alone in her bedchamber. Augustus bid her goodbye, with a promise to call on the morrow, and at last had the courtesy to make a grudging wish that her indisposition would only be a very temporary one; but if he had wished the moon to be of green cheese, and they two its only inhabitants, Arabella would not have realized what he had said. She made some sort of reply, and burst from him and away up the stairs.

Caroline, who had met them as they came into the vestibule, watched her in astonishment. Good manners made her ensure that Augustus did not leave without due civility, but she was even more surprised to find that he did not know the reason for Arabella's distress. He was at a loss.

They had just seen Captain Wilmott and his new mistress in the Park, most elegant! One hoped it would be possible to meet her at a Ball, or Rout! Soon after that Arabella had seemed to be ill, had not seemed to attend; and had at last begged him to bring her home . . . Caroline said so gratefully how much she appreciated his kindness that he settled down in his chair, and looked like staying, joining in her praise of his thoughtfulness. She tried to steer the conversation to Derbyshire, in which she was interested; but without success. Instead he told her of all the people they had passed in the Park, in great detail, until she was tired, and her patience worn out; then at last, as Richard entered and the clock chimed six, he went, and she was free to go upstairs to her sister.

. . . . . .

The first fury of weeping was over. Arabella had had to face the fact that she had loved Captain Wilmott far more than she had realized; that was one part of it. In the Inn—that Inn in Superior style, with its neat chaises, good post horses, and steady drivers, and super-excellent goose and game pies—she had suspected his motives; how she made herself suffer after, thinking she had suspected him mistakenly! How much more did she suffer now, knowing that she had not been mistaken!

He was a scoundrel. There could be no doubt of it. He had not more than a competence from his family, she had learned that, and had thought it the reason why he had not courted her openly and honourably, and made an offer. Where had he got the money to set up an establishment and a mistress? But that wonder was the least of it. Spurned by her, she could not be surprised if he turned to another woman. Had he started to pay attentions to an heiress in order to make his fortune, she would not have been shocked. But this . . . she said as much to Caroline when her sister entered.

"You would not have minded if he had paid his attentions elsewhere, for money?" said Caroline slowly. "Is that really your reasoning, Arabella? Can I believe that of you? Then your vanity would have been left untouched. Is it of such importance? Poor, poor Arabella . . . you could believe him mercenary, and would prefer that to knowing him lecherous, to save your vanity? Either way, he is shown to be without principles. How I wish you had never met him. But I did not know your heart was touched. I thought you had fancied, and then forgotten him. What about Mr. Nadis? You have led us to believe you would marry him."

"I did—I will," was the answer.

"And yet—thinking of marrying Mr. Nadis—Captain Wilmott's desertion has caused you all this pain? Or is it something else?"

"It is compounded. His mistress is Phoebe."

"Not Phoebe Hunt."

"Yes."

Caroline sat on the bed with a thump. Arabella spoke from the shelter of her handkerchief.

"All the time he was making advances to me—more advances than you knew of, Carrie—he must have been making them also to Phoebe . . . courting the mistress and seducing the maid . . ."

"And you never suspected?"

"Never."

Arabella thought, but did not feel like expounding on the subject, that no one was likely to discover anything about Phoebe which she did not wish them to discover. That self-possessed young woman—no, no longer self-possessed, now she belonged to Captain Wilmott, rot him—would never give away her thoughts or private actions; she could hide a secret like a bowlful of thick cream could hide a golden chain. Poor Joel! He was not master of his fate; if she beckoned he would follow, entirely her creature, no matter what she had become, and Richard's boots would be left unpolished.

Richard, when she met him later in the evening, made no comment on the matter, and ignored her swollen eyes; but he did remark casually, that he had heard Captain Wilmott had won a vast amount of money lately at the gaming tables. That explained, but it did not help. An enriched Wilmott could have paid his court to her. It could only mean that he had come to prefer Phoebe, and this was no comfort.

She wondered how Augustus Nadis would react when he knew who the lady was that he had admired so much, and she did not have to wait long to find out.

The following day he called to ask them to join a theatre party and as they were about to drink tea, he stayed, and Richard, in his open fashion, told him of their discovery that Captain Wilmott's mistress was Arabella's former maid.

"Indeed," said Augustus, stirring his tea in a thoughtful manner. They all waited for some word of censure. "That would be where she learned her ladylike airs, of course," he said, bowing slightly in Arabella's direction. For at least a minute she did not realize that he intended this speech as a compliment; she thought it an insult.

"She is indeed a charming woman," he said further. "I am sure that her parties will be delightful." By now they were all staring at him.

"But do you approve, then, of such behavior?" asked Caroline in surprise.

"Well, one cannot exactly disapprove, you know; mistresses are all the thing; vastly elegant to have one; almost expected, you might say, and such a taking little thing! What would Society be without the Demi-reps?"

Caroline wondered if he would have talked so if Jane or the Russetts had been present. How quickly the amiable Derbyshire squire had taken on the mantle of the Dandy! She could not think of him as she had done formerly. Her notions of propriety were too formed, too immovable—subterranean passions might arise, to be sure; but to admit them! to flaunt them! as though they were a matter of pride, and not for heart burning and for shame. She looked across at Arabella, wondering what effect this complaisance towards wrong behaviour was having on her. Arabella's eyes were fixed on Augustus, who was happily drinking his tea, with every elegance of gesture which could be employed in that ceremony. For once, Arabella's thoughts were not apparent in her expression. Her features looked as though they had set into marble. The lips were folded together, the gaze rigid. Caroline almost looked round to see if someone had contrived to bring in a Medusa's head, and turn Arabella to stone. Her expression, as she looked at the man she was proposing to marry, was ice itself.

Chapter Eight

Cornelius Watts had not heard that soft voice, with an undertone like steel in silk, say of his address, "I have memorized it," and of contacting him, "The time is not yet." Therefore he had let Mirabelle slip once more into the back of his mind. His Mirabelle had died long ago, and the Earl had given the present-day Mirabelle her legacy and that was the end of it. But it was not the end of it.

He went into his office one morning, on hearing that a young woman had asked to see him. Young lady, the clerk had almost said, but he had corrected himself in the very act of beginning the word, to young woman. She stood against the window, but as there was no sun, and the day was dull and grey, filling the room with a dull grey light like fog, showing every detail yet with a touch more like death than life, Cornelius was not dazzled, or unable to read her expression. He came forward courteously, noticing her fashionable dress, her slim figure, asking how he could be of assistance to her. Then he came to a stop, and stood, saying,

"Good God!"

"Yes, Mr. Watts, I see you know me."

He flushed with anger, and his first thought was of turning her out. But he was confused, and so for a few seconds said nothing. She took the initiative, saying,

"It is not what can you do for me, Mr. Watts, but what can I do for you."

"There is nothing you can do for me." He did not understand her remark.

"I know a good deal about you, Mr. Watts. You are much respected for an upright man; your success rests on that reputation. Now if the world knew of you what I know, they would not care to put their affairs in your hands."

He was stung into heat.

"The world can know everything of me. Does know everything. My reputation is above your reach."

"You think so? Would they be so pleased to know that you are a seducer, who, having got an innocent girl with child, could leave her, abandon her? That the wretched girl took shelter in a house of ill repute, before her miserable death? What of your school for young women? What if the world knew that you founded that school only so that you could educate in it your bastard daughter?"

"What do you mean?" His voice was catching in his throat.

"You know what I mean."

"No, I do not. I am not guilty of these crimes you accuse me of. If you spread such tales around Society—if that is your intention—you will waste your time for, whatever rumours you have heard, they must be of someone else."

"Oh, no. You covered your tracks well, but not well enough. Will you deny lodging in the house of Goodwife Green, at the same time as a French Emigré and his daughter?"

He turned on her a look of pure astonishment.

"Do you deny that she was called Mirabelle, and that you were in love with her?"

"I don't deny it."

"Can you deny that you deserted her when she was with child, and that she finished her life miserably, crying out for you?"

He turned away from her, and walked to the fireplace and back again, in an agitated rush of movement.

"It cannot be true! She went back to France. There was no child! How could there be?" Then, as if his rapid brain began to recover from the shock of her words, and began to weigh and measure this extraordinary interview, he snapped into alertness and started to act quite differently.

"So, Miss—Madam—Hunt, you know all this about me. May I ask where you got your information? What is your price for secrecy, for I take it that is your errand?"

"Oh, my facts are on the best authority. Your friend Madame Eglantine could confirm them. I am glad you have decided to be sensible, it saves so much trouble—it goes against my conscience, of course, to allow you to go on deceiving so many good people about your real character. Very much against it."

"I'm pleased to hear that you have one." He saw her eyes darken stormily and regretted his tactics. He abandoned them at once, and tried to speak in a fawning manner.

"My—daughter—who you say was educated in our training school, which you have guessed was started merely as a blind. Oh! how astute you have been, Miss Phoebe—what was her name, now, and what do you say has happened to her since?"

"Oh, I have all the facts. She is Ann Ducros, and you have apprenticed her to a milliner."

It appeared that her conscience could be lulled to sleep by a payment of money. Payment would amount to confession that the accusations were true, and almost certainly lead to further demands, but Cornelius paid. When he was alone her words ran through his brain like fire. He had bought time. Mirabelle—she had gone to France. What possible connection could she have with Madame Eglantine? And Ann Ducros; he remembered the girl well. She had been a thin, quiet creature, very good with her needle. Mirabelle's daughter? But what did it all have to do with Phoebe Hunt? It was strange how different she had seemed to the docile maid he knew well from Welby House. Self-possessed, positive; if he had been guilty of her accusations, had been a weaker man, he would have found her menacing. As it was, he longed to rush into action, always his solace. But what action? His business would certainly suffer if this story got about, and it had enough truth in it to make it difficult to explain away. After all, he had recently found out that Mirabelle had not returned to France as early as he had thought. He shuddered as he imagined the Duchess of Doncaster, the Marchioness of Harome, the Earl of Epworth, hearing these tales. No doubt they would lose nothing in the telling. The training school, which he and Waveney had started after such long and careful consideration of the best ways to help the destitute who had no chance of learning skills and pro- viding for themselves, would certainly be thought to be a source of paramours—he could guess what talk would make of it. Wa- veney, with his young family dependent on him, might be harmed and dragged down as well as himself. He—who had always tried to follow the example of Mr. Valiant-for-truth—to submit to extor- tion, or to see his good name destroyed! But the thought that hurt more than anything was that, if he could believe a fraction of the story, Mirabelle had been destitute and needed him, and he had not known.

Christmas seemed very near. Caroline and Richard had sent gifts to Dick, who was not to come home until the summer. Dick was happy at his tutor's, and would not miss the family as much as his small sisters and brothers would miss him; so it was determined that the children's Christmas should be the nicest possible, to make up for it.

They were going out shopping; the girls put on their cloaks and bonnets, and picked up their little fur muffs, and waited for Caro- line, who was trying to get away from Baby Charles, who did not intend to let go. At last she freed herself from his clinging fingers, and walked firmly to the waiting group. But they were still not ready, for Arabella was arguing with Henry, who wanted to take his hoop. At last Arabella gave in, and they all walked briskly through the streets to the sound of the ring of iron on stone, and Henry's shouts for joy when he gave a good hit, and his cries of disgust when he caught it awkwardly on the rim, so that it wheeled crazily out of control.

Among so many shops, their attention was drawn in every direc- tion at once; but the first they paused at was a butcher's, filled with great joints, and in the background they could see sides of beef and mutton, waiting to take their turn upon the counter; the poulterer's was crammed with hanging birds; turkeys, pheasants, snipe, herons, woodcock, curlew, plovers, wild duck; hares hung among them; piled on the floor were rabbits by the score for the poorer families; the pork butcher's was in its element with great ropes of sausages flavoured with herbs, bowls of tripe and chitterlings, piles of bloodpuddings, steaming fresh from the boilers, pork pies like Norman castles, pigs' heads cut in half and gorily displaying their half tongues and half brains, so that little girls turned their heads away and only peeped out of the corners of their eyes, while Henry gazed boldly and wondered how it felt to be a pig. York hams hung in all their self-confident glory; bacon stood on the sides of the benches ready to be sliced by the knife; pigs' feet steamed in vulgar succulence. There was a crowd of ragged boys hovering by the pork butcher's, entranced by the plenty. Arabella fancied that she saw her little friend of her early morning walks, but it was not he; she gave one of the boys a farthing on the strength of this chance resemblance, and he rushed to buy some pigs' tails, and busied himself sucking them.

They moved on to the pastrycooks, and Martha, who had a sweet tooth, pressed her nose to the glass, savouring the vision of delicate marchpane, formed into all manner of delights; Christmas cakes, as big as chargers; plum bread, in great loaves; mince pies, in piles (as high as a house, declared Martha), each shaped like the manger.

"They are that shape," explained Caroline, "to remind us of Christ's birth."

Tiny biscuits starred the front of the window; Martha wished her breath did not mist up the pane so, she could hardly see . . .

The confectioner had a row of sugar pigs, pink and white, chasing each other along the bottom of the window, with a box full of sugar mice behind them; Caroline whispered to Arabella and then went inside for a minute, as the children waited impatiently, wondering if, on Christmas morning, they might find . . . perhaps it was too much to hope, to get anything before morning service, but after . . . and of course, there could hardly be a Boxing day without Christmas Boxes . . . might a tiny sugar mouse find his way into one?

Arabella was glad of her fur muff as she waited. The frost was nipping her fingers. She thought how many people she now knew in this London which had seemed so strange—but so exciting—in October. Famous people were no longer names, but flesh and blood. She could point them out, with pleasant superiority, to a newcomer; "Oh, yes, that is Lord Chesterfield, Lord Farendon,

His Royal Highness"—but he of course was unmistakable. If a newcomer had but seen one of the scurrilous prints, they would recognize him.

There were all the others, too. Not far away her former maid was languishing in a love nest with Captain Wilmott—down by the river Mrs. Ringrose was no doubt busy with her very best pies for the Christmas trade, and Isaac Sutherland and his good wife were living their austere and beautiful life as the endless Thames lapped their water steps; the boy she used to see on the street and give a penny to—how would he be faring without that help? How full the town was with people, and she knew all sorts and conditions of them . . . Augustus Nadis would be just completing his two-hour toilet, and tying his neckcloth; Mr. Watts would be up to his ears in papers and parchments; the world of her acquaintance swayed and swung about her, interlocking circles . . . she moved to one side as the brawny cats' meat man strode along with his malodorous basket on his head.

Caroline came out and they went on their way.

"I want to go to Mr. Whiffin, the tea dealer," she said. "But perhaps I will go tomorrow, or send William."

The brightest colour in the road was the fruiterer's. Out of the open door came a smell of such delicious freshness that the pork butchers seemed coarse, and the confectioners, cloying. Polished pyramids of scarlet apples and golden oranges, wicker baskets of chestnuts, were there, Christmas Pearmains, Russetts, Pippins.

"Those are like the corner tree gives, at Curteys," cried Lucy. "Look, Mama! Aren't they Wheelers' Russetts? Can we have some?"

"I've got a box of our own, dear; I'm saving them for Christmas Day."

"Scarlet Nonpareils! So crisp and juicy! Shall I buy some, Sister?"

"Tangerines!" Martha's eyes were like saucers.

"Perhaps there might be one of those, for a good girl, later on."

"I've never seen so many nuts," said little Kitty. "Those are walnuts, Mama, I know; and those are hazel nuts, like we pick from our hedges; but what are those long ones?"

"Almonds, dear; you haven't seen them in their shells before."

"Let's roast chestnuts!" cried Henry. "And snapdragon, Mama; let's play snapdragon."

"What would Christmas be," agreed Arabella, "without snapdragon?"

It was difficult to go on past the fruiterer's.

"Would it be extravagant," Caroline was eagerly eyeing the golden bunches of muscat grapes nestling in their cotton-lined baskets, "to have just one bunch?"

"Two bunches!" cried Arabella, taking Henry's stick and hoop from him and bowling the hoop at random across the pavement, narrowly avoiding the stomach of an elderly gentleman, and bumping into a sweeping boy carrying his brushes. The boy looked longingly at the hoop as it tumbled over and made gradually decreasing spirals until it settled on the pavement, and Henry ran to rescue it. Arabella thought that at this rate they would never get as far as the bookshop, but she knew that she could always come again without the children. Their pleasure was worth the forfeiting of today's purchases.

The toyshop was so magnificent to the children that at first they were awestruck, but the silence gave way to whispers and then to rising chatter.

"Have you seen it?" Lucy asked Arabella, her eyes like blue stars. "Have you seen that doll? Oh! Isn't she lovely. A blue silk dress, and an opera cloak, and that travelling trunk, with all her underpinnings in it . . . you can see them, because they've left its lid open, there's some tiny pantaloons, can you see them, Aunt?"

"Do you think that if I save all my pennies, I can have a hobby horse like that one, Mama?" Henry's hoop was in temporary eclipse.

Martha and Kitty were chattering together like two small birds, and Arabella just caught the gist of it, among Oh!s and Ah!s. She smiled, remembering when she too had measured happiness by such trifles. How did she measure it now? What would it take to make her feel for one moment that unclouded joy? She thought of Augustus Nadis, and the pleasure of driving with him—then she thought of his attitude to Phoebe, and the world of fashion, with its endless anxiety that one should always be in the swim . . .

Caroline caught her eye.

"I'll look after them for a few minutes—run along, Bell, the bookshop is just at the end of the street." Bell obediently ran along.

She rapidly bespoke for her present to Caroline, a copy of Miss Owenson's new novel, *Woman; or Ida of Athens*, and for the three little girls, *The History of Pineapple Pie*, *The Alphabet of Goody Two Shoes*, and *The Butterfly's Birthday*. She went as far as the one and sixpenny version of *The Butterfly's Birthday*, because it looked so much nicer, coloured, than the plain copy at one shilling.

She rejoined the others, her task done, and they made a few purchases as they walked towards home. The errand boy from the fruiterer's was to follow after with their order of Pines, "Such fine juicy ones!" Caroline had said; and the toymaker had understood, by subtle hints from Caroline, and surreptitious pointings, and significant looks, which toys he was to pack up when the children were on their way, and to send to Welby House.

Afterwards, that outing lingered in Arabella's memory. For the rest of the day she kept thinking of it—the children's eager faces, the plenitude of the shops, the church bells and the chime of great clocks, measuring the time as it wore away towards Christmas; the crowds in the streets of young and old, rich and poor; it settled down like a bright fragment into her mosaic of London Memories, which gave her more pleasure in times of reverie than the lush countryside of her youth had ever done.

Christmas; a calm, peaceful day; the air full of church bells, as they walked along to morning service; the streets were filled with smiling people, and the frost in the air defeated the dirty slush of the preceding week, and made the fine London pavements for once clean to walk upon. Muffs, and warm bonnets, with the children's curls tumbling from underneath, were the favoured wear, and Arabella, in the simple bonnet which had once been overburdened with trimmings, showed the vulnerable nape of her neck above her fur tippet.

"Marry me," breathed Nathaniel Eeles into Arabella's ear, as they came out of church; she laughed, and shook her head at him, and he went off with a sigh of despair.

The Russetts called on their way to somewhere else, as so often; Jane drew Arabella on one side for a minute to tell her, with vibrating joy, that she had just had a letter from Robert Spencer, such a dear, dear, letter . . .

"I wonder how they all are, back at Curteys," said William, meaning just one pair of grey eyes; at least he knew that everyone on the estate would be having a good Christmas, for Master had ordered a bullock to be slaughtered, which would give every family a stone of beef; and Fred Wilson had been told to give a sack of potatoes to such as were in need of them, and if there were any without firing, to see they got some coals . . . Coals! They would be blessing his name at Curteys, his and his lady's. The old men and women crouched over the luxury of coals, with the potatoes and beef in the larder, would feel like kings and queens.

A calm Christmas, before the gaiety of Boxing Day, when Lucy could hardly believe it when she was given the doll in blue silk, complete with travelling trunk; she still had her old wooden baby from so many years ago, and she felt she had to solemnly introduce the new doll, and reassure the battered old toy, with an affectionate whisper in her ear, that she was not being supplanted.

The noise Henry made with his new hobby horse had been deafening, and Mr. Watts, who seemed rather quiet and out of sorts, had wondered how Richard stood it without a word to the boy. Martha and Kitty were so busy with sugar mice, and a most enchanting baby house, that they hardly had any time to spare, as they told everybody importantly.

Caroline, at some time unknown to Arabella, must have gone to a bookshop, for she brought out and presented Crosby's *Fortune Telling Pocket Book*. This not only helped in the telling of fortunes, but was full of enigmas, charades, new steps for old dances, poetry, and Pleasant Talks, which were meant to be spoken aloud and which Arabella announced she would read out, one a day, after dinner. This sounded like a penance, but they had a great deal of fun that evening with the Pocket Book, and the children went to bed flushed and laughing, and convinced that there had never been and would never be again, any other Christmas as good as this one.

Christmas had passed by without a sight of Mr. Nadis, and

Caroline wondered at his absence, looking at Arabella, and trying to guess from her expression whether she was missing him. He came, however, with the Russetts, to an evening party, and greeted Arabella in his usual manner, she appearing as pleased to see him as ever. He distinguished her with his attentions, and if they were a little more mechanical—if there was a slight coolness between them which had never been there before—no one but he and Arabella guessed it.

She listened with a grave face to his conversation. He was all criticism, tonight, of the clothes of the other people in the room; they were in the Egyptian Saloon.

That jacket was too tight a fit; such and such a lady had chosen her ribbons badly; Arabella made very little reply, even when he hinted at the perfection of his own tailoring—and she should have responded with a compliment—and when he praised the delicacy of her own gown, she smiled in silence. Augustus went through the women who were present, grading their charms by the style of their clothes, ignoring native graces of mind or body; and in discussing the men, did not question amiability or sense, preferring to admire those who were best dressed and scoff at the others.

Arabella wondered; where was the charm she had always before noticed in him? Where the gay conversation which had made their acquaintanceship so lively? Perhaps the fault lay in herself. This was the man she was prepared to marry. Was she fickle beyond redemption? Or had she only now learned to know him?

"Jane," said Arabella, when they were alone on a sofa behind the exotic screen, "are you fond of Mr. Nadis?" It had struck her that Jane had been very quiet about her friend's relationship with that person.

Jane hesitated.

"Do you and I ever hide our feelings from each other?" Arabella urged.

"Do you still intend to marry him, Bell, and become my cousin?"

"He has not asked me. Perhaps I do."

"Then I can say nothing, except to wish you happy, and be glad that we will be permanently connected. The estate in Derbyshire is one of wild beauty, and the house is snug and comfortable."

"And the husband? He goes with the house and estate, you know; there is no having one without the other; and his wife will see little of Derbyshire, for his heart is set on one half-mile of London."

"Then—I must say, Bell, and if I lose your friendship, remember it was you who asked—then I own I have always found him dull. Worthy and amiable, but I do not want a man to talk forever on the cut of a gown . . . Now Robert—Mr. Spencer—is, as you know, a Latin scholar of some note, and an excellent sportsman, and his conversation would keep one entertained through the dullest winter."

"Your mother's training is not all lost, Jane. You require intelligence in your husband."

"I look up to Robert for his learning, and I love to hear him talk. But he does not talk—as you know very well—like the people my mother admires. There is liveliness and spirit in his character; which I need. I am glad to admire my husband, Bell. When we are married, I will forget my own books, but am gratified that he is respected for his studies."

"You are still certain that you will be married? Lady Russett's veto has not made you think differently yet?"

Jane did not answer for a while. Then she said,

"Do you think it is possible to love more than one man, Bell? To really love two men?"

"I think so! If one is a good while after the other. Or if one loves them in quite different ways. There are so many different ways of loving. Then, who said love was necessary for a match? Some of the happiest marriages one sees are arranged between the families. If Lady Russett arranges a match, have you the strength to refuse?"

"Can I love anyone but Robert?"

Jane had no time to answer further. The card tables had broken up, and the servants were bringing in the refreshments; and in spite of all Arabella's early doubts, Caroline's suppers were counted among the best in London.

Chapter Nine

There had not been much delay between Phoebe's visit to Mr. Watts' office and his journey to see the young girl called Ann Ducros. He entered the milliner's establishment with the benevolent air of a friendly alderman and enquired how she was doing, and nodded blandly when told that she gave every satisfaction. In the training school she had been quiet and hard-working and her employer was pleased to have her, and suggested that if any other such young women were produced by the school, she would be interested. Staff of good calibre were hard to find.

"I'd like to have a word with her, if I may," said Mr. Watts, and among beams of goodwill from both himself and the milliner Ann was called and told that she might stop work for a few minutes and take the air with her benefactor.

He questioned her kindly, about her early life, her parents, her upbringing. All things that had been gone into when she joined the school, but then he had not taken particular notice, once satisfied that she was a suitable case for help. Now, as he talked to her, he was keenly searching her face for some likeness to Mirabelle, and every syllable, every inflexion, every movement of her features, seemed to be engraved on his memory. Her hair was golden, but a dull gold, not that living, gleaming gold of Mirabelle's; her figure was slight and her movement graceful; she was sixteen, and so could be counted a woman; but it was not the

grace of movement of Mirabelle. Her eye was blue, but it was a
lifeless blue; her voice gentle, but not gentle enough. She had
been brought up by foster parents, had been told her mother was
dead, had had visits from time to time by someone who brought
money, and said she had been a friend of her mother's; a large
lady, very bright; a Madame Eglantine.

Still cheery, still benevolent, Cornelius Watts parted from her
at the door of the shop, with a few words about being a good girl
and going to church on Sundays. He hardly knew what he was
saying, except that the appropriate noises were being made, both
to Ann Ducros and the milliner; and as Ann re-entered the back
room, so full of muslins and threads and feathers and other thin
pale girls, she gave him a little wave of her slim hand which was,
for that flash of time, pure Mirabelle.

He walked away sad and puzzled. In this situation who was
there he could talk to? He thought of Arabella; talking things over
with her was becoming a cherished habit. But she was too young
—too madcap—not yet the woman he thought she might one day
become; Caroline! Who else? No need to mention the visit of
Phoebe. No need to mention the suggestion that Ann was his own
child. He was confident that could not possibly be true, but even
the idea must be kept from getting about. These things, true or
not, spread by themselves, like thistledown in the wind. He could
tell her that he had discovered—or thought he had discovered—
that she was the daughter of an old friend; that was enough to explain his wish to help her, and not see her languish in the back
room of the milliner's until she was carried out in a coffin. Too
many young apprentices with that pale candlelike look ended that
way. Caroline would know just the right thing to do.

Arabella, feeling a little grey and unhappy about Augustus Nadis,
and her relationship with him, looked forward to seeing Mr.
Watts, his bright smile, his ready flow of talk, his interest in her
opinion and the minutiae of her world. But he disappointed her.
Caroline seemed to be the only person he wanted to talk to; it was
very obvious. He schemed to get Caroline alone, and when he did
Arabella could hear them, talking earnestly for a long time, and
then the next time he came it was the same again. She was re-

minded of the first evening, when he had wanted to talk about his garden. It had been plain that he thought a great deal of Caroline's opinion, and very little of Arabella's. Very little of Richard's either, come to that. He was a provoking, detestable man!

It was unfortunate that, on a day when he was to spend the evening with them, Caroline should be called away as soon as she had refreshed him with a cup of tea. There was some domestic crisis which, Mrs. Jackson felt, needed Caroline's attention. Richard was out walking with the Admiral and not expected back for another half-hour.

Mr. Watts was left, for the time at least, alone in the Egyptian Saloon with Arabella, and she was in no mood to amuse or entertain him. Augustus Nadis had not called; Captain Wilmott and Phoebe were still creating a dazzling impression in Society, and she hardly dared go anywhere for fear of meeting them.

Nothing would have been as welcome as quiet misery, indulged in alone in her room, with perhaps the relief of snappish behaviour towards her maid.

Cornelius showed no sign of regretting Caroline's departure. Instead, he settled in his chair, crossed his legs, cocked his head on one side, and looked up at her as she stood playing with the silver toys which ornamented a side table.

"How are you, Miss Hill?" he asked. "I do not think you and I have had the opportunity for a talk this past week. Did you see today's news-sheet?"

"No, sir. I have had neither time nor inclination today for such reading."

"But it would have interested you, of all things! You did not know, then, of the boat, loaded with copies of the *Moniteur*, which was turned adrift from Calais?"

"No, sir, I did not." Her shortness did not seem to deter him, for he went on:

"It floated nearly across the channel when it was picked up by one of our fishing boats and brought into Dover."

"Do you mean it was deliberately set adrift?"

"Of course." She was not usually, he thought, so obtuse.

"But what was the point of it?"

"The point," said Mr. Watts, beginning to wonder what was

the matter with her quick mind, "was to tell us Napoleon's point of view. The *Moniteur* was full of news of French successes in Spain."

She looked at him enigmatically, and suddenly felt a strong desire to upset and annoy him. He, after all, was present, and Augustus Nadis and Captain Wilmott were not. And had he not been neglecting her shamefully for the last week?

He, in his turn, was looking at her, in admiration. The slender waist, the dark head poised on her neck and shoulders as gracefully as a flower on its stem, the shadowy eye, veiled by its lashes and at present almost mournful with some emotion he could not divine, her profile, so clear-cut against the background of the gloom of Egypt, seemed to please him, in spite of her lack of interest in the floating boat with its load of newspapers.

"You come here often, Mr. Watts," she said, opening war with a deceptively quiet fusillade.

"It is my pleasure."

"But I do not think you come with the purest of motives. I have surprised your secret, sir. You are in love with my sister."

His face had been as cheerful as a speedwell. But as she looked, it changed, became hard, remote. He did not reply immediately.

"Your sister!" he said at last.

She was afraid of what she had done. The change in him terrified her. The atmosphere between them, so friendly over the past few weeks, was suddenly hostile. The enormity of her remark became the more obvious, the more she thought about it.

He rose from his chair, and the air seemed to vibrate with unspoken thoughts, but what they were Arabella could not guess.

"You accuse me of being in love with your sister." He turned on his heel, and walked away across the room, and then spoke with only his profile presented to her.

"Could anyone know your sister, and not love her, Miss Hill?"

Arabella was still combative, exalted in a mood she did not understand. If her life had depended on it, she could not have left him alone and let the matter rest.

"We all love her, for her goodness and kindness, but that is not to what I refer. You have a dishonourable passion for her."

"How dare you, madam!"

"I would dare anything to protect her and her reputation."

"You goad me with these accusations! What are my innermost feelings to you?" He turned towards her, and his eyes were so intense that she could not meet them. "Who are you, so careless with your own reputation, to pretend to defend another's?"

His energy, always so abundant, vibrated in his anger. "Do you realize," he went on, "what disrespect you have shown your sister, in supposing her the object of such a passion?" His voice had dropped, but although low, it was clear, and every word burned Arabella. "I must try to forgive you this indiscretion, because you are young and foolish. May I suggest, that instead of malicious imaginings with regard to Mrs. Welby, you try to imitate her in sense and propriety?"

But you have not denied it, was the thought that rang through Arabella's mind. With all this heat, you have not said that you do not love her! And she could not have said why this gave her such intense pain.

Mr. Watts drew himself up, braced his back, and seemed to regain command of himself. He had not lost control like this with Phoebe, whom he despised as he might despise a viper to be crushed. At any day she might trumpet to the world that he had seduced and deserted Mirabelle, and then Arabella would believe the worst of him, as everyone would. She would think herself justified. For some time neither of them spoke. Arabella did not dare to. For a while she had believed he was going to strike her in his fury; then he had moved away, but his voice had whipped across the room.

"I will try to behave courteously to you in public," he said at last. "You and I must both try to appear as though nothing had happened. But, Miss Hill, I must always regard you as one on whom one cannot rely for ladylike behaviour."

From him, she felt, this was an ultimate loss of esteem, as though he had detected in her the unseemly oaths and lack of delicacy of a fishwife.

He left the room, turning only at the door to say,

"Please excuse me to Mr. and Mrs. Welby," before closing the door behind him with quiet finality.

Alone, Arabella wondered just what she had done. The devil in her was satisfied, and she began to review her action. She had been unladylike. She had behaved unforgivably. She had goaded him. Now she felt as though she had been kicked by a horse, or had fallen from a precipice, so that the wind was singing in her ears. Was it possible that she had witnessed in him such intensity of feeling? How could Caroline—in spite of everything, Arabella still thought her dowdy—how could Caroline inspire such passion? When she herself had inspired nothing . . . except now, surely, Mr. Watts' loathing and reproach . . .

In that hour in the Egyptian Saloon she went again and again through the words which were printed on her mind, saw his movements, as he turned haughtily away from her, and then paused. Regret swept over her, and shame; but the devilish exhilaration of battle which had prompted her was slow to die, and she went through a mixture of emotions which she could not name.

Why had she behaved so—why lose, for some impulse to show power over him, the growing friendship—interest—he had been showing towards her? For there had been such interest, and it had had value for her. And now it would be gone—and all because she had observed tenderness in his manner towards Caroline, and because this week it had been Caroline he had been seeking out, and not herself . . .

She shrugged her shoulders with sudden hard air which did not suit her.

So? What did it matter? It was a husband she wanted, and what did the friendship and respect of one older man matter? Old? Well, was not near forty old? Men of his age were not in her field of consideration as husbands, although of course one might ask them to be godfather to one's children. And a rich old bachelor like Mr. Watts might be a very good godfather. That was what it was. She was sorry—yes, she admitted it—to have lost his respect. But her sorrow could only be for the loss of a potential godfather for the children of herself and Augustus. Arabella gave a little nod to herself after this exercise in self-deception, and left the Egyptian Saloon to go to her bedroom. She had been right about the Egyptian Saloon—it was never dull—and she had lost the impulse to weep, or to torment her maid.

"Where is Mr. Watts?" asked Caroline, when they gathered to-

gether in the dining-room. "I thought he had come for dinner."
"I heard him go, as Joel was taking off my boots," said Richard.
Caroline looked puzzled. "I left him in the Egyptian Saloon
with Arabella . . . Bell! Have you upset him?" Arabella shrugged
her shoulders carelessly, and Caroline compressed her lips and
looked displeased. But at that moment Lucy came into the room
to join them for the meal, so she said nothing more.

Lucy was learning to meet the smaller obstacles of Society. A
sweeter, more innocent face never wrestled with the problem of
what to do with a cherry stone, or the bone in a piece of fish.

When she was in bed, Arabella's thoughts returned to the
events of the day, and she found herself unable to sleep. A mood
of introspection was unusual for her. She considered her own character, and with a flash of insight saw that to be wilful and capri-
cious might frighten, instead of attract, a man; and that a suitor
magnetized by her vivacity, might hesitate at her peremptoriness.
Mr. Watts could not have castigated her more than, in that sleep-
less night, she punished herself. Well, life must go on; she must
appear as bright and happy as ever; but it seemed to her that she
had recently lost a great deal, and gained very little.

Chapter Ten

"I am getting up a theatre party," said Augustus Nadis, "to visit the Olympic Pavilion tomorrow evening; can you all come?" His glance swept the assembled company, from Lord and Lady Russett to Jane, Arabella and Caroline.

Lady Russett assented graciously. Lord Russett cried,

"And what is it this time, Nadis? Before Christmas you bustled us off to Drury Lane to see 'Venoni,' or—what did they call it—"

"Or 'The Novice of St. Marks,' Papa," said Emma.

"And Bluebeard after; good enough stuff, for a social evening; but it is still running, is it not, and I for one do not wish to see it twice."

"No, nor I," said Augustus quickly, "although they are now following 'Venoni' with 'The Devil to Pay' . . . which would be quite different, you know; but I was suggesting the Olympic Pavilion, as a change from the Lane. They say it is a very spectacular production, opening tomorrow."

"I did so love that play we saw when we first came up, do you remember, Papa?" asked Jane, smiling sentimentally at the recollection. " 'Kais, or Love in the Desert' . . . oh, those choruses of Arabs and Pilgrims! How romantic they were! And the costumes were so very exotic and pretty—"

"That was at the Lane," said Emma.

"Are you all joining me in going to the Olympic Pavilion tomorrow?" said Augustus, exasperated, trying to return to the previous point of the conversation.

"Of course," put in Caroline. "We will come with you with pleasure, Mr. Nadis. The horsemanship at the Olympic is said to be superb."

"Yes, yes, Augustus," added Lady Russett. "We will be pleased to come. The Twelve Days have never dragged before as they are doing this year. Perhaps it is with Jane's illness, but Town seems very tedious; there is a deal of Nothing Doing; one might as well be at Littlethorpe Park."

By half-past six on the following evening they had taken their places at the Pavilion. Caroline was a good deal tried by Lord Russett's fashionable insistence on being late, because she was herself congenitally disposed to be early, and she was convinced, as the minutes ticked by without the arrival of the Russetts, that he had somehow got himself into the Sanspareil Theatre which, after all, was very close, and was even now settling down to watch "The Ghost in the Rigging, or Woolwich in an Uproar," followed by, "The Red Robber, or The Statue in the Wood."

She was reassured only two seconds before the beginning of the piece, by their arrival.

Augustus had been in his place, next to Arabella, long before, and was busily engaged in pointing out the persons of note who were arriving, in the pauses between going over the playbill and anticipating the delights of the evening. He would have to become much more blasé about the theatre before he would risk missing a second of a performance. There was an interest in seeing a piece which was on view for only the second time in fifteen years; none of them were likely to have seen it before, and it promised entertainment of the most delightful kind.

"A serio comic capricio!" said Richard. "Then we will not know whether to laugh or cry, Carrie. 'The little World!' Aye, the world is indeed little, as none know better than those who have sailed across it . . . yet a few yards can be impossible to cover 'Or *Ombres Chinoises*!' Well, China I have never seen, so I will regard its shadow with interest."

It was a most dramatic production, and all of them forgot their surroundings, forgot their companions almost, in the spectacle before them. There was music, song, dance, and brilliant imitative action; although the bill had promised a hundred-and-twenty pieces of scenery, the constant changes made the number appear even more, and Caroline wished that the children had been older, and invited, as she was sure they would have loved it. The dialogues were interesting, the songs pretty, and they all thought that the machinery animating the whole must be remarkably clever.

Then they relaxed and watched the Equestrian Exercises, involving the whole company, and amazed by their skill, Caroline remembered that during the earlier parts of the day the Pavilion was used to give tuition in horsemanship, and she wondered if lessons would benefit the children. Mr. Smith's Flying Act of Horsemanship drew gasps of admiration, and she changed her opinion, for if little Henry saw such an exhibition, she knew that he would be experimenting at home and falling off, and not gifted with Mr. Smith's astounding powers, he would be bound to injure himself.

This part of the evening concluded with the grand spectacle called "French Intruders, or, The Maid of Portugal," and then there was a quieter interlude, during which they listened to Mr. Johannot, rendering for the second time, "Abraham Newland's Ghost," and "What a beauty I did grow," and Miss Bloomgreen singing on this, her second appearance, "Just like Love."

Augustus took advantage of this quieter interlude to talk to Arabella. He was in a state of rapture at the elegance of the waterfall effect produced with his neckcloth by a nobleman in a seat opposite, but the lady accompanying him was severely censured, and described as a "fright," although Arabella had been thinking what a sweet face she had.

"Those ribbons!" cried Augustus, in admiration. "What an excellent choice of colour, to match such a dress! Do you have that lady's acquaintance, Miss Hill?" She followed his eyes, and found he was admiring a young woman in the extreme of fashion, who was flirting with her fan, and coquetting with a dandy who was attending her. The face was pretty, and the dress, no doubt, the latest, but Arabella decided she preferred her own shimmering net, and simple opera cloak of ivory silk, lined with the pink of a baby's palm, and trimmed with swansdown, to such extravagances of colour and shape. Besides, the young woman's face was hard, heartless even, and did not attract her. But Augustus' attention had left the young woman of the ribbons, and travelled further, to an elderly duchess, well known to them by sight, who, he announced, "looked like a stork" and was "not fit to be seen."

Arabella had a disquieting sensation. She felt that whatever the personal worth of the persons who passed before him, Augustus saw only the outward show. The dandy who wore his estate on his back was admired; the family man, who dressed simply and sat with his modestly clothed wife, was condemned as not worth looking at.

All around she saw much to interest; the poorer people were now entering, as it was half-price time, mingling with the richer; among them were some fashionables who had decided to come halfway through the evening; everywhere she saw the innumerable facets of the human character; envy, hatred and greed were mirrored here as well as the more obvious simple happiness of the evening, the glad looks among family parties, the secret looks of lovers, alone among the crowd in their private worlds; the heavy stupidity of the drunken officer who had just made his way in; the timidity of the young milliner on perhaps her one outing of the year, tucked in a corner and shrinking from notice. There was so much to see! But Augustus saw this not at all. He saw the soiled ribbon, the creased coat, the worn stockings, or the elegant gown, the new type of trimming, the coat with a fit equalled only by his own . . . they might, Arabella felt, as well have been worn by dummies as human beings, except that the bodies within could also earn his praise or censure. They could have twisted spines or spindle shanks, or be fine, upstanding figures of men, or graceful women. There was no doubt who Augustus considered as the pick of the audience. He felt very satisfied with himself, and with her; Lady Russett and Lord Russett earned his approval; Jane and Emma were "passable," and if he was silent on the subject of Caroline, at least Richard's boots came in for praise.

Arabella grew thoughtful. Would this conversation satisfy her for the rest of her life? Had she been wise to decide that she could be happy with Augustus? She thought over again his reaction to Phoebe's defection. Many times since that afternoon she had dwelt on it; but now she could hide from herself no longer that she had serious doubts about Augustus' ability to make her happy. She knew she could make him happy; she could see with crystal clearness just what it required, what would be expected of her, in what ways she must be content to behave to produce his happiness. There would be no stint of money to make her miserable; an excellent table, an elegant home, expensive clothes, these would be things she could take for granted . . . it was fortunate that the next part of the programme was beginning, or her mood might have caused remark, for she could no longer keep up her side of the conversation.

The last part of the evening was a performance, for the second time in four years, of the popular serio comic Pantomime of "Quixote and Sancho, or Harlequin Warrior."

It was not enough to have Mr. Crossman as Harlequin, and Mr. Cook as Quixote, Mr. Norman as Sancho, and Miss Bloomgreen (her second appearance on any stage) as Mirth, and Miss Greville as Florella, and Mrs. Parker—the redoubtable Mrs. Parker —as Columbine; in addition, in the course of the Pantomime, two squadrons of Horse took the arena, to show various evolutions of ancient warfare.

By the time the show was ended, it was very late, and they were hungry, and tired of sitting still. It was with pleasure that they all went on, as agreed beforehand, to Mr. Nadis' rooms, for a supper; and then, at his suggestion, they went to a masquerade, dressed in dominos of his providing. Arabella was amazed at Lady Russett. Such frivolity! Usually she frowned on evenings so purposeless, devoted merely to pleasure. The only conclusion was that some streak of motherliness had been aroused by Jane's illness, and she had come to give her daughter pleasure, for Jane loved all kinds of spectacle and had been as happy as a child, and eating and masquerading in the early hours of the morning had all the charms of novelty to her.

Normally, Arabella was sure, the Russetts would rather have stayed quietly at home with their own music and their books, than endure such entertainment. It did not occur to her that the normal forms of social politeness meant something, even to them, and that they wished to retain their connection with Augustus;

also that her own relationship with him was the subject, in the Russett family, of speculation. There were the estates in Derbyshire, and if Augustus had no heirs, they would pass to the Russett line of the family . . . and perhaps Arabella had done Lady Russett justice, perhaps for once, she wished to please Jane . . .

Augustus had noticed Arabella's withdrawal from talk, he had seen her lack of agreement with him; some little remarks of hers had jarred on him, and he was not altogether pleased with her. During the supper and the masquerade, when they had talked again, and danced together, he had felt reassured, but for him, too, clouds had crossed the sunny certainty he had previously had of her.

Dawn—an early but winter dawn—had begun to break before they thought of going home. As they came out on to the street, taking off their dominos and sending them home to Augustus' chambers by his footman, they found that already they could see quite well, well enough not to need the services of a linkboy. In the workaday light they felt all the hectic gaiety of revellers, their feet still tingling to the rhythm of the dance, their bodies still wanting to be rotating and whirling.

"Let us walk home?" cried Augustus. "Why not? Through all the people who are out already at this time in the morning. You might surprise your maid, Mrs. Welby, just risen and scrubbing the steps; or a footman; your cook, Lady Russett, by the time we arrive, might be buying her cresses, or getting her chimneys swept. Come! Let us end the night by strolling home."

Lord Russett shook his head.

"Lady Russett is quite tired enough, Nadis, in your service this evening. I have already sent a messenger to fetch the carriage. Can we give you a lift?"

"I thank you," Richard answered. "We will be obliged."

"Is no one to accompany me?" cried Augustus.

"Caroline," said Arabella, "would you allow me to do so? I do not know how it is, but I too have a fancy to sample the morning air; Mr. Nadis, I am sure, will not mind taking me to Clarges Street. It is barely quarter-of-an-hour's walk, and if you arrive first, and instruct Mrs. Jackson, perhaps she would heat a little bouillon to set Mr. Nadis on his way home again."

Caroline, after thinking a moment, could not raise any objection. All around them other revellers of both sexes were to be seen, setting off, some separately, some in each other's company on foot. She agreed; meaning looks were exchanged among the Russetts; and Arabella and Augustus, with a dance in their step, set off on their short journey.

They talked little. Both, although they would not have admitted it, were beginning to feel the effects of a night of revelry; their heads did not feel as clear as they might have done, and their feet, still moving with the spirit of the dance, were unexpectedly tripping over cobblestones more often than they thought. The remarks they did exchange were mainly about the show at the Olympic; the amazing acts of horsemanship performed by Mr. Smith had perhaps impressed them more than anything else in the evening, and they went over his acts in their memories, with little exclamations of "how marvellously he . . ." or "and when—it was superb, if you remember . . ."

Absorbed in just getting along without showing tiredness, and in this chat, they were unprepared for a sudden outbreak of cries and noise, and the eruption of a small whirlwind from a set of area steps, which whirlwind, precipitating itself across the pavement, hurtled into Arabella, almost knocking her over and adhering, with remarkable tenacity, to her skirts.

Hardly had she recovered her balance from this contact than a force—if the first was a whirlwind, this, being slower and heavier, might perhaps be termed a tidal wave, except that it was difficult to think of anything as clean as water in connection with it—a second force emanated from the area steps. This proved to be a very large and angry chimney sweep, with an upraised stick in his hand, and a very ferocious expression, which led one to the conclusion—and correctly so—that the first small whirlwind might have been his climbing boy; and so, looking down, Arabella discovered, it was.

"Gie 'im 'ere," said the sweep.

"I beg your pardon?" said Arabella.

"Help!" cried the little boy. For he was a very little boy—not, Arabella judged, above five years old. At least, she thought he said "help!" but it was rather difficult to tell, as his face was buried in her opera cloak, of ivory silk, trimmed with swansdown, and lined with the pink of a baby's palm . . .

"My dear Miss Hill!" cried Augustus. "Your clothes! My man, you will be held responsible for this. You will have to compensate the lady. Her clothes will be soiled beyond redemption."

"Not my fault," growled the sweep. "Fine folks shouldn't be walking about at this time in a morning, stopping honest folks as has to earn their living getting on with their jobs. Come on, Ben. Let me 'ave 'im, Miss. Your Ladyship. Ma'am."

Arabella had been looking down at the boy, who appeared to think that as long as he retained fast hold of her, he was safe. She saw that, although it was such a cold time of the year, he had no stockings, his shirt and jacket were both so old as to afford no warmth, and he was blue with cold. Perhaps, she reasoned, he had taken his warmer clothes off to climb the chimney. Holes at elbows and knees showed those joints to be covered with sores, some old and forming calluses, some newer and still red and weeping. He was such a little boy!

"Climbing boys have to be eight years old, don't they?" she asked the sweep.

"Oh, yes. 'Tis Act of Parliament, Madam. Eight years old."

"He's very small for eight."

"It was his mother said he was eight, Ma'am, when she sold him to me. And that was six months since."

"Sold him?"

"Asked me to take him prentice. To teach him to be a master chimney sweep, Ma'am. Three pounds, I gave her," said the sweep piously, adding on fifty per cent.

"Come on, Miss Hill," said Augustus. He was standing with a look of distaste on his face. The sight of soot on her cloak was almost too much for him. "You must get home and set your maid to clean your cloak as fast as may be. What is your name, my man? If it is impossible to clean, Miss Hill will send you the bill for a new one."

Arabella, heedless of the soot, had put her hand on the boy.

"But, Mr. Nadis, I want to know why! Why was he running away? Come, Mr. whatever your name is, why was he?"

"My name is Black, Ma'am, 'tis a proper name for a chimney

sweep, because people remembers it. Why, he was only running away because he didn't want to do his job. We all started as climbing boys, I keeps telling him that. None of us liked it at first. But if you're set to learn a trade by your kind parents, Ma'am, learn it you must; and the only way to learn it is to do it. Now, come here, you," and he made a grab at Ben.

"Let's look at the chimney he wouldn't climb," said Arabella.

"Miss Hill!" Augustus' voice rose louder in protest. "Your cloak! You seem to have no concern for your cloak! How can you be seen like that? On the rest of the way home it is nearly sure someone will see you! He is but a child! He must take his chance!"

"The gentleman's right, Ma'am. There's plenty more where he came from. Plenty to sell their seven-years' service for twenty or thirty shillings. I paid more for him, see, just because he is little, and can get up chimneys the others cannot . . ."

"In the country," observed Arabella reflectively, "our servants seem to sweep the chimneys quite well, with a heather brush, or a broom, or by climbing themselves, up the very wide ones."

"Oh yes, Ma'am," said the sweep, sidling round Arabella so as to take a grab at Ben. "Oh, and wouldn't we like to do the same? But since there was so much sea coal burnt, chimneys have been built narrower and narrower, and there's many a one with a forty-foot run only seven-inches wide; now how can it be cleaned without a climbing boy? And the cook is waiting."

The cook had appeared, and was standing by with folded arms.

"This chimney's smoking," she remarked, "and are you going to sweep it or aren't you? For if not, there are other sweeps with boys who will."

"The chimney will be hot if you've lit the fire," said Arabella.

"That's why he won't go up it, the little devil," said Mr. Black. "Just because there's been talk about young Will of Blaby's . . ." He caught Ben's legs with a cut from his stick, and the boy howled and took closer hold on Arabella.

"Miss Hill!" put in Augustus Nadis. "I cannot countenance this. Either you let that boy return to his master, and walk on with me, or I must be compelled to leave you."

"What happened to Blaby's boy?" asked Arabella, ignoring Augustus.

"Well, these things happen sometimes—it's nature. He died. But boys do die."

"And the world well rid of pauper children," said Augustus, who was standing now two yards off.

"Did he die in a chimney?"

"Well, where else was he to die?" said Mr. Black with contempt.

"Miss Hill, will you come? The concerns of this good man are none of yours. You might be seen at any moment. I beg you . . ."

Arabella turned and looked at Augustus as though she had never seen him before.

"Mr. Nadis, do you value a human life less than my cloak?"

"A child is soon replaced; such a cloak is not."

"Does it not concern you—" she remembered something she had heard Mr. Watts say—"that while the House of Commons was abolishing Negro Slavery this year, its own chimneys were being swept by little boys of four, five and six years old, sold, as this boy was sold, into duress far worse than any slave?"

Augustus in his turn looked shocked.

"My dear Miss Hill, such things are no concern of a lady! You really must not mention such matters. They are not spoken of in polite society. There is no need for you to concern yourself with any such thing! You must not—I pray you will not—ever mention such matters again. Let go the boy; come home; we will endeavour to forget this."

Her face was stormy.

"If that is your opinion, sir, then we must part company. You may leave me. I must value a life above a garment, and will take the boy back to Welby House. Mr. Black, here is two guineas; you have already had six-months' work out of him. I only pray that his legs are not too distorted to prevent him growing to a normal height."

"What point?" said Augustus. "Take him, and there will be another in his place before nightfall. What good can such a rescue do, except to prove to me how little you value my opinion?" He had still not made up his mind to go and to leave her. But she was made of sterner stuff.

"Go, sir," she said, and taking Ben by the hand, dragged him with her along the street. He came willingly enough, hardly able to believe his good luck.

Augustus hesitated. For things to come to such a pass! He had thought his future settled, although lately, he had had his doubts . . . but he had seen no one to match her . . . for a while it seemed as though he might go with her, climbing boy and all. But as he looked, she laid a clean white glove—so far uncontaminated —upon the boy's head, and tipping it back, looked into the young eyes, made bleary by soot; then putting his head down again, she let fall that hand to her side, making a mark at a position on her cloak so far unsullied.

A gallant on the other side of the road, swaying home after a night at the tables, peered at her, and, raising his eyeglass, looked her over from head to foot with undisguised amazement. It was too much for Augustus. With a catch of the breath that almost amounted to a sob, he turned on his heel and began to walk rapidly away.

The bouillon, which Mrs. Jackson was warming in readiness for Mr. Nadis' consumption, went into the empty stomach of Mr. Black's climbing boy. Then Arabella, weary and distressed, gave him over to William's care and went to her rest.

Had she done right? To put this scrap of suffering humanity before her own cloak, and Mr. Nadis' prejudices? She could not say. Caroline, who had to be told of the episode—she could hardly be kept in the dark, with Arabella coming in soot besmeared, and with the weary, crying child clinging to her hand—had looked grave. She had not condemned, and had looked at the small Ben with pity, and confirmed Arabella's opinion that he could not be more than five years old at the outside, though he was so dirty, poor, innocent blackness, that it was hard to tell much about him. But on hearing the way Augustus had gone off, she had looked even more serious and sorry. The association had promised well, and she began to wonder if Arabella would indeed become an old maid, or marry one of their neighbours in Linchestershire, as she so often said she would. Either way, Caroline did not think she would be happy. A temperament such as hers, ardent and active, needed worthwhile occupation and stimulus to fill its days. Having thought this, Caroline went on to acknowledge the possibility that, after all, Mr. Nadis might not have brought Arabella lasting fulfilment. To put the needs of another before their own was, she saw now, a capability Arabella had, but he had not. Would it not always have been leading to friction between them? Would Arabella have knuckled down to the quiet docility which is sometimes necessary to keep the allegiance of a selfish man?

Nothing had been seen of Mr. Watts since the interview with Arabella in the Egyptian Saloon. They assumed that he was kept busy by pressure of business, but Richard, who needed to see him about a tenancy agreement, went over a few days later to the City, and found his way in among the old lanes and alleyways to the chambers of Waveney and Watts.

Cornelius had been in a curious state of paralysis of the will. If Ann Ducros was Mirabelle's daughter, he wished to give her his protection; to do so it might be an advantage to be believed to be her father. On the other hand, he knew that he was not her father, and he shrank from discovering more. He could not conceive any connection between the lovely well bred girl he had known, and Madame Eglantine and Phoebe Hunt. The more he thought of Phoebe, the more repelled he became. Yet on the other hand, the very real damage she had the power to do to his career should be spurring him to find out the truth of the matter. He was also deeply unhappy because of his rift with Arabella. He could not think of his loss of control, his display of anger, without the overpowering shame and guilt of one who regards such exhibitions as uncivilized.

She had proved herself, he thought, to be unworthy of the growing feelings he had towards her, but he should not have responded by behaviour equally bad. And he missed her . . .

He was delighted to see Richard, and, after they had dealt with business matters, ordered coffee and prepared to relax and chat. On Richard's casual mention of Arabella, he stiffened, and asked coldly,

"Miss Hill is still with you, then?"

"Yes, did you think otherwise?"

"I have been expecting every day to hear of her engagement to Nadis."

"I'm afraid that it may be off, after all. Not that I was so much in favour of the match; but Caroline thought it an excellent one."

"And I agree with her. Excellent. Their values seemed to be in accord."

Then Richard went on to tell Cornelius of the gradual cooling of the relationship which had been taking place ever since Augustus had approved of Phoebe, instead of disapproving; and related their visit to the theatre, when all had, once more, to the casual observer, seemed to be going well; he mentioned the decision to walk home, the encounter with the distressed climbing boy, who had taken refuge with Arabella; and Mr. Nadis' eventual abandonment of her, and her return accompanied only by the child.

During the story Cornelius had listened in silence, though with obvious interest. Sometimes he seemed to be about to speak, but stopped himself. As soon as Richard paused, he could restrain himself no longer.

"I honour her!" he burst out. "How many Englishwomen would have done such an act! How many would have disregarded their finery in their compassion! I have been unjust to Miss Hill. I have not understood her character. You know, Welby, many women will urge on a chimney sweep to haste, so that dinner is not kept waiting because of a blocked-up kitchen chimney, and not care if he beats his climbing boy. I have heard them call a sweep's boy lazy, and all the time pet and indulge their own children."

"I know you are interested in the climbing boys."

"Interested! We meet regularly to try to help them—some invention to sweep chimneys is what we need. Jonas Hanway tried to improve their fate, but we must learn to do without them."

"Yes," said Richard slowly, "at least a few years of freedom and happiness, before the toil of life."

Watts did not hear him.

"Not," he went on, "that Miss Hill has, by rescuing one child, done anything to benefit the hundreds in London; it will take the law to do that. But she has done a Christian and humane act, and put herself, in my eyes, above the majority of women. What is she proposing to do with the boy? She must not let him loose on the streets, or he will be stolen back again."

"No, no, we realize the danger. William, our manservant, who had the job of bathing him and finding him a bed—at last he shared his own—has taken to him, and is tending him for now. He is as gentle as a woman, and it is doing him good to have something to occupy his thoughts apart from his longing to get back to Curteys and his sweetheart."

Mr. Watts' immediate decision was to go to see Madame Eglantine, so that he could clear up the mystery of Mirabelle; but before doing that, he obeyed his heart, and went to Clarges Street.

Arabella and he met with constraint on either side. He did not refer to the way in which she had acquired Ben, or mention Augustus Nadis; but he enquired gently after the boy's physical condition, and she answered brightly and pleasantly. Ben's kneecaps had been twisted out of place, and it was doubtful if his legs would ever be straight and as reliable as those of normal people; but his bleary eyes were looking better already, and a little flesh was coming on his bones.

"Would you like to see him?" she asked.

"I would like it of all things."

"Then come downstairs to the kitchen. He is a docile, affectionate boy," she said, leading the way, "and a diligent creature—it must have been real terror that made him run from his task."

Ben, who had been helping William with the silver, ran to Arabella as soon as she appeared; she sat down in a chair by the hearth and pulled him up on to her knee.

"Ben Small, I've called him, sir," said William to Mr. Watts. "We can't find out his parentage, and the apothecary told Miss Hill as he would never grow up to proper size, because he must have been half-starved as a baby."

Mr. Watts had been watching Arabella with the boy, and he noticed the motherly way she held him in her arm and asked Ben what he had been doing, and the trusting expression on the face of the child; he answered William only with a smile and a nod. Perhaps, he thought, perhaps . . . but before he put his thoughts into words, even to himself, there was the question of what had happened to Mirabelle.

Chapter Eleven

The Marchioness of Harome had decided, having already given a Ball and a Rout that winter, and feeling in need of still more gaiety, to announce an Evening Squeeze. Her invitations—as always —were gladly taken up. Mr. Watts, unfortunately, had to send his apologies, as urgent business called him out of town; the Welbys, however, were coming, and their protégée, Miss Hill.

Caroline looked over her rose-coloured gown, and decided it would do; Richard's best evening coat had a button loose, and Arabella had caught the hem of her shimmering net, but half an hour with the needle put those matters to rights, and, with the extravagance of French gloves decided upon, and two pairs of satin slippers ordered, one pair pure white for Arabella, and one with sprays of flowers in embroidery for Caroline, their preparations were made.

They were early, and hardly half an hour had passed before Arabella, finding it dull, as most of the company had not yet come, decided to escape to the bedroom where she had left her reticule and cloak, to re-pin a curl which was dangling on her shoulder. At the Ball—in this very room—Captain Wilmott would have murmured that it looked bewitching; but in her present mood it annoyed her. She was, as Caroline put it, full of the megrims.

The corridors were long, and dim; the drugget on the floor was old; Arabella felt surprised that the Marchioness, so lavish in her public rooms, should pennypinch in other places. It was quite a difficulty to see one's way. She did not see a large figure come out of a door some yards off because of a bend in the corridor; but she heard a cry, and a noise of something falling, and she ran forward round the bend to find a large elderly lady prostrate on the floor.

Arabella rushed forward in concern. At first sight she assumed the figure to be that of an old governess, or retired nurse, and Charles Hill had brought up his daughters to show all possible respect and consideration to those in situations less fortunate than their own.

To a Dowager Duchess, Arabella might have been pert, even saucy; to this pathetic figure on the floor, she went with tenderness.

"You have fallen!" she exclaimed unnecessarily, and bent to help the large lady to her feet. It was not easy. Now that she was nearer, she could see better, but there didn't seem anything to get hold of, strong enough to sustain such bulk. The black garments were thin and fluttery. But, to the sound of groans and gasps from the fat lady, Arabella gripped her, regardless of propriety, under the arms, with her strong, young hands. This was not sufficient; she had to slide her arms right round the other's body, and with all her strength combining with the other's struggles, contrive to raise her. At first Arabella kept tight hold. It did not seem at all sure that she was firm on her feet. But in a few minutes the puffs grew less, and the groans stopped, and the bulky figure remarked in a breathy voice,

"It's all right now, my dear. You need not grip my waist quite so tightly."

Surprised to find that the elderly governess, nurse, poor relation, or whatever she was, was under the impression that she still had a waist, Arabella let go.

"Are you sure you're all right?" The other gave a deep sigh. "Can I help you back to your room?" She was answered by a shake of the head. "Is there anything I can fetch for you—a cup of water, perhaps? A glass of wine?" There's plenty, she thought, downstairs. I'm sure they won't grudge a drop—or even brandy— to a poor old woman who has had such a heavy fall.

She had kept hold of one large arm, as the poor old soul was trembling, and Arabella did not like to let her go altogether; she did not seem fit to be left.

"Help me in here, if you will; I think I must sit down awhile before going any further."

Arabella held open the door and guided her through it; in the bedroom—her mistress's, perhaps, the furnishings were too rich for a servant's—she helped her to sit on a comfortable chair. "Don't rush me," said the older woman—and then Arabella decided to fan her and to refresh her by the current of air. She used her own white silk fan which, in the half-light, created its own little radiance of silver flashes from the delicate pattern of silver sequins, shaped like tiny flowers and minuscule leaves. There was no doubt that the nurse—or governess—was severely shaken. Such a fall is serious for someone so heavy. Her chest heaved, and her high colour came and went, rather alarmingly.

But before many minutes had passed, things looked better. Her breath steadied, and she looked at Arabella in an alert way. They had lately been in such close physical contact! The feeling of Arabella's arms was still about her body, the sensation of being heaved up to lean against the slender girl was still so recent; they knew each other's corporate being as only sisters, or mothers and daughters, usually do, yet they were strangers.

"Do I know you, child? I don't recollect. The Marchioness really must do something about her drugget. Only this morning I would have fallen if I had not caught hold of a table, which was none the firmer afterwards; and now, if it had not been for your timely assistance, I would have been lying there yet! Once off me feet I have the devil's own job to get up again . . . my heart is steadying, but I thought it would pound its way out of my breast . . ."

Arabella replied gently. She was still feeling very concerned about her companion.

"I am a guest tonight of the Marchioness. She is giving an Evening Squeeze, and my sister and brother and I are invited; but it was dull, with so few arrived, so I thought to readjust my hair." Arabella could still feel the lock of hair which had escaped from her silver comb, and she thought more had slithered down after it, due to her struggles in the corridor. She stood patiently under cross-examination, as she would not have done if she had known that the bearer of so much unnecessary weight was in fact the Dowager Duchess of Doncaster, the Marchioness' mother, and a byword for her severity with young people.

"You are a good child," said the large lady. "What is your name?"

"I am Miss Hill, sister to Mrs. Welby, and daughter of Charles Hill of Hill House in the county of Linchestershire."

"And a very well-brought-up young woman too. I wish more of your generation had their wits about them and came forward with a ready hand to help those in difficulties . . ."

Arabella began to fidget. How often, she knew, she had been thoughtless, or inconsiderate, and irked by her father's infirmities. She had laughed at the eccentricities of his friends. How easily she might, in other circumstances, have likened the stranded lady to a whale, made some witty remark to Jane, and passed by, leaving others to help! She felt too conscious, now, of her past faults to accept this praise.

The other saw that her young rescuer had become thoughtful, and wanted to know more of her before she left the room.

"Are you unmarried still, child? Not even engaged? Have none of our gallants snapped you up?"

Arabella laughed, and her natural high spirits reasserted themselves.

"They have not, ma'am. Perhaps the fact that I have but three thousand pound may account for it, for 'pon my soul, I don't know how else they resist me! I had expected a duke, or prince of the blood, at least, to have been at my feet ere this . . . A gentleman's daughter! And with three thousand pound! You must admit the charms of all those heiresses, and peeresses, with whom Town abounds, should have paled in comparison. But it seems they have not. I fear I will return to my father's house a maid, and marry Mr. Steel, one of his friends, as I often threaten!"

"I don't think that will be necessary, child." The large person had recovered from her fall, enough to smile at Arabella and pat her hand. "Somehow I think you will not want for suitors. Now! I am too shaken to come down tonight."

Arabella could not help looking surprised. This governess—or nurse—spoke as though she had been on her way to join the festivities; surely she would have felt out of place?

"Pray tell the Marchioness for me that, thanks to her old worn drugget, I am too shook up to come; but perhaps she will send me up a little comfort of some kind to my room."

"What name shall I give?" asked Arabella hesitantly.

"If you just say Susan, she will know."

Tidy again, and with her silver comb securely in place, Arabella returned to the Squeeze, and found the Marchioness.

"Ma'am," she broke in on the conversation hesitantly, and had some stony looks for her trouble, "I have a message from an elderly person who said her name was Susan, to say that she is not coming down tonight; she is shook up from a fall."

Having carried out her purpose, she bobbed slightly and backed away.

"An elderly person who said her name was Susan?" the Marchioness looked at her young guest in surprise, and quickly excused herself to her companions.

"A fall? Is she much hurt?"

"Just shaken, I think, ma'am."

"I must go at once! Thank you, Miss Hill, for telling me. An elderly person, who said her name had to be given as Susan!" The Marchioness rushed out of the room.

The stir she had raised was puzzling; but Arabella, seeing that the scene was much livelier than when she left it, forgot the whole incident. She would have been surprised to hear the conversation in the Chinese bedchamber, between the large lady and the Marchioness.

"I like that young woman," said the Dowager Duchess decidedly. "She had sense and compassion; rare virtues in the younger generation of today. What about her for Giles?"

"Giles?" repeated the Marchioness.

"Giles! My grandson! Your sister's child! He has got into this entanglement—now, if we can introduce him to Miss Hill, I'm sure she would suit him, and she would certainly suit me."

"Her dear friend, Jane Farley, Lord Russett's daughter, is eligible, too."

"Hm! You know I don't like the Russetts!"

"But she is not like the rest of the family! Not at all!"

"What is wrong with Miss Hill?"

"Nothing at all, except that she has less fortune. Her sister is married to my dear Marmaduke's youngest sister's son."

"Invite Giles down, Julia, at once. I will write, too. Introduce them. Fortune is not important in this case. I have taken a fancy to Miss Hill, and my poor Laura is worried to death."

Giles, Earl of Epworth, was a young man of exceptionally pleasant and compliant disposition. He was at present in high disfavour with both his mother and his redoubtable grandmother, and being so made him unhappy. When the command arrived, to go to London and pay his court to Arabella (with a side mention of Jane) he thought he saw a way out of his present difficulties, and at once prepared to go.

Susan, Dowager Duchess of Doncaster, having issued her instructions, left Town to spend the rest of the winter in a sheltered, sunny manor in Cornwall. She had not a doubt that when she returned in the spring it would be to find her grandson married to her young friend of the passageway.

The Earl took his usual berth with his Aunt, and this time let her take him into Society, and introduce him to the Welbys and the Russetts, to Arabella and to Jane; and they all liked him at once. It was regarded as a distinction to meet the Earl, as most of the Welbys' circle were not so highly born; but more than that (in the Welbys' opinion) he was a very prepossessing young man.

"How pleasant to meet someone in his position who remains unspoilt," said Caroline. "He has twenty thousand a year; but there is no trace of pride, or condescension, in his manner; he is one of the gentlest and most friendly people I have met since coming to Town; do you not agree, Richard?"

"He is too quiet—perhaps shy; but I think well of him."

"He wished particularly to meet Arabella."

"Oh, well!" and Richard said no more, showing only by his look that he thought any possible match would be an excellent one.

Caroline was surprised to hear from Lady Russett that the Earl had also had a desire to meet Jane.

The courtship of Arabella by Mr. Nadis was now tacitly considered over. Somehow it had dwindled away, after the events of the theatre, the masquerade, and the chimney sweep; he had visited less often, and gradually stopped coming at all; she in her turn had shown less and less interest in him; had ceased to direct towards him the sparkle of which she was capable; and in the end, they were acting towards each other almost with indifference. The Evening Party at Welby House was the last occasion on which anyone could have been deceived into thinking that matters were on the same footing as they had been, a month or six weeks before.

Caroline had been sorry to see the change. Augustus, as he wormed his way into fashionable circles, had altered, she felt. The interesting squire from Derbyshire was becoming no more than any other young man about Town, and she had preferred him as he had been when they first met.

Mr. Nathaniel Eeles had never been a serious contender for Arabella's hand; he might write poems, but any Cloe or Phyllida might be their goddess. Arabella knew that, when she was not present, he promptly forgot her. When the Earl arrived in Town she was well on her way to disillusion. Caroline thought that in certain lights she could detect a few lines, as delicate as silver point, round the large, beautiful eyes, and the generous mouth. To strangers she seemed to bubble with life, as much as ever; only Caroline and Jane noticed the difference. Jane, too, was different. Since her illness she was more serious, and less giddy. Her softness of manner, which charmed all the men who met her, was as beguiling as ever; but her artless flirtatiousness seemed to have left her.

The Earl, however, had arrived; and, like the Prince in a fairy story, all things were expected of him.

Cornelius Watts had, at the first opportunity once his decision was made, gone to try to get at the truth through an interview with Madame Eglantine. He thought at first that the house was closed up; the window shutters were fastened, although it was midday. But a servant answered his knock, and took him into the back room, as before.

Madame had, in the three months since he had met her,

changed considerably. Her skin hung in folds, as though she had shrunk in the wash, and it had not been able to adapt itself; and she seemed to have lost all her assurance. She looked furtively round the room on entering, as though something nasty might be behind the door. Cornelius was surprised. Having nothing to be ashamed of himself, he had no comprehension of the effect blackmail can have on one who has very real cause to fear exposure. His manner, when he spoke, was much less arrogant than in the previous interview, when he had been merely filled with loathing of her position in her profession.

"Madame Eglantine," he began, "I have had a visit from a girl, Phoebe Hunt, and she mentioned you."

"Phoebe Hunt? Oh—I had forgotten that was her name."

"You had forgotten—then you call her—"

"Mirabelle."

"I see . . . we understood—my friends the Welbys and I understood—that she was a lady's maid. Are you suggesting that she . . . ?"

"Oh, she was a lady's maid, right enough, but young madam is greedy; she thought she would make more money by being a harlot. So she came to me; she was with me six months, then she robbed a customer's pocket, and ran away. The next I knew of her, she was here again, fine as you please, threatening me."

"I see—she had found things out, while she was with you—I won't ask what."

Madame turned from him with a groan, and a helpless gesture with her left hand; he was surprised to feel pity for her. Whatever she had done, the punishment was bitter.

"Why did you call her Mirabelle?"

"I told you—I always have a Mirabelle."

"And when one girl goes—for whatever reason—the one who takes her place also takes her name?" The woman nodded.

"I didn't come to talk about Phoebe Hunt; but she mentioned you. You see, nearly twenty years ago, I knew a girl called Mirabelle." Madame Eglantine looked up at once, and her face had a different look, one that could almost be called tenderness.

"When you first came, and I read your name on that piece of

paper," she said, "I almost ran after you—because of Mirabelle. But you were too late—sixteen years too late."

"I was told she had gone to France," he said, "and when two or three years later, I was in a position to marry, I wrote to her father; but he replied that she was dead."

"She knew you had been deceived," said Madame Eglantine sadly. "You were never blamed. She always knew that you would have helped her, if only you had known. We tried to find you, but London is a big place."

"And she had a daughter?" Madame sighed deeply.

"I might as well tell you everything. If Mirabelle has been to see you, you will need to know the truth! And you have a right to know it. First of all, you know that Mirabelle Ducros was being courted by a man of rank?"

"Yes, I heard, but only recently."

"He seduced her. Her father had thought it was marriage he was after, but no such thing. When she was ruined, he cast her off; but by then she was bearing a child."

"If only I had known!"

"She thought of you, as I have said. Her father told her she had disgraced him, and that she was dead to him. He went back to France, and left her here."

"Destitute?"

"Quite destitute. She came to live in a room in the same house as me; that's when I got to know her. There was never anyone like Mirabelle."

Cornelius agreed, silently.

"I had the chance to set up here, and she came with me. Oh, you needn't look so shocked. What is a girl to do, with no trade? Work this way, or starve!"

"I'm not shocked."

"Not that she ever did much work, she was too ill. Too delicate a constitution. She died soon after."

Cornelius remembered Phoebe's words, "she died in misery, calling for you . . ."

Madame Eglantine seemed to read his thoughts.

"I did everything I could to look after her. At the end she often spoke of you. Her baby girl was fostered out, and I saw to it that she didn't want. Then—strange how things happen—her foster parents got her into your little training school, and I hear she's now apprentice to a milliner."

"She is."

"It was because of her that I started always calling my girls certain names. Just to say her name reminded me of her."

"And I suppose you told Phoebe the story?"

"Yes, because while she was here she bore the name."

"I think she can't have been listening with her usual attention. She thought I was the father of the child."

"She would twist it to suit herself. Is little Ann doing well?"

"Don't worry about her. You have done your share; I'll see to it that she is never in want."

Cornelius stayed longer than he had intended, and left at last with a strange reluctance. He had the feeling that he would never see Madame Eglantine alive again, and that she was fast sinking into a fate, perhaps destined for her, but none the less one of horror.

"If there's anything I can do—" he found himself saying, as he took his leave. For the first time she smiled.

"I am past help. But Mirabelle cannot hurt you. Phoebe, I mean, since that's how you know her. But if ever there is anything you can do for me, I will let you know."

"I owe it to you, for looking after Mirabelle Ducros and her child."

"I will not be afraid to ask."

She was to ask, and he was to see her again; but by then she was dead.

Chapter Twelve

Arabella had of course heard of the Earl of Epworth long before, and when he came to stay with his aunt she expected to meet him, as they saw the Marchioness often; but the fact that he had asked to meet herself and Jane! Now there was a compliment no maiden could resist! As soon as she had heard of it, some of the spring had come back into her step, she began to peer into mirrors at every opportunity, and, if she had not started to sing again, then she was at least heard to hum, quite distinctly, once or twice.

Their first meeting had not been in the glitter of a ballroom, or under the shaded lights of a gambling party; it had been over a dish of tea in the full light of day; and Lady Russett and her Lord, and both their daughters, had also been there. Even Emma Farley made efforts to be light and affable. Jane was all modesty and sweet refinement, which in the presence of her mother was the most that could be expected, and Arabella seemed to have recovered her old liveliness, and had looked up at the Earl with interest as he was introduced.

He was an unusually tall, thin man, with an eyeglass; a long, well-bred face, and thin, light-brown hair. When he had bowed politely over her hand, she had already felt that she liked him, and when she heard his quiet voice, with a slight hesitation, not strong enough to be a stammer, she was charmed.

For an Earl, he was very unobtrusive. His very way of sitting was gentle, and his clothes drew no attention to themselves although, with an eye trained by Augustus Nadis, she realized that they were of the best fabric and impeccable cut.

Jane and Arabella could not have helped being flattered by the way the Earl constantly deferred to their wishes when they met, which was often, for he went out of his way to get to know them. Lady Russett accompanied them frequently, and her eagle eyes picked up every favourable nuance of his behaviour to Jane, while Caroline dwelt with equal eagerness on each sign that he was attaching himself to Arabella.

It was indeed hard to tell who had the preference.

"Well, Jane? And if he offers, what of Robert? Mr. Spencer, I should say."

"I could say to you," replied Jane with spirit, "what of Mr. Nadis? Is my cousin thrown over for a man of higher rank?"

"Jane! This is unlike you. You must be aware that your cousin and I no longer seem to suit . . . surely you are repeating your mother's words."

Jane was silent for a while. Then she said,

"I confess that she has said such things, Bell, that I was ashamed to hear them. But you nettled me."

"Not goaded, Jane? Or was that the word you really meant?" and Arabella's voice dropped and she turned half away. Jane was too absorbed by her own problems to notice her friend's reaction.

"How can I—I answer you—about Robert—oh! Bell! we have been having such scenes! I could not tell even you. Such threats! I did not know that Lady Russett could sound like a fish wife . . . if the Earl offers, and I will not give up Robert, she will cast me off, and I will have no home, no family. If I persist in what my Lady calls my unfilial, undutiful love for Mr. Spencer—I will be her daughter no longer. Of course I love Robert, will always love him, while the breath is in me; but—I have not heard from him these three weeks, and he is no nearer preferment than he was a year ago. Can you wonder if I hesitate? If I think, can I bear to marry, without love, but with liking? For I do like the Earl, more than any man I have met, except Robert; always and forever, except Robert . . ."

"I cannot wonder," replied Arabella sadly. "We must wait, I see. Time will show us what is to be."

"If only, Miss Hill," said the Earl as they were dancing together, "I could show you our park at Arden Priory! You would like it of all things. If my mother were to invite you, now, would you consider a visit?" The slight hesitation in his speech caught at Arabella's sympathy, and she replied, perhaps more warmly than she had intended,

"How delightful! That would indeed be a pleasure."

"Do you think, Miss Farley," said the Earl as he carried an oyster patty to her, "that you would care to visit Arden Priory, if my mother should ask you? I know that you would find the gardens a delight, even in this season, and it would give me great pleasure to show you the beauty of the grounds." He sat down on the secluded sofa beside her.

"I have often heard Arden Priory spoken of, with the utmost praise," answered Jane. "To visit it would indeed be a privilege." With a soft glance she took the patty, and looked round for Arabella.

Caroline heard the flying patter of feet with dread. She too had received a letter from the Countess of Epworth, and knew the occasion of Arabella's haste. But she had only a few moments before Arabella, dressed only in the flimsiest of wraps, hurtled herself on to the bed.

"Child! It's lucky Richard has already risen—you are more naked than the statues in the Exhibition yesterday. Yes—" as Arabella waved the letter of her own in Caroline's face—"I have got one too . . . I don't want to disappoint you, my dear. You should go, and I would be all too willing to accompany you. Only . . . I don't see how it is to be done . . ."

Arabella's breath had returned. She took no notice of Caroline.

"Jane is invited too, dear sister. Still he cannot decide which of us he is courting, aggravating man! How delightful a visit to Arden Priory will be! Perhaps his mother is to look us over and decide between us. Which will she prefer? Jane's fairness, or my brown? The complexion of a wild rose, or the richness of a Gloire de Dijon? Yes—" as Caroline shook her head disapprovingly—"I am vain. Since my poet compared me with that incomparable rose I am indeed vain . . . Arden Priory and twenty thousand a year! A most eligible match, Caroline! And why can you not go with me, when the Countess commands your presence?"—leaning over from her perch on the edge of the bed and affectionately kissing her sister—"for Jane and I can hardly go alone. You could not countenance such disregard for the proprieties, it would smack of the marriage market . . . why, Carrie?"

"When you catch your breath, Arbel! I might be able to tell you. That's right, my dear. Are you warm enough? Put this counterpane round you. How pretty your hair is."

"Yes, Carrie," said Arabella impatiently.

"I'm coming to it . . . one does not talk of such things to maidens . . . I am again with child, and although with Charles, I felt well, I have already had such sickness with this one that the thought of such a journey at the moment makes me shudder, even a journey to Arden Priory, which I would dearly love to see. In a few weeks, they tell me, I should begin to feel better; but at the moment it is hard enough to get up at all, and look after the household affairs."

"Oh, sister!" Arabella's eyes were wide with concern. "You should have told me, so that I could be a help, and not a hindrance. I can order meals very well, you know I have been giving Mrs. Hunt her instructions these five years. And I can be economical, I assure you. I can order beast's cheek, and marrow bones, as well as turkeys and lobsters. You should have trusted me, Carrie, and not struggled on with illness when you could have rested. We will write immediately and tell the Countess that we cannot go, and the whole of the dreams—foolish fancies—which we have been building, will evaporate as the phantoms they are."

"We will do no such thing. If I cannot go—and I fear I cannot —Lady Russett must give up her Mechanics Institutes and think for once of her daughter."

Arabella had slid off the bed, and gone to the door. She paused, with her hand on the knob.

"Are you getting up for breakfast, Carrie, or shall I take your place?"

"At least I must look after Richard's coffee, although I fear I can eat nothing. We will talk about it again downstairs, and ask Richard's opinion. But I fear it must rest with Lady Russett."

Mr. Watts called, in passing, with no intention of staying, to speak for a moment with Richard on business, and Richard told him of the turn events had taken. The promising situation Arabella was in seemed to come as a shock, Richard thought, to Cornelius. He responded to Richard's praise of the Earl, but in a subdued manner. When he was urged to stay longer, and come upstairs to join the family, he agreed, and they entered the breakfast-room together. The remains of breakfast were still on the table; no one but himself would have been allowed entrance so soon, except Jane; and it was not long after his own arrival that that young lady herself drew up at the door and, rivalling Arabella in her precipitation, almost fell into the room.

"You have got one too, Arabella! Oh, good morning, Mrs. Welby, Mr. Welby, my duty, madam . . . good morning to you, Mr. Watts . . . oh! Arabella! Do we go?"

"That rather depends on Lady Russett, Miss Farley. I am not well, and am afraid it will be some weeks before my illness abates. Do you think your Mama would accompany you and Arabella?"

Jane's face fell, and the brightness faded from it. Caroline had often noticed that the mere mention of her mother was enough to reduce the girl to an appearance of stupidity, and wondered once more what kind of treatment the child had received, to produce this effect in the woman.

"Indeed," Jane faltered, "I do not know . . . her work is so very important; she would be reluctant to interrupt it with a visit to the country in winter."

"Her child's future, and happiness, must be important to a mother. It is vital that this young man, who has been paying both of you such marked attentions, should have the chance to make his intentions clear. No sensible woman would marry only for money and an establishment, but, combined with the Earl's attractive person and gentlemanly manners, any mother would be pleased to see her daughter so well settled. Your future well-being would be assured. There could be no fear of future want, or straitened circumstances, and on this earth that is an unequalled blessing."

While Caroline had been giving her little sermon Cornelius had been reading her letter, which was a polite, even warm, invitation to her to bring her youngest sister and Miss Jane Farley to Arden Priory for a stay of some weeks, with Richard too. The children were not mentioned, so it could be assumed they were not included.

"May I make a suggestion?" he said. Everyone listened.

"It happens that I know the Earl and Countess quite well, both as friends and in business. They have given me a standing invitation to spend time under their roof whenever I am in the area. At present Waveney and I are not as busy as usual; it is quite possible for me to take a holiday. May I offer my services as an escort and—dare I say it—chaperone, to the two young ladies? Even if you had not said that you are unwell, Mrs. Welby, you have not your usual colour, and look, if you will forgive an old friend, in need of rest. You can rest if I take the responsibility for Miss Hill and Miss Farley from your hands for a while. Mr. Welby will care for you, and with only your children to concern yourself with, I think we can be sure of seeing you your old self again when we are back in Town."

Richard and Caroline looked at one another. Could they accept this offer? For themselves, there could be no question. A few weeks without the need to entertain, no balls or card parties, just a few select friends and their family, a few weeks to be alone together, to grow used to the idea of a further addition to the family, this was all so desirable. They felt quite happy to allow Arabella to be escorted anywhere by Cornelius Watts. But what would Lady Russett think on the matter? It was significant that no one asked what Lord Russett would think. He left the upbringing of his children to their mother, although an overloud laugh on their part, or a careless use of knife and fork, brought down his wrath immediately.

No one raised any objections to the scheme. Jane, after her first look of surprise, was, in a few minutes, smiling timidly at Mr.

Watts; she was not afraid of him, and felt she would go with him as willingly as with Caroline.

"I hope Lady Russett allows us to go with you, sir. I am grateful for your kindness, in giving up your time to us."

He bowed over her hand.

"The kindness will be all on your side, in allowing me to escort you." He sat down beside her and they began to talk about the proposed visit.

Arabella looked over at them, and noticed Jane's head inclined towards Mr. Watts, and his bending towards her, in a very friendly way. She was so used to considering him an admirer of her sister, that this put him in a new light. In a twinkling she was filled with novel feelings she did not choose to put a name to. Was he, in fact, such a suitable person to escort them? Should not Lady Russett begin to make enquiries as to how many thousand a year Mr. Watts had? After all, he was eligible! Not old—she could no longer consider him old; middle-aged, perhaps; everyone past thirty was middle-aged; oh, no, it was ridiculous. But they did, at this moment, look so very satisfied in each other's company! And what of Robert? she mentally asked her friend. She could understand the worldly considerations of the Priory overshadowing a childhood love so very opposed by her parents. But Mr. Watts was no belted Earl or figure of romance! It could not be borne! The situation must be put a stop to at once. She danced over to them, and cried playfully,

"Mr. Watts! I declare if you escort us I will make a condition. Why should you have the pleasure of our company if you do not pay for it? You must pay a forfeit, indeed."

He responded gallantly.

"A forfeit for a lady's company! There is nothing too difficult. I will even bite an inch off the poker, or turn round five times blindfold. Demand away."

"Why," she said, gently touching his hair with a fingertip, "only grandfathers are now powdering their heads. You must become a gentleman of fashion, sir; you must be polled; give up this old-fashioned and messy custom, and accompany us in a Brutus cut, or not at all."

"Arabella!" cried Caroline, "you go too far!"

But Mr. Watts did not seem to be offended.

"Why, Miss Hill, I had not dreamed my appearance was of such importance to you! Are there any other changes you would like me to make? Shall I cut off my coat tails, or the frill from my stock?"

"We must walk before we run," returned Arabella. "The second time we go on a visit with you, I may go on to make further requirements; but for the present, I will confess myself satisfied, if you crop your hair."

He rose to go.

"Needs must, when the devil drives; I have business to attend to; this early call as I was passing is in the nature of a luxury, and if I have to call at the barber's too today . . . let me know, as soon as you can, Welby, what Lady Russett says, and I will arrange my absence with Waveney. Your servant, ladies."

The ladies could not rejoice at the invitation to Arden Priory, until they knew whether or not the two would be able to go; so Jane set off back to Russett House to persuade her mother, with a tactfully worded note from Caroline tucked in her muff.

"I shall have to leave Ben," said Arabella sadly. "Do you know, Richard, he is learning to read quite nicely. He knows his alphabet already."

"He will miss you. But he can go on learning. William will teach him."

"He looks forward to seeing me." Her sadness was real, for she felt each passing emotion keenly, and she was fond of the small former chimney sweep, and saw him every day; but the interest of the proposed visit reconciled her to leaving him behind.

Lady Russett, vexed to death with Jane's obstinacy, handed her custody to Mr. Watts with relief; and with some last admonitions, to the effect that she would accept the Earl or be no longer her mother's daughter, washed her hands of the matter and forgot Jane in the fascination of congenial occupations.

The visit to Arden Priory, then, was settled. Margery, Arabella's maid, was to serve both of them, and was sent off beforehand with the trunks, travelling post; Jane and Arabella were to go with Mr. Watts in one of the Earl's carriages, which he insisted on putting at their disposal.

Caroline had given Richard a glance full of significance, at hearing of this gesture; and he had to admit that it looked, at the very least, as if the Earl's intention was to marry one of the girls, although his observations of the young man had brought him to the conclusion that he was not in love with either.

It was the day before the journey. Cornelius Watts had had his hair cut as required, and, as he was near to Welby House, decided on an impulse to go in and see Arabella's reaction to his new appearance. He was looking forward with mixed feelings to the visit to Arden Priory. Weeks of Arabella's company now seemed very desirable, although once it would have been the last thing in the world he wanted. But the visit was not to be made with his pleasure in mind, and he was going to have to stand by and witness another man courting Arabella, and the probable end was that she would marry the Earl and go from his—Cornelius'—reach forever.

As he knocked on the door, Cornelius admitted to himself that even that was better than staying in London and not knowing what was happening, and he knew that he could not put himself forward when Arabella had such a dazzling chance of advancement. He had no hesitation in putting her interests, as he saw them, before his own.

Mr. and Mrs. Welby, William said, were out; but Miss Hill was in the Egyptian Saloon, if Mr. Watts cared to go up. She was not alone; her former maid, Phoebe Hunt, had called to see her.

Cornelius had entered the door in a mood of light-hearted cheerfulness, but this left him instantly. He climbed the stairs as a terrier who has scented a rat. By the door of the Egyptian Saloon he paused, and then turned the handle very gently, and eased open the door. Phoebe's voice, dulcet and poisonous, reached him. It was a monologue. Arabella—he could see her as he slid silently into the room—had her head on her arms, and was sobbing wildly. Phoebe's back was turned to him, and for a moment he thought of felling her with one blow from behind, but the transitory impulse left him as his mind focused on her words.

The impression of the first words he had heard, as he opened the door, was of goose and game pies, and it seemed strange that Arabella should be in distress over such a comestible; but he had only caught the tail end of the discourse. Phoebe left it and went on, with graphic exaggeration, to detail what she could reveal of an episode in which, it seemed, Arabella had acted the pander by introducing into Jane's bedchamber a young man in women's clothing, and had seen to it that he and Jane were not disturbed for the requisite space of time. There was also the matter of secret correspondence with an officer, letters which could be produced— most indiscreet—as Phoebe built up an airy labyrinth, a tissue of lies built to gleam with the putrescence of evil—but evidently, from Arabella's sobs, with sufficient basis of truth to damn her forever in the eyes of the world. Once these were the gossip of London, Cornelius knew, any hope of the Earl of Epworth as a husband became impossible. She would be shunned, an outcast to return to the country in disgrace. His first decision was that she must have her chance; her chance of her grand marriage; that must not be spoilt by this viper she had nourished in her bosom. He spoke, and broke the spell binding the two girls together.

"Don't you think, Miss Hunt," he tried to infuse into his voice respect, if not servility, "that if you were to wait until Miss Hill returns from her visit to the home of the Earl of Epworth, which she may well do as his affianced bride, she would be able to give you a recompense for your silence much more worthwhile than she could at present? At present, you see, she is nothing; just a young girl like many others in Society; but as the fiancée of the Earl, how much more would she lose by your hands! How much more reason would she have to thank you for your restraint in not publishing her true story!"

Phoebe had whipped round at his first words, and stood looking at him with unspeakable malevolence on her face. He remembered once more Madame Eglantine's cry, "she is one of the damned!" Damned indeed. Phoebe had not realized Arabella's hopes with regard to the Earl. She did not know that Cornelius knew she had no hold over him whatever, and that her threats were to him like cobwebs. So she smiled, thinking that he was in her power, and acknowledging the truth, if things were as he said, that she would do better by waiting.

After that it was only a matter of time before Cornelius managed to get Phoebe out of the room, and on her way. Arabella did not stay long, after her. He got one grateful glance from the swollen red eyes, one sensation of soft-scented warmth fleetingly pressed to his shoulder, and she was gone, running upstairs to her room. In all the whirl of sensations which engulfed him, one thought, like a splash of sunlight on a sullen sea, made him smile. She had never even noticed his Brutus cut.

The next morning, very early, about four of the clock, Jane, who had slept the night with Arabella, stood waiting in the vestibule. Arabella was in the nursery, giving the sleeping children a goodbye kiss, but soon she came flying downstairs to join her friend.

"Bell! How can you dash about so, at this time in the morning?" Jane was pale, sleepy, and cross. Had it not been for her mother's edict, nothing would have induced her to undertake a journey which involved rising at such an hour. Arabella was at her best in the early morning, and after the distress of the previous day—she had said she had a headache—she had bobbed up again like a cork. Phoebe's presence made London suddenly hateful to her, and she was glad to be leaving it.

"Why, are you not excited? Has Mr. Watts not yet come? What can be keeping him? I will just go downstairs and call goodbye to Ben."

"I can hear a stir outside," said Caroline, who had followed Arabella.

It was Mr. Watts. Joel Tomkins flung open the door, and there was a figure swathed in the obligatory greatcoat, and sweeping his hat off to salute the ladies, revealing . . . that the long powdered hair had gone.

"Sir!" cried Arabella. "You have given me my wish!"

"Mr. Watts!" Caroline was all amazement. "Come over here, by the lamp. Why, my old friend! You have never given in to her girlish whim? Now how will all your clients repose confidence in a man with such an air of fashion?"

He groaned. "That is exactly the danger of following the trend! No one wishes to deal with a man of business who does not appear a sober sides. But I hope all their confidence did not rest in my hair. It should have a surer foundation."

"I have offended you," said Caroline contritely.

"It is vastly becoming," put in Jane's timid voice.

"Vastly, indeed," and Caroline tried to make her voice as enthusiastic as possible.

And it did suit him. His hair proved to have a crisp way of waving, and curling up at the ends which were brushed forward, resting becomingly on brow and temple.

"Shall we go? It will take all the horses are capable of to pull a coach so far in one short winter's day."

There was a last flurry of kisses and good wishes, and the travellers were in the chaise; the horses strained forward in the traces; the wheels began to move; they were away, clanking merrily down the quiet street, and taking the road away from Clarges Street, away from Piccadilly, away from London.

With Arabella it was always the next thing on life's programme which mattered. She did not regret leaving the London she had struggled so hard to visit. It was overshadowed, at present, with the sad news from the Peninsula, and poisoned for her by her interview of yesterday with Phoebe. That was something she hardly dared to think about. The construction which could be put on her light-hearted actions, the shame which would follow disclosure, were both so frightful that she could not think of them.

Her gay weeks in society, the agitations, the slow disillusion, the happinesses and distresses, she deliberately put out of mind. The journey, Mr. Watts' haircut, the possibilities ahead, were all important.

The day was declining to its close as the carriage drew within sight of Arden Priory. The small party had chimed together well, in talk and temperament, on the journey. Mr. Watts and Arabella had never raised their meeting of the previous day; it was as though it had never been. The last hours, though, were wearisome, and they had stopped talking. Suddenly they drew to an unexpected halt, and Cornelius put his head out of the window to see what was amiss.

"Would you like to have a breath of air, ladies? It looks as though one of the horses has gone lame. The road is clean and dry."

They stepped down on to the road. It was a quiet country

place, and the scene around them was of woods and fields. Mr. Watts went forward to the horses, and Jane and Arabella looked around them.

They had travelled for some time through light woodland, the road running through apparently endless trees, all bare and dark. In following the bends of the road it had not been possible to see far ahead, and after a while the prospect had bored them. With the beauty of spring flowers, Arabella could imagine that to travel through the wood would be a charming journey; or in the heat of summer, when the shade of the trees would be delightful; but in a cold carriage in winter it was not interesting; there was very little wildlife; birds were few, and although they had seen a fox, he had made off quickly.

They had just emerged from this long expanse of woodland, and were a few yards from the edge of it. The road now sloped down into an open valley of fields, and then up again to a large stone building, where it appeared to end. Behind this distant building rose bare shoulders of moor. Arabella shivered involuntarily, and looked round for Jane. Jane was standing a little way from her, and her pale clothes outlined her against the dark backdrop of trees, seemingly impenetrable, through which they had come. Snow began to fall, and flakes drifted down around that isolated figure. Arabella's thoughts tormented her. Whatever she had done in the past few months seemed to have turned to dust and ashes. Oh, why could Lady Russett not have consented to Jane's marriage to Robert, and none of Arabella's foolish mistakes would have been committed? But no doubt she would have committed others, equally foolish . . .

She turned and looked towards the stone building, Arden Priory. From their position, they could distinguish its windows, and its doors; even at this distance, its silence struck an unwelcome chill into their hearts.

The only sound apart from those made by their own group—the shuffling of the horses, and the murmurs of the men—was the distant bark of a dog.

The bark went on and on, monotonous, repetitive, and the short, sharp sounds seemed to rise, each individually, into the frosty air.

Arabella wished—she was sure the dog belonged to Arden Priory—that someone would let it out, or let it in, or give it a bone, or a kick, anything to stop that endless barking.

Jane was visibly shivering, and the snowflakes were beginning to cling to her hair.

Arabella walked up to Mr. Watts.

"What is keeping us?" she heard the note of querulousness in her voice with unease. It was a note she disapproved of in other voices, and she had not expected to hear it in her own.

He straightened his back, and turned towards her, and she felt instantly restored to normality by the sight of his face.

"It's all right. You might like to climb back into the carriage now. This near horse had a stone in his foot, and went lame; but now it is out; he will make shift to pull us farther. The other three are tired, but well."

Arabella thought of retorting crossly that it had taken a long time to discover and remove a stone, but she was too grateful for his care of her to be sharp, and too awed by the forbidding silence of the place, the persistent barking of the distant dog, and the lifelessness of the house ahead of them, to speak naturally. Was this the adventure she had longed for? It was chilling. There was no one in the house, she was sure. No one to meet them; one solitary curl of smoke rose from a chimneypot to refute her, but the dog barked on. The woods pressed behind them as though they were listening, and the bare rise in the distance seemed to be holding its breath.

Chapter Thirteen

The London they had left behind them was overcast by the gloom of the news from the Peninsula. The full realization of the extent of the tragedy had not yet come to the people, but rumour was busy, and to a soldier such as Captain Wilmott the news that was available was sufficient. A hard-fought and bravely contested action of three hours—he knew what this meant, and that many of his friends and brother officers would have fallen; the complete repulse of the enemy, so that the British Army could embark unmolested—what was this but a retreat? A rearguard action, to cover the scuttling into their ships of the remnant of armies who had, through that winter, suffered incredible hardships?

The death of Sir John Moore seemed to be the last straw in the disaster, but there was no doubt that his heroism and leadership had saved a slaughter of British troops. Captain Wilmott sat sprawled in an elegant chair in Phoebe's boudoir, hardly speaking and no longer responsive to the idea of the outing they had planned for the evening. He had tried to explain to her what the news meant to him, and from her quiet listening and serious expression thought she shared his mood. She cancelled their previous arrangements, and ordered supper for two to be served in her room. Phoebe was nothing if not good at her job. Her thoughts, as always, were her own.

. . . . . .

Mr. Watts looked round at the listening woods, and the bare rise of moors.

"I shall be glad to get on . . ." he said. "Come . . ." he held open the door of the carriage. "A little supper and our beds, will do us the world of good."

With a cheerful blowing out of breath from the horses they began to move forward. The front nearside horse was still limping, but he went on bravely. As they drew closer to Arden Priory it appeared just as lifeless. It was not until they stopped at the door that there was a sign of a human creature. How the thought of visiting the Priory had thrilled Arabella! But when she entered it, her one longing was for light and warmth, and she felt as though she were entering a tomb.

The Earl and his mother were in the sitting-room, where the firelight played over walls which held the warmth within them, like a shell. These stone walls—almost a yard thick—held out all sounds; the barking of the dog, the stillness of the woods, the faint rustle of the descending snowflakes.

"You're here!" Giles jumped up and came towards them, his hands outstretched.

"Bring our guests to meet me," said the Countess languidly from the sofa.

Arabella and Jane stretched their frozen mouths into smiles. Cornelius as usual was brisk and to the point.

"Devilish journey, Epworth! The young ladies never complained, but they must be very cold. I wish you good evening, Ma'am. I hope I see you well?"

"My health is indifferent, Mr. Watts. The winter tries me. I wish I had my mother's spirit and constitution. How the war goes on! I tell her that when travel is easier, I will winter with her in Paris, or Florence. Pray tell those young women to come over here. I cannot be running about after them."

Arabella and Jane, who had been waiting only for the chance to be presented, came forward.

"Ma'am."

"Your servant, Ma'am."

The Countess looked at their meekly bent heads.

"I'm pleased to receive you. My mother has sung your praises, and you are acquainted with my sister, I believe."

"We were several times at Harome House this winter, Your Grace."

"How she has the energy to bother, I don't know." The Countess was silent, and Arabella had the opportunity to observe her. Whatever she had expected, it was not this. On the one hand, she had never seen such beautiful eyes in a lady of the Countess' age. They were a light grey, and in that were like her son's; but their shape, and the way they were set, was very lovely; the rest of her features were dainty, and lost in the plumpness which seemed to envelop her. Her head was small, with a corona of baby-fine, light-brown hair, hardly showing grey, but she was of so large a figure that it was not surprising that she was reclining on the sofa, instead of rising to welcome her guests. Yet Arabella saw that she had neat ankles, and her feet, lifted into view on the end of the sofa in a perfection of dainty slippers, were beautiful, if ever feet were beautiful. The delicate arches and finely-shaped bones looked too frail to support the Countess.

"You, Miss Hill, are a country gentleman's daughter, I understand? And Miss Farley is the daughter of Lord and Lady Russett . . ."

"Yes, Ma'am."

"That is satisfactory—I have already heard of your families. You are neither of you connected with trade? Not the least connection with trade?"

"None at all, Ma'am," the girls sounded surprised.

"None of your money comes from cutting up and selling cloth, Miss Hill? Muslins, or linens? Or dealing with cheeses, over the counter?"

Jane bridled a little at this, but both answered together, "No, Madam."

"So you went to my sister's balls. I am not well enough to bother. There are no balls in Arden. Well, well, Giles; hand the young ladies to Mrs. Bridge, and when they have tidied themselves we will be able to dine. It is much later than our time already."

Arabella left the room feeling reproached. Was she so untidy?

Had it been so inconvenient to wait half an hour for their dinner? But she said nothing as she followed Jane and the housekeeper down the long stone-flagged corridors. Before they had gone two yards the warmth of the sitting-room was gone as if it had never been, and the icy air which struck them made the candle flicker, and shadows mop and mow against the wall. They seemed like imprisoned spirits, begging for a life of their own, but condemned again to darkness when the candle had passed.

The girls were sharing a room on the first floor, and on entering, Arabella went to the window, pulled the curtain aside, and opened the shutter, peering out into the gathering night. She could just see the woods through which they had travelled, dark and soft against the skyline, and the pale streak which was the road. A snowflake drifted across the window and she closed the shutter again and turned back into the room.

"Didn't we have enough of that dreary stretch of countryside when we were out in it?" asked Jane.

Arabella, oppressed and unhappy, tried to sound like her normal self.

"Dreary! You come to a Priory, and call it dreary! My dear girl, where is your Gothic imagination? Call it Horrid; Fearful; Awe-inspiring; but dreary, no!"

"Well," conceded Jane, "it was Horrid, then, if you will have it so. But cold and dreary is what I thought it. The Alps, fearful with Banditti, are more my idea of the horrid."

"And instead of Banditti we had only that wearisome dog; hush, can you hear it still?"

"No, I can't, or I would not stay here another minute," said Jane, putting out her hands to the fire. "Come, Bell, change your dress; I'm ready. Margery is waiting to comb your hair, and we must hurry."

Although Arabella did not feel the cold as Jane did, and on her own account would not have had a fire for general sitting by before November, the chill in the corridor had got into her bones, and she was glad she had brought all her shawls. They were soon running quickly back along the corridor, glad of the candle and each other's company, and re-entering the sitting-room.

Mr. Watts gave the Countess his arm, and the Earl hesitated.

He looked first at Arabella and then at Jane. His mother turned and watched him sardonically.

"Bring 'em both, Giles," she commanded, and went on ahead. It was doubtful which had the precedence, so with a young woman on each arm, the Earl entered the dining-room.

Where the sitting-room was neat and modern, the dining-room was much lower than eighteenth- or nineteenth-century fashion. It was wide, and stretched far enough for the magnificent dining table to look small. The fireplace was carved into an ogee arch, with crockets and turrets, and over it was a painting on the plaster of the wall. Arabella was seated in a high-backed, carved chair opposite to it, and little by little the faded colours began to make sense to her. At first she thought it a mere motley. It was a painting of a dance of men and women, with red and blue and green and gold; amongst them, dancing too, was the skeleton of Death. It drew her eyes; but she had to take part in the general conversation; no one else was so directly facing the painting. Looking down at the table, she thought it must have been hewn from Priory oaks, and polished with beeswax of the monks' bees; it was so dark that the light of the candles vanished into it as though snuffed out. The floor was made of oak boards as wide and shining as those of the table top, and the plaster walls bore traces of patterns and figures, partly covered by whitewash. Only the panel over the fireplace had not been whitened over.

Jane tried to fill the gap left by Arabella's silence by chattering, and Mr. Watts supported her, his laugh ringing out, rousing Arabella, and animating the Earl. Even the Countess made a few lugubrious remarks.

"How charming the Priory is!" Jane said. "Miss Hill and I do admire the Gothic. So romantic! Tell me, Madam, do you have a ghostly monk? That would fulfil one of my school-girl ambitions."

"To be sure," murmured Arabella. "No Priory is complete without a ghost."

"What's that, Miss Hill? You must speak up. You are so far away down the table. No, Miss Farley; we do not have a ghost. What a fanciful idea. To actually want ghosts! All that went out long ago. There may have been ghosts when the monks were here, it is just the kind of old-fashioned thing they might have had; but one really could not put up with them now."

Jane was snubbed, but Arabella went on, dreamily.

"But would it not have been romantic, Madam, to have—say—a great carved chest, containing the mummified remains of a bride of an olden time, crept in to hide in a wedding game, and never found?"

"Not romantic at all," replied the Countess, shaking her heavy chins. "Such a waste, you know."

"Or perhaps a cellar, with one wall newer than the rest, where a nun was walled up alive for loving a man?"

"Your imagination runs away with you, Miss Hill. This was the home of monks, not nuns. And it is unseemly in a maid to talk so boldly of love."

"What does youth ever think of?" interposed Mr. Watts, giving Arabella a warning glance, but she was too carried away to notice.

"Do you not hear unearthly bells at midnight? Or, looking at the ruined arches, see a pale figure flit by?"

To everyone's relief the Countess laughed.

"My dear! How droll you are! I can see why my mother liked you. The quaint and amusing always appeals to her."

"Madam, I was not aware that I had had the honour of meeting the Dowager Duchess of Doncaster."

"Why, Miss, did you not help her up, when she fell down in a passage?" After a moment's pause she went on, "And now you may help me up, for my back is troubling me, and help me into the sitting-room. No, Mr. Watts, remain seated and finish the wine with Giles. Miss Hill's support will do admirably."

Arabella was all amazement at what she had heard. But as she supported the Countess, she was reminded of the lady whose name was to be given as Susan, and who had been so very difficult to raise from the ground. Their way of walking and of holding on to her was very similar. She wondered why she had never realized the relationship.

They settled round the fire, and the Countess picked up her netting.

"Don't you young ladies work? I am never without my netting, in spite of the state of my health; or, in the morning, my work for the poor. It is calico petticoats, at present, for the savages in Africa. Young people should always employ their time usefully."

"We have brought our work with us," explained Jane. "But after such a long journey, we thought we might, with your leave, retire early."

"You will not wish to go this half hour?"

"Until then, to look at the flames leaping from your fire will content us."

Arabella opened a small square pianoforte she found on the other side of the room. Her fingers began to pick out a tune, one note at a time, as Jane, sinking down by the fire, watched spurts of blue-green flame, shooting among the red-gold.

Softly the notes of music filled the room, as the Countess netted placidly. The Earl and Mr. Watts came quietly in to join them, and half an hour passed pleasantly before the footman came in with hot water and wine, leaving them on a side table, and Epworth mixed them himself to suit the different tastes of the company.

Arabella let her tinkling tune fade away, and closed the lid of the pianoforte. She took the drink the Earl offered her. How affable he was, how welcoming; his speech gentle, his manners impeccable . . . he had gazed for a moment into Jane's eyes, as he gave her her glass, and now his eyes met Arabella's with the same look, so that as she reached out to take the wine she blushed and her hand shook. Which of them? Did he mean anything, or nothing? His mother, watching the byplay from the sofa, looked pleased, almost smug. Mr. Watts appeared not to have noticed, but when they bid him good night he was so unlike his usual self as to be curt, in fact rude.

"What's wrong with Mr. Watts?" They had gone with breathless haste along the corridor and up the stairs and into their bedroom.

"I don't know," said Arabella thoughtfully, although she was sure she did know. "He is nearly as provoking as the Earl; to suggest bringing us! To cut his hair at my command! To be pleasant and attentive all the way—and he can be very pleasant, and very attentive—and then to be so surly! I declare I have no patience with the man."

"Probably he was going to have his hair cut anyway," said Jane philosophically, jumping into bed. "Come on, it's cold out there, and this bed has had a warming pan in it."

"Having it cut anyway?"

"I've noticed a lot of these staid older men are giving way to fashion—long hair and powder are so completely out. It must be short or nothing—and as they discover how easy it is to dress, why! more and more of them are doing it."

"I might have known he did not do it to please me. And he offered to escort us to help Caroline. There is nothing he would not do for her. Thank goodness she married Richard! For I could not bear Mr. Watts as a brother-in-law."

Nothing came from Jane but a sleepy hmmmm, and the fire was dying down, casting shadows on the wall almost as grotesque as the shadows of the corridor. Arabella blew out the candles, and climbed into bed.

Whichever way her thoughts turned was unhappiness. If the Earl proposed to her, she would have to come to some sort of settlement with Phoebe; and would she ever feel safe again? Would the persecution be a constant threat? She could not understand the reactions of Mr. Watts. How much he had heard of the interview with Phoebe, she did not know; but instead of treating her as an outcast, he had rescued her from Phoebe and been kindness itself. Surely he must despise her! But he was not going to expose her, that was obvious. Yet tonight—for no reason—he had been abrupt. In anyone else, she would have thought he was jealous of the way the Earl had gazed at her. Arabella leaned out of bed to lay her hand on the wall. Beneath the pretty paper she thought she could feel the coldness of stone. She had leaned so far out it was difficult to recover and get back without overbalancing and tumbling on to the floor, but she managed, and snuggled down into the billows of the feather bed.

How long they had spent in that coach! Hour after hour. She could almost imagine she was still moving, the curtained bed swinging along the highway, with the stone wall at its head encasing them, as the trees had done; and so fancying—with an imagined Mr. Watts being, first delightfully attentive and then as curt and offhand as he had been in the sitting-room—it seemed to Arabella that she had scarcely slept at all, when Jane was shaking her, and saying,

"Bell! It's morning!"

Chapter Fourteen

"After church," said the Countess, "Giles will show you round the Priory. I hope we will hear no more of your nonsense about ghosts, Miss Hill, but you will find the building interesting. Now, can you all be ready to go to service in half an hour?"

The drive to church was pleasanter than the girls, still close to their long drive of the previous day, had expected. The little village church lay in a fold of the landscape between the Priory and the village of Arden St. James; it was built of grey stone, and was simple, almost severe. The party from the Priory had approached the building from the back, and not down the yew walk which the villagers took, so they were seen for the first time by the congregation when they walked into the large, old box pew belonging to the family. The girls were glad that it was set sideways on to the nave, so that they could see the congregation.

In many village churches over the countryside there must have been much the same mixture of old and young, men and women, most of them showing by their physique their service to the land. The younger men stood up in their strength like oak trees, their muscles straining the cloth of their jackets; the old men were bent and twisted, but their skins were tanned, and their eyes clear. The bonny, pink-cheeked young women looked as if they were in charge of babies and dairies, chickens and pigs, and the old ones, thin or fat, looked as though they could still do a day's work to be

proud of. Arabella felt she could have been in the church at Sax-
elby, or Curteys Percy, or Littlethorpe; except that these moor
folk had a tougher look than those of the deep, rich meadows, as
their countryside, with its bony landscape, was tougher. They were
built to endure.

A few of the flock looked as though they had indoor lives; in particular Arabella noticed an elderly woman who might be a gentlewoman of small means, and a young girl beside her, whose bloom
and beauty lit up the pew she sat in as though a finger of light
had come through the window and picked her out.

Arabella turned to the Countess.

"Who is that young woman?" she asked. "The pretty one in
the grey bonnet. Is there another gentle family in the village?"

"There is not," replied the Countess curtly. "And that is a most
undesirable young person." She looked angry, and said nothing
further. Arabella, abashed, asked no more. But she looked over at
the other pew, and would very much have liked to have met the
undesirable young person in question. As well as having a pretty
face, it was such a very sensible one! Her dress was becoming
without being showy, the bonnet modest, the beautiful hands
held the prayerbook with grace. As the congregation sang, the undesirable young person joined in, swaying slightly, still looking
pretty as she sang—such a very difficult achievement! Those hands
did not look as though they had ever scrubbed a floor, or pounded
the washing in a dolly tub. That complexion had never been exposed to frosts, or harvest sun.

"You still have Widow Hawkins and her niece in the church, I
see," said the Countess sternly to the Vicar as he ushered them
out of the building.

"They are parishioners, Madam; I cannot turn them from the
church door. Your Grace's dislike and disapproval, I own, should
be enough for them to seek to worship in another parish, if they
had feelings of such delicacy as yours, Ma'am. But alas! it seems
they will not go elsewhere to oblige you. Widow Hawkins has
been a regular attender since she was baptised in this very font
fifty-five years ago. I fear I cannot ask them to go elsewhere. It
would mean a journey of several miles, your Grace."

The Countess snorted in answer to this, and the Vicar visibly trembled; but he smiled and bowed as he saw them to their carriage. Arabella wondered what would happen, but Cornelius Watts, seeing the expression on her face, came to her side, and, falling behind the others on the pretence of showing her an interesting tombstone, he explained,

"I have been to church on several occasions during the past twelve months at Arden St. James, Miss Hill; and the conversation you witnessed between the Countess and the Vicar has been repeated each time, and is likely to go on. Mrs. Hawkins owns her little house in the village, and she and her niece live on her annuity, and the money left by Miss Hawkins' father. This small income suffices them. The Countess may dislike them, but she has no power over them, and the Vicar knows it, so they are like to have the same arguments each Sunday forever."

"Why does she dislike them?"

Cornelius shrugged.

"Who knows?"

The Countess, missing them, turned round at the carriage steps and called imperiously.

As the weather was fine and sunny, they began their tour of the house on the outside, as soon as they got back, the girls still in their boots and cloaks, bonnets and muffs. On the previous day the house had seemed forbidding, frightening. Now the sun brought out the gold colour in the stone walls, making them glow like honey against the snow, and conjuring a sparkle from the deep-set windows. They were not sorry, though, to go inside again, and take off their wraps.

With the Earl leading them, they were soon lost in a maze of rooms. They were used to smaller houses, built in the classic manner, and could not understand this building, where one suite of rooms opened out of another, while other groups sprang at random, it seemed, from corridors. The corridors themselves were unlike any they had known before. They had steps, and corners, for no apparent reason; opened out into the width of a room, with seats and fireplaces; or narrowed to a yard in width and six-feet high. Some doors were panelled with linenfold carving, and the stone rose to a gothic arch over them; others were rectangular and plain; still others were flanked by carvings from the age of the first

Elizabeth, or beautiful Italianate gilding. The Earl knew exactly which sections of the building had been built in which century, or which notable architect had designed this wing, what previous earl had brought such and such a doorway back from Florence.

Even in the sun, there were aspects of the Priory which the girls did not care for. They ought to receive a delicious thrill from the Justice Room, or the Black Chamber, or the dining-room, which was properly called the Momento Mori Chamber; but they did not . . .

The Justice Room had been the scene of trials, and justice had been promptly carried out, down a shaft into the cellars—and the Justice Room was on the upper floor. The Black Chamber, never used within living memory, had a low ceiling and wainscot stained black with soot and smoke—they hurried away, as though a fiend were at their heels.

Neither of the girls found the pleasure in being in Arden Priory that they had expected. They went back to the pretty modern morning-room, built on to the sitting-room by the Countess as a young bride, and told the Countess that they thought it the nicest part of the house. She looked at them with a sardonic gleam in her eye, but said nothing scathing.

"You are not seeing it at its best," she said reflectively. "It is a welcoming home to us; and very fresh and beautiful in the spring and summer. The monks always chose these out-of-the-way places for their religious houses; and the uplands are hard, stern places to those who have lived all their lives in the lowlands. Linchestershire is a very lush and pleasant place, I know; and at first you will not appreciate such a very different form of beauty."

The next two weeks passed cheerfully away. The girls avoided the Justice Room and the Black Chamber, and grew used to the paintings in the dining-room. Arabella picked out more and more of the subject of the painting as she sat opposite it day after day. The theme struck a chord in her heart. Death in the midst of life! How near they had come to losing Jane, after the ill-fated adventure on the river! She would never forget . . .

The young woman they had seen in church, Miss Hawkins, was in the village street of Arden St. James when they passed through on a drive to a local beauty spot. The Earl stopped the carriage—

the Countess was not with them—and got down to speak to her, but Arabella and Jane could not hear what was said. They thought perhaps he was apologizing for his mother's enmity, for the scene they had witnessed on the first Sunday was repeated each week. Arabella thought it ill-bred of the Countess, and was sorry, for she was growing to like her very much. They were a cheerful house-party, and schemes for enjoyment took up their time to the exclusion of anything else.

Arabella and Jane then had an experience which worried them, and almost induced panic in Jane.

It was a cold day, but dry, with only the crisp snow underfoot, barely two inches thick where it lay deepest, and blown off altogether from the higher sections of ground. The sky was brilliantly blue, and the breeze was slight. There were no plans for the morning, so the girls decided to walk to the village. The two men were taking out their guns, and this arrangement suited everyone. The Countess intended to sew calico for savages on her sofa. The two men went off after partridges and the girls, in boots and furs, also left the Priory. They walked slowly on the quarter-mile to the village, for there was much to look at and exclaim over; last year's nests in the hedgerows, lingering berries on the hawthorns, and rushes, each bearing a tiny flag of ice to show which way the wind had been blowing when there had been a freezing fog.

They were almost into the outlying walls and farms when Jane, who had been growing quieter over the last few minutes, said that she was sure they were being followed. Arabella looked round and saw the figure of a man behind them, but saw no reason for fear. Other people had a right to walk the footpath. But as they traversed the last few yards into the village, she saw the reason for Jane's concern. If they stopped to look into the hedgerow, he stopped; if they hastened, he hastened. But now the village street was about them. They began to look into the window of the only shop, and the man disappeared altogether up some side lane. There was little in the shop window to interest them, and Arabella was thinking about turning for home, when she realized what a state of agitation Jane was in. Since her illness, her health and spirits had never really recovered their healthy tone, and this was the longest walk she had performed without rest. The agitation she had felt over the man behind them had wrought on her nerves to such an extent that she was quite unfit to go on. While they stood by the window, a customer within the shop, Miss Hawkins, the beautiful girl they had seen in church, had noticed through the glass that something was wrong. She came out with her purchases and spoke to them. Her voice was sweet and her manner gentle and refined.

"Excuse me," she said to Jane, "but you do not look quite well. May I offer you rest in my house before you go any farther?"

"I thank you," Arabella was relieved. "Miss Farley is a little faint; she has been ill, and has not yet fully recovered her strength; and we—" she laughed self-consciously—"felt a little panic at the thought that we were being followed."

They looked back along the road, and the young man was standing some way off, gazing over the fields. He was dressed like a farm labourer, and his face was hidden by a large-brimmed hat.

"That young man has been staying in the village for a few days," said Miss Hawkins. "I expect he is looking for work. My house is just here." Supported by Arabella and Miss Hawkins, Jane managed to walk to the house, enter, and sink into a chair. Arabella was worried by her friend's weakness; but she was sure that with the spring she would recover her old strength. Such an illness could not be recovered from under many months.

Miss Hawkins sat down and talked to them, and Arabella wondered why this girl and her aunt were held in such dislike by the Countess. They learned that the late Mr. Hawkins had been a draper in a nearby market town, and until his death his daughter had helped him in his business. She talked pleasantly, and when Jane felt a little better, offered to walk back with them to the Priory.

This time there was no pausing and lingering to look for tiny treasures; they walked on as briskly as Jane could manage, and in no time were in sight of the Priory. Miss Hawkins stopped, bid them goodbye, and ran off in a sprightly manner back towards the village. Once, nearly out of sight, she turned and waved to them.

This was enough adventure for that day. If they had not seen the young man again, in church on the following Sunday, Arabella would have forgotten the matter; but he was there, behind

Miss Hawkins and her aunt, at the very back of the church, half behind a pillar. Arabella might have missed seeing him, if Jane had not seemed so disturbed by the fact that his gaze was fixed on her. Peering into the shadow of the pillar, Arabella could not make out his face, for his hair was very rough, and tumbled all over it, and his coat collar was high. She was troubled by a recollection, or half memory, but could not place where she had seen someone similar before.

It was on the Monday that things moved to a crisis in the Priory.

Arabella had, in the course of conversation, mentioned the portrait of Lady Kitty at Curteys Court; the Earl had exclaimed that there was a painting by the same artist at the Priory; she did not recall it, so he offered to show it to her. They went to the room where it hung—it was a charming small portrait of the Countess as a young woman—and Arabella duly admired it; then they lingered a little.

"Have you grown to like the Priory?" asked the Earl. Arabella was surprised that her first dislike had been so obvious.

"How could I not? When we have had every comfort and luxury, and the society of friends," she answered.

"You would not object, then, to spending your life here?" he said, in a low, meaning voice.

She hesitated. Was this a declaration? If not, it was more positive than anything he had previously said.

"Anyone, given the opportunity, could live here very happily," she said at last. She felt this was temporizing. But she could make no plainer answer. She could hardly say, "Yes, I will be your Countess," when he had not asked the question. But if that was not what he meant, what did he mean? She was agitated, and began to doubt the truth of her answer. Would she indeed be happy to spend her life at the Priory? A vision rose before her of Piccadilly, the cheerful rush of carriages, the crowd of people, and she felt in her heart that she would cheerfully exchange the sombre glories of Arden Priory, and the bone-bare beauty of Arden St. James, picked clean by the moorland wind, for the motley fascination of London, even the meaner streets, even the maze of old lanes and ancient dwellings, like a nest of Chinese boxes, round the offices of Waveney and Watts.

The Earl said no more, and they were both very quiet as they returned to join the others in the morning-room.

It was not until late afternoon, when Arabella was alone in the bedroom she shared with Jane, that something further developed. Arabella was deciding what to wear in the evening. Her gowns had all seen the light of Arden Priory candles so often, that she thought everyone must be tired of the sight of them. If only there were a handy haberdasher's, where she could spend a shilling or two on new trimming! Before she could make up her mind, Jane burst into the room.

"Oh, Bell!" she said, and sank, panting, on to the bed.

"What is it?"—there could only be one thing to produce such agitation—"has the Earl made an offer?"

"Nearly—as good as—almost! We were alone, Bell, in the sitting-room; and he asked me—he asked me—whether I could spend my life happily at Arden Priory."

Arabella gazed at her friend in astonishment.

"This is unbelievable! Is there more?"

"Is that not enough? I said I would be happy to spend my life here. Oh, Bell! Robert! My Robert! What of Robert?" and Jane began to cry.

What of Robert, indeed? Then Arabella said,

"But that is exactly the question he asked me, this very day, in the white drawing-room. He has gone too far in this game with us . . ."

Now it was Jane's turn to look astonished.

"He asked you . . . oh, Bell . . ."

Arabella took her by the hand.

"We are going to confront him," she said. And, pulling Jane behind her, she set off in search of the Earl.

He was alone, as it happened. Mr. Watts was out walking, and the Countess, complaining of a headache, had gone to her room. The Earl turned round at the impetuous entry of the two girls, both agitated, Jane's yellow ribbon flying with the haste of their movement.

They came to a standstill in front of him, and Arabella, not stopping to think, burst out,

"Your Grace! You have been paying attentions to both Miss Farley and myself. Which of us is it that you love? Which of us do you hope to marry? For it is not well done in you to court both of us! We cannot stand it, we cannot, indeed."

Giles looked, first astonished, and then—changing by degrees— he began to look ashamed. At last he turned away from them. He had been standing with his hand on the mantel; now he lowered his head until his forehead rested on that hand, gazed into the fire, and said in a muffled voice,

"I am afraid all I can do is to beg your forgiveness. It is true. I have paid attentions to both of you, and, indeed, admire you both exceedingly. But—now I must confess it—I love another."

"Another?" was all Arabella could find to say.

"Another?" repeated Jane, bewildered.

"Another," said the Earl again. "I am deeply in love with Miss Hawkins; and she has been kind enough to say that she is not indifferent to me."

Arabella and Jane could think of nothing to say. The Earl continued,

"You will wonder at it; you will think it strange. I have hated playing a deceitful part, and am glad it is over. In your eyes I must be damned forever, but it was not my wish—I was forced into a position where I did not know what to do."

He turned towards them, and they could see he was in the grip of powerful emotion.

"You must forgive me! Sit down, and I will explain." They sat, and he began.

"I am deeply in love with Elizabeth—with Miss Hawkins; when my Mother and Grandmother knew of it, they would not hear of a marriage. Then the Duchess met you, Miss Hill, in London, and suggested you as a bride. I was at my wits' end, and thought only of getting a little peace, so I came to Town, and began to court you. By also paying attentions to Miss Farley, I hoped neither of you would take me seriously—the last thing I wanted was to hurt either of you, only to gain time. I hoped one day my family would

relent, and I could be joined in marriage to my dear Elizabeth
. . . forgive me."

"And what does Miss Hawkins think of all this?"

"She is being very forbearing about it . . ."

"I freely forgive you," said Jane, all impulsive warmth, "for I
am in the same position; there is a young man—we grew up together—who, I confess, I love dearly; and I have done as much
wrong, in bowing to my family and allowing your advances, as you
have in making them. My family will not allow my marriage, either."

He looked up and, reaching out, clasped her hand in his.

"God bless you, Miss Farley!"

"And I," said Arabella thoughtfully, "though I have not
plighted my troth, and could not have refused my consent, sir,
had you asked me to be your wife—yet I am glad that I do not
have to make my home in Arden Priory."

"Your forgiveness is more than I deserve!"

"We like Miss Hawkins; we met her in the village," volunteered Jane.

"You have? I know you would have liked her—no one could
help it, except my family, and that is because she is poor, and
used to serve in her father's shop."

"Perhaps we can meet her again," said Arabella.

The Earl looked pleased.

"Why not? And why not tomorrow? She has sent me a message
—I am to meet her in our usual place, in the forenoon. Why not
come with me, and get to know her better? She will like it, of all
things."

They agreed, for the time being, to try to appear the same together, as before; but that evening, in Arden Priory, three hearts
were lighter than they had been for some weeks past.

Jane, once more free to think of Robert, without the fear of
being forced to marry another, could have sung with relief; the
Earl who, apart from being under the thumb of his relations, was
a good, true kind of man, was free from his load of deceit; and
Arabella? For she had no Robert, no Elizabeth, to absorb her
hopes; only the sadness of past foolishness, not the expectation of
future joy. Why did her heart sing because she was not going to

marry the Earl? Why did her fingers on the piano keys perform a joyous sarabande, and swing into such a country dance that the china shepherds and shepherdesses wanted to join in and dance along their painted shelf? Why did she play in such a way as to make the Countess think a Ball in Arden might, after all, be possible? Oh, why indeed?

Chapter Fifteen

The following morning the Earl set out to keep his tryst, and Arabella and Jane were to follow a quarter of an hour later. They were excited by the novelty of the situation, and looking forward to seeing Elizabeth again; Jane was soft eyed and sentimental as they set off for the Hermit's Grotto.

The Grotto had been built by the Earl's grandfather, and decorated by his grandmother, who had pressed shells into the inside walls of the little structure while the plaster was still wet, and then added details to the design she had made by putting in pieces of rock crystal and other semi-precious stones the family had collected. No hermit had ever inhabited it. Now it was quite hard to find the entrance, it was so overgrown with shrubs, and it was not fresh and gay any longer, but rather gloomy and dark; but sitting in the inner part, close together, they found their host and his love. There was a small fireplace, and some rustic furniture.

If anyone, knowing one of the three girls was to be a Countess, could have looked down on the scene as they met, Elizabeth Hawkins would have been picked out to be the chatelaine of Arden Priory. She stood, serene, graceful and stately, stretching out her hands to Jane, all tremulous softness, and Arabella, who showed in every movement her eager, questing spirit.

"I think you have a surprise for my guests," said the Earl, when the first few emotional minutes were over.

"Yes, indeed," and Elizabeth looked at Jane very kindly. "You remember the strange young man who followed you to the village? It turns out he is not a stranger to you. Do not be alarmed, Miss Farley; in disguise, it is Mr. Spencer." "Robert!" It seemed to the onlookers that even before Elizabeth had brought out her sentence, Jane had jumped to the realization of what she was going to say, for her hand had flown to her heart. "Where is he?" were her next words; "Oh! I knew in the church, when he was looking at me so; but I would not believe it."

Elizabeth moved as though she were going out of the Grotto, but Jane read her intention, and rushed out in front of her, to meet Robert as he came out of his hiding place. She ran towards him, and flung herself into his arms, bringing him to a sweet stop, in front of anyone who might be passing by, quite uncaring.

A little later they came back into the Grotto together, with their arms round each other's waists, and one glance at their faces was enough for everyone to know that all was right between them.

"But why come in disguise, Robert?" asked Jane at last. "You quite frightened me. I thought it was you, but could not believe my eyes, with this rough hair and funny hat. And the way you followed us!"

"I was hoping to manage to speak to you alone. A University friend in London wrote to tell me that you were to marry the Earl, and had come to visit Arden Priory; I could not stay in Cornwall and let it happen; I thought Arabella might be encouraging you to marry someone else—"

"How could you, sir!" cried Arabella. "After what I did for you!"

He grinned boyishly. "I ought to have known better. But I thought if Jane told me with her own lips, that she had given me up, then I would rather not encounter anyone else."

"Why not just walk up to the front door?" cried Arabella, the forthright.

"I did not know what to think; I was trying to find out the lie of the land before doing anything rash. Who was it taught me the arts of disguise?"

"How unhappy you must have been," said Jane softly.

"I was," he answered, and they were silent, gazing into each other's eyes.

"What a pity it is," said Giles, looking sadly at the lovers, and holding Elizabeth's hand in his, "that we cannot marry and be happy."

"Why cannot you marry Miss Hawkins?"

"Why, Miss Hill, you know that my grandmother and mother will not countenance the match."

"Are you—do you mind me asking—still in any way under age, or in their guardianship?"

"No, I came into the Earldom absolutely."

"Then why not disregard your family's disapproval? Why not take out a licence, marry Miss Hawkins, and proceed to be happy?" The Earl looked at Arabella as though thunderstruck.

"And you, Jane. It is doing you no good trying to please your mother. You and Robert are both over twenty-one; again it is only your parents who keep you apart; make that two licences, and we will have a double wedding."

"But the Countess?" said the Earl.

"Do not tell her, until you have made her the Dowager Countess."

"But Lady Russett?" said Jane and Robert together.

"Do not tell her either. You are not happy, Jane, in the social life of London; I advised you against marrying on a small income, but I have changed my mind. You would be better off with Robert than being thrown at the head of every fashionable parti who comes on the scene."

"As to the income," said the Earl, "what is the problem? I believe you are in orders, sir. Have you not obtained a living?"

"I have a curacy, sir."

"One of the livings in my gift," said the Earl reflectively, "is to become vacant, because the incumbent has been offered a stall in the Cathedral; he takes it up in a few months, and I have to find a successor. It is the small village of Old Arden, and the tithes are not large; but if it would be of interest to you . . ."

"It would indeed," put in Jane, before Robert had time to reply. Where Robert was concerned, she was neither weak nor timorous.

For a while they were silent, trying to comprehend the change in their fortunes. To marry! The more they thought about it, the more it appeared the best—the most sensible—solution to their problems. All the reasons, youth and hope said, were for marrying, parents notwithstanding. The most docile of children rebel against parental pressures, when their own needs rise imperiously and compel them.

"It would have to be secret," said the Earl at last, still in dread of his mother's wrath.

"It would be, if you got a licence; if you can trust the vicar not to rush to tell your mother, you could be married in your own church here in Arden St. James."

"The vicar would say nothing," put in Elizabeth.

"Then you could present the Countess with a *fait accompli*, and her successor."

"We could all honeymoon here, and go on a tour later in the year," said the Earl, who, freeing himself of the burden of family disapproval, was beginning to think and plan.

"Who would be the witnesses?" said Robert.

"You could be witnesses for each other."

"Or you and Mr. Watts could be witnesses for both of us," remarked Jane.

"I think not," said Arabella. "It is hardly fair to involve Mr. Watts. He is in high favour with the Countess, and it would be a pity to prejudice her against him. If it was known that he was in ignorance of the affair, he could remain in favour with both her and the Duchess of Doncaster. I will have to stay away, to keep the Countess happy in your absence."

Everyone agreed with this; the two couples were to stand witness for each other.

"Spencer," said the Earl, "you and I will go and see to the licences. We will meet here tomorrow, and fix any details that have occurred to us in the meantime. Now, I can't help thinking, if we are to keep the secret, we ought to part. Tomorrow at four; my mother always sleeps then."

They all parted very happy, and the next day there was no reason to be any less so. The licences were prepared, and the day after the next was fixed as the wedding day. The Earl had brought with him a bottle of wine, and some glasses, hidden in the pockets of his coat, and Elizabeth had brought a mysterious cloth which proved to be full of muffins, and a large pat of butter; so that when Robert—who was very good at that kind of thing—had lit the fire, they used a forked stick and toasted the muffins, and had such a party as the little grotto had not seen for many a long year.

As they sat round and beamed at each other, Elizabeth sprang a surprise.

"You remember in my note asking you to meet me yesterday, I said I had two surprises?"

"Yes," replied the Earl. "Spencer was the surprise."

"Mr. Spencer was one of the surprises. The other was not told."

"Do tell!" cried Arabella. "There is nothing so nice with muffins as surprises."

Having got everyone's attention, Elizabeth went on, looking at Giles.

"Did I ever tell you I had a half share in a lottery ticket?"

"I think you did, though wasn't it in December, when we were both so unhappy. I thought no more about it."

"I won a prize." Elizabeth's voice was expressionless.

"But the lottery was drawn before Christmas!" exclaimed Jane. "I remember, for I had an eighth share in a ticket. The thirteenth, I think, of December."

"Yes," said Elizabeth.

"And you have waited all this time to tell me!" the Earl sounded piqued.

"There did not seem much point in telling you, when you were in such trouble with the family, and I had my reasons for waiting."

"Good," said the Earl. "You will have some money of your own. Not that I would ever grudge you anything, but independence is a good thing in a marriage. Watts can draw up a settlement."

"It is ten thousand pounds," went on Elizabeth.

"What!" they all looked at her.

"I told nobody, except my aunt. If your family could not accept me as I was, I did not want them to change their minds just because of the money."

"No, but . . ." and the Earl sounded rather rueful. "Miss Hawkins with ten thousand pounds, would be more acceptable to them than Miss Hawkins without."

"And that is why I did not tell you until you decided to marry me in spite of them. Now I know that I am not influencing your decision."

The Earl got over his chagrin at being kept in the dark, and was comforted by the thought that his family would accept Elizabeth more easily. Everyone was delighted for her.

"She is what he needs," thought Arabella. "She has strength and strongmindedness. She will give him backbone," and she went on to plan her strategy for keeping the Countess occupied on the next day.

It was difficult, but not impossible. Mr. Watts, as usual in the mornings, was busy with letters, and the Countess was in a mood to miss the other young people. Giles said he was driving Miss Farley to the village to see the first lambs, and for a minute Arabella was afraid that the Countess would decide to go too. Jane slipped down the stairs and out to the carriage without the Countess seeing that she was wearing her very best walking dress, which was too elegant for a lamb-viewing expedition. Arabella saw her off, with an expressive handclasp, and a beaming face. As soon as the carriage was moving away, Arabella had only to return to the sitting-room and parry the Countess' curiosity. Why had she not gone to see the lambs? She said she had a slight indisposition and preferred to sew calico this morning . . . she talked so hard, and so entertainingly, that the Countess, if she had pondered the matter, would have stopped believing in the indisposition. The *tête-à-tête* did not have to last long; barely an hour after leaving the house, the carriage was back again.

Jane entered, leading Robert by the hand.

"Madam," she said, "may I introduce Mr. Robert Spencer? We have just become man and wife, in your little church of Arden St. James. He is a clergyman, and we have had an attachment for many years."

"What? You are not old enough, child, to have had anything for many years. What will your mother say? Did she know of this?"

"I fear not, Madam. My husband and I are both of full age, and have taken the matter into our own hands."

"You had no right to do so, Miss Farley—or Mrs. Spencer, I suppose I must say—while you were under my roof. It puts me in a most unfortunate position."

Mr. Watts had come in, and was standing quietly in the doorway. It seemed to Arabella that he was looking at her, rather than at Jane. No sooner was this little scene over, than the Earl, with Elizabeth, came into the room. The Countess rose, heavily, intending to say,

"What is that woman doing here?" but she was forestalled by her son.

"You may not have heard our neighbour's good news, Madam. Elizabeth has won ten thousand pounds in the December Lottery."

Such craft! thought Arabella, mentioning that first. Perhaps Elizabeth put him up to it. The Countess, taken aback by her son calling the young woman by her christian name, said dubiously,

"Then perhaps she and her aunt will be considering leaving Arden St. James, and living in Town."

"She has already left Arden St. James, Mother. She has done me the honour of becoming my wife, and I have brought her to live at the Priory."

It will never be known if the ten thousand pounds softened the Countess, or whether she had secretly resigned herself to the thought that this might happen. Her reaction was not as fearful a thing as had been expected. She threw herself on the sofa and had hysterics, and her maid had to be fetched, but it could have been much worse . . .

At the Earl's words, Mr. Watts had looked astonished, and his eyes had gone quickly to Arabella's face; as soon as he could, he crossed to her side, and said in a low voice,

"Did you know of this, Miss Hill?"

"Yes, sir," and for once her eyes looked, with close proximity, directly into his own. They were in a room with five others, but in that instant they could have been in the middle of a desert, and one soul spoke to another.

"I set it in motion," she answered him. "I really believe that, but for me, they would still be lamenting their inability to marry."

"You are not distressed? You have not been deceived, or deluded?" his tone was sharp; his concern for her was sweet.

"Not at all, sir. In fact," she admitted, smiling up at him playfully, "I am relieved rather than otherwise. London calls me. I have heard the sound of Bow Bells, and am longing to return to them. Whatever the consequences," and, thinking of Phoebe, she raised her chin and looked resolute.

He looked at her again, then looked thoughtful. For a while they both watched the Countess having hysterics, but neither moved to help her.

"When you wish to return, I will take you," he offered.

The Dowager Countess' maid arrived, and took charge of her, and the Earl went to see Mrs. Bridge and arrange about suites of rooms. He showed his own apartments to Elizabeth, and she agreed with him that they would do very nicely for them both, and that the Dowager should retain her far grander apartments as long as she wished.

Between Arabella and Mr. Watts nothing else was said just then; but things had altered between them.

"So you have supplanted me," said the Dowager, dangerously, later that evening.

"Please do not say so, Madam. I wish to be a true daughter to you," was Elizabeth's mild answer.

"Humph!" was the only reply she got, but she shot a glance at her daughter-in-law which was not entirely antagonistic.

"Ten thousand, did you say, Giles?" she asked once, and, assured that it was so, said nothing more. Perhaps she felt that for her own sake, it would be wise not to make an enemy of this young woman her son had married.

Chapter Sixteen

They had been at Arden Priory scarce a month; it hardly seemed possible, but it had been so short a time. So much had happened! Miss Hawkins and her lottery ticket; Robert Spencer and his living; the double wedding; so much!

The Dowager Countess of Epworth was at present snoring in the sitting-room, her netting slipping from her hand. Somewhere in the grounds, looking for the first snowdrops, were the two happy young couples.

Arabella was alone in the morning-room with her canvas work; she was stitching a new cover for the seat of her father's favourite chair, which had originally been worked by her mother, and was now quite worn out. He said that, if he must have a new one, it had to be as like as possible to the old; and so it would be.

She had sorted out her wools, and bent industriously over her frame, with her right hand hidden under the work, ready to meet the needle pushed through from above with the left hand, and return it to the surface. Mr. Watts entered the room. He paused, looking over at her as she sat near the window; she raised her head and smiled, pleased to see him. He walked over and dropped into a chair beside her.

"I like to see you stitching," he remarked after a few minutes. "It reminds me of the times I used to watch my mother, when I was a boy." She did not answer, but looked up and smiled again, and he sat on for some minutes.

They now knew each other well enough to sit without speaking, each happy in the presence of the other. He tried to read her emotions in the shadowed grey of her eyes, but then relaxed and stretched out his legs comfortably. She thought it unusual that he did not fill every moment with talk, as he normally did; she had often noticed that one always knew where Mr. Watts was, if one were to pause and listen; there were not many times when he sat as he did now, without a word. But she was glad that he felt so much at ease with her that they could have as comfortable a time as this.

Gradually he became attracted to the contents of her workbox and picked up, one by one, the small ivory accoutrements—undoing the miniature beehive that held the finest thread, moving about the flat ivory discs, with silks wound across them from one indentation to another of the engrailed rims. Picking up her tiny scissors and one of the skeins of wool, he began to systematically demolish it, snipping off half-inch lengths from the end, until a shower of segments of brightly-coloured wool fell on to the carpet, and stuck to his riding breeches, and lodged themselves inside his boot-tops.

"Mr. Watts," said Arabella gently, "if you must waste my yarn, pray use this colour. I have so very little of the garnet red." She handed him a hank of dove grey, but he started, as though woken from a dream, hastily put down the scissors, and what was left of the wool, and went to lean on the jamb of the door, and look out into the garden.

Far away among the melting snow could be seen glimpses of the four young people, running and calling to one another through the bushes at the edge of the plantation.

"I just came to tell you that I am going away for a few days," he said at last. "I will be back, of course, to take you home again as I promised. Is it next week you have decided to go?"

"I thought so . . . you are going away?" For the instant no other thought was possible. Then, "Do you go by stage?"

"No; it is quicker to ride; I am borrowing a horse of the Earl's. You know his generosity—even to a Cit! But to one who has married a daughter of Trade, perhaps these distinctions do not matter."

Arabella had not realized before how much he could be hurt by the haughty behaviour of the aristocracy towards him and his fellows in the powerful circles of the City. Why, they could buy and sell most of those dandies! But he was vulnerable to those slights he seemed to ignore, she knew that now, and wondered that it had not been obvious before. Realizing the greatness of his heart, his forgiveness of her own faults, the time and money he spent on people he tried to help, how could she have supposed him so thick-skinned as not to notice the veiled insults of such people as the Russetts? Following on that thought—might she herself not have hurt him, times without number—before she knew his worth?

Mr. Watts gazed for a few minutes more out of the window, then, asking her to bid farewell to the others on his behalf, he pressed her hand briefly, and with a nod and a word of farewell, he was gone.

It seemed to her that he had not wished to leave her, and to find herself alone, although she had been content enough before he joined her, was no longer enough. The place on the carpet where he had been standing to look out of the window, the little pair of scissors, the scatter on the floor of brightly-coloured snippets of wool, were suddenly become dear to her, because they spoke of him. The pain of parting was too sudden. Putting her handkerchief to her eyes, she found she was weeping; how she had always hated endings and partings! Beginnings and meetings were what she liked. They might never again be together as they had been in these past weeks and, for a moment, apprehension of what might happen to her on her return to London struck her. It was hard to recover her usual optimism. If only Mr. Watts had not gone! She had to admit to herself that she had grown to care very much for this brisk, dignified man.

After a while she regained enough self-control to go on with her embroidery, and even managed to proceed quite quickly with it, distracting her thoughts by telling herself how much the chair-cover would please her father.

They were six that night at the dinner table, and Arabella

found that she was just as lonely as she had been in the morning-room. After all, a lover is not good company for anyone but the beloved; and two sets of lovers at one dinner table, gazing mutely into each other's eyes at every opportunity, were enough to put a blight on any meal. Nor could the Countess be counted as good company. To be sure she had told Arabella at length about the state of her tooth, which had stopped her sleeping a wink for a week. To someone within earshot of the drawing-room that after-noon this statement was hardly credible . . .

Arabella smiled and sympathized politely. Mr. Watts would, she felt, approve of her behaviour now, if at no other time. She wished he could see how very ladylike and considerate she was being, under the very trying circumstance of having no one of any sense whatever to talk to. She looked at the Earl, who was smiling fatuously at his Countess over the salt cellar, and decided she must have been very foolish to ever imagine she could care for him.

The party moved together into the sitting-room.

"We miss Mr. Watts," remarked Giles, and Arabella restored him to favour immediately.

"Yes," agreed the new Countess, "he is such a bright, friendly sort of person."

"But very vulgar," put in the Dowager, settling herself on her sofa. "That laugh of his! One can hear it everywhere. It is vulgar to laugh out loud, and particularly in such a very hearty manner."

"I like to hear him laugh," Arabella could not help saying; "and I thought you liked him, Madam."

"So I do; he is always so solicitous about my health. Mr. Watts really cares how I am feeling, and always tries to make me com-fortable."

"It is like him!" said Arabella in an undertone. "He is the same with me—even when I vex him. Always concerned with the wel-fare of others."

"He is a little man," said the Earl, who stood six foot three in his socks.

"But not a *very* little man," replied Arabella.

"With plain features," said Jane mischievously.

"But animated," replied Arabella.

"He sings well," put in Robert.

"And with great energy," said the new Countess, "as he does everything."

There the conversation seemed to have ended. They sat a while in silence, feeling that the evening was incomplete without Mr. Watts; but by degrees talk began again, and Arabella went over to the small, square pianoforte whose soft tones she had grown to love, and filled the room with imprinted arabesques of melody, as the lovers chatted together, and the Dowager dozed by the fire.

"I declare, Miss Hill," said the Dowager Countess, as supper was wheeled into the room, "I don't know when I spent an evening so pleasantly. That is, since your dear father died, Giles. He used to read to me, and that was also very pleasant; one did not need to make any effort, you know, just to listen; and if one happened to drop off, well, he was usually still reading when one came to again."

Arabella decided she was bored with chicken wings and had no appetite for patties. A little wine and water, she declared, would suffice. The party broke up early, and she was glad. She had had the pleasure of Jane's presence, and could enjoy the sight of her happiness; she liked Robert Spencer; the Earl had become a favourite companion; and she was growing to like his wife almost as well as she had always believed she would. But there was no one in the company to whom she came first . . . and it had seemed to her lately that, in spite of everything, Mr. Watts put her first, above the others.

The Dowager was concerned only with her own welfare, and Arabella was a convenience to her, not someone whose company was sought after for its own sake. How bright his presence would have made this firelit evening, while the rain fell gently and persistently outside on to the melting snow! Well, she must be content. No doubt she was nothing to him, although her heart whispered that she was; perhaps his attentions were no more than politeness—but she missed him, and was lonely.

On her way to bed, Arabella paused in the embrasure of the window on the stairs, her candle flickering in her hand, and looked out. He hadn't said where he was going. To Town? On business to a country estate? He was not as a rule so reticent. He had the habit of telling her of every one of his actions, however small, as though to do so gave him pleasure. He could hardly have finished his journey in one day; though the days were getting perceptibly longer. Perhaps at this instant he was laying his dear curly head on some pillow at a wayside inn, with the horse stabled snugly outside, and no thoughts of her. Pah! Why should he think of her? What was she to him but a naughty child? A romp, a madcap? But he might think of her, for he might find a snippet of garnet wool clinging to his boot-top, or caught in the fold of his breeches—

"Bell!" called Jane from along the corridor. "Do go to bed, dear. You will catch a chill, and that will displease the Dowager. She does not like anyone to be ill but herself."

Arabella left the embrasure and went, shivering, and not sorry to undress, to blow out her candle, and to slip into a warm bed.

In his wayside inn, Cornelius Watts was sitting, looking at the tiny scraps of garnet wool in his hand . . .

After two lonely days, which gave Arabella time to realize to the full how much she needed him, Cornelius Watts rode back to Arden Priory on the evening of the third day, brisk and cheerful as ever, and ready to set out again after only the briefest of rests, to take Arabella back to London.

Whatever might be the outcome, she was on fire to be gone. There was something in her spirit which could not be at peace among moors and fields; only when she was enfolded by the parallel lives of many thousands of her fellow beings, by the stir and bustle, the endless variety, could she achieve the inner tranquillity, the sleep of the hummingtop, the centre of the vortex.

Jane gave her a letter to Lady Russett, breaking the news of her marriage, and asking that her old maidservant be sent to join her. Arabella offered to leave Margery behind, but Jane refused. In case Lady Russett, in her anger, refused to send her own maid, Arabella promised to see to it that the girl knew of Jane's whereabouts and had the money to reach her.

The trunk was packed; the Earl offered his carriage as far as the nearest Posting House—for they were travelling by public coach— and the next day saw all ready for their departure. A last walk

round the grounds, a last half-hour playing on the pianoforte for
the Dowager's pleasure, a last embrace for Jane and farewells to
the rest of the party, and she was accepting Mr. Watts' assistance
into the vehicle, and they were away, waving from the window as
long as they could see the group at the door of Arden Priory. Since
his return, Arabella had noticed that Mr. Watts was suppressing
excitement; she did not wonder what its cause; his presence made
her happy. Margery's company put a damper on conversation, and
he easily stonewalled Arabella's veiled enquiries about his absence.

When they transferred into the public coach, and the Earl's
carriage was dismissed with thanks and half a guinea for the
coachman, matters were a little better. Margery was in an outside
seat, but they were not alone for, in the interior, as well as Mr.
Watts and Arabella, there was a roly-poly gentleman from Oxford, with a snuff-stained waistcoat, and an elderly lady of forbidding appearance, so that all conversation must be of a public and
formal character. Mr. Watts' face was expressive of something,
but Arabella knew not what; he was endlessly attentive to her
comfort, and polite to the other passengers; but he had a screwed-
down air, as though at any moment he might explode with whatever emotion he was containing.

It seemed to be a happy emotion, though sometimes clouds
crossed his face as though across a sunny landscape, expressions of
doubt and seriousness. But they were chased away again by cheerfulness and suppressed gaiety.

Arabella was in almost the best of spirits. Perhaps for her, too,
there were graver moments; but this was, for whatever reason, a
day on which the sun shone, colours were bright, and the winds
were sweet with the breath of spring.

At the next stage the man from Oxford got out, and two stages
after, the forbidding lady followed his example. They were alone.

"Shall we have Margery inside?" asked Arabella.

"I think not," replied Cornelius abruptly, and she said not another word. For the first time with him, she felt a strange embarrassment. As the wheels began to turn, they were both silent. She
cast about in her mind for something to say—any commonplace
remark would have done; but nothing occurred to her. Then, in a
low voice, he said,

"Miss Hill, you once accused me of being in love with your sister."

Whatever she had half expected him to say, it was not this. To hark back to that time! It was too unkind, really it was! She turned her head away without answering, with a flush rising to her cheeks. Yet his voice had not been angry—gentle, rather—he went on, as though she had answered.

"Do you not consider," and she found that he had taken her hand, and was touching each finger in turn, as one touches a baby's toes, "do you not consider, that it is your duty as a sister to protect Mrs. Welby from the threat of such an improper passion? Do you not think that you owe it to your sister to put such a possibility out of court, once and for all, by marrying me yourself?"

Arabella looked round quickly. His face was tender, and he was sitting very close, and he was still holding her hand . . .

"After what you heard about me?" she said.

"Spencer explained about his visit to Jane," he replied; "and Phoebe threatens me too. You can leave the contest with her to me."

Her feelings changed, from embarrassment to surprise, then to joy, then to complete happiness; then she replied, with a little archness,

"You feel that it is my duty?"

"There is no doubt of it," he replied gravely.

"Why, Mr. Watts, I declare you are holding my hand!"

"I intend to go on doing so."

"But if I were to agree—you would realize that it is only because of the great love I bear my sister . . ."

"That is understood completely," he smiled.

"And of course, to stop you marrying anyone else," she looked at him sternly, "anyone else whatever . . ."

A wheel of the coach went into a pothole—Arabella slid, and most unaccountably found herself in Mr. Watts' arms.

"Sisterly duty is so very important," she murmured, just before he kissed her.

It was some very satisfactory minutes later that Arabella, with her head on Mr. Watts' shoulder, and one of her hands playing with the crisp curls behind his ear, whispered,

"I wonder what my father will say."

"He seemed very pleased about it when I rode over to ask his leave to address you."

"So that's where you were!" and she looked up at him saucily.

"That's where I was," he replied, very low.

Such contentment was rarely carried by the Quicksilver coach in its journey from Ghent to Aix . . . the remainder of the stage passed in the most delightful embraces and low spoken endearments, until at the next post inn they had to pull apart, and Arabella to hastily re-arrange her hair and compose her face to meet the new passengers who were piling in, filling the interior completely. She and Mr. Watts sat opposite to one another, and if the last stage had been delightful, this one was not much less so. To glance at each other was to remember the happy scene just lived through, and to look forward to its renewal very shortly; to converse in calm and reserved tones had a teasing deliciousness, deceiving the other passengers while they enjoyed themselves with their private knowledge; and such conversation was useful.

Arabella was able to ask for family news. Mrs. Hunt, she heard, had been very much stricken by the news about Phoebe; but Mr. Hill had done his best to talk her out of useless grief, and she was gradually becoming less miserable an object.

This brought her own former unhappiness to the forefront of Arabella's mind, and her brightness dimmed a little; but not for long. Soon she was glancing at him again from under her eyelashes, and demanding some slight attention with a frivolous request, glorying in her new-found power.

William, nodding sleepily as he waited to meet them with the Welby carriage, saw at once from Arabella's radiant face, and from the tender way in which Cornelius handed her from the coach, how things were with them. He tried to beam his approval in a respectful manner, but soon his face looked longer than ever. The sight of their happiness only made him long for his Hannah. If he had known that on the previous day Isaac Sutherland, in one of his periodic journeys round the country, had attended the Melton Meeting, William would hardly have slept that night, and would have given his cause up for lost.

After Meeting, Isaac had been invited to speak to the assembled Friends, and after giving them news from other parts of the country, he had happened to mention that William Pigeon who they knew well, was now an attender at his own Meeting in London.

"I fear," he had said heavily, "I fear for this young man, Friends. He serves with a family who indulge in courses of viciousness—who care naught for sin—and does not remonstrate with them. He does not struggle for their souls. He does not set an example to them. Should I take back to him your censure! Your blame?" he paused rhetorically.

Hannah, who had been caught unprepared by this attack, was on her feet before she had time to think, declaring, in her clear, high voice,

"William Pigeon is a good man, Friend Sutherland. There isn't a better in Linchestershire. Any sin is abhorrent to him. Where are your wits, Friends? We all know the Welby family are God-fearing people. Who can stand up and say nay to that? We reject your censure, Friend Sutherland. Your impression of them must be founded on misunderstanding. Our message to Friend William Pigeon is our Love in God, as a true Christian."

She became conscious of the complete stillness of the Meeting, and their eyes on her; she blushed; she became silent; she sat down. Never before had she spoken in Meeting . . .

Isaac Sutherland looked over at her very kindly.

"Well, Friends? we have heard our Sister?"

There was a general murmur from the older members, and at last, urged on by two of the others, one rose.

"In this matter, Friend Sutherland, we agree with our Sister Hannah Sharpe. We do not join you in censure. Our message to William Pigeon is, 'God's strength and Love go with thee; and come back soon, God permitting, to join with us once again.' "

Hannah realized that she had committed herself, and in everyone's opinion she had now plighted her troth to William; and she had better send him a message to tell him so . . .

Caroline and Richard were surprised at the turn of events; but they were pleased, and the more they thought about the match between Arabella and Mr. Watts, the more they liked it. "How long have you known?" Caroline had asked; and, later, Arabella said to Cornelius,

"How long have you known that you loved me?"

"Not more than a year."

"Now tell me the truth, for a year ago you thought me perfectly odious, and perhaps I was! Richard has told me some of your speeches about me, sirrah, so we will have no dissembling. How long since you ceased to think me the most detestable of young females?"

"Oh, when you bought the black bonnet."

"Sir! Now when?"

"Well . . . it grew upon me unawares; I was going about my business, with no thoughts of marriage, and Love grew unnoticed until, even though I tried to deny him, he would out."

"Before we went to Arden Priory?"

"Yes, before then."

"But you offered to take us! Knowing that the Earl was making advances!"

"If you were going to become a Countess, at least by being there, I would know the worst at once. Not that I enjoyed it."

She looked gently at him.

"You could have asked me to marry you, before we went to Arden."

"And wronged you by so doing. The chance of an Earl does not come every day. What had I to offer, compared to his magnificence?"

It took some time for Arabella to convince him that, in her eyes at least, he had everything to offer . . .

What happened to everybody else?

Ann Ducros was removed from her apprenticeship at the milliner's and appointed as needlework teacher in the training school; her place was taken by another girl from the school, in the back room full of ribbons and feathers. Once teaching, and with a dowry tucked away by gift from Mr. and Mrs. Watts, she was able to meet suitable young men among whom she later found one to marry.

And Phoebe? She had a confrontation with Cornelius which

put the fear of God into her to such an extent that she never indulged in blackmail again. But, regrettably, it must be told that she went on from strength to strength, rising, in a horizontal position, ever higher, both financially and socially; abandoning Captain Wilmott once his gambling win had been spent or settled on her, she took other lovers until—having at last achieved immense wealth—she began to desire respectability. It was then that the faithful Joel at last came into his own, and they were married, whereupon Mr. Phoebe was as happy as it was possible for him to be, and to her assorted sons and daughters were added some of his own. Phoebe ruled her family of tall, devoted sons and meek submissive daughters with a rod of iron, and none of them ever dared to go against her wishes. Until, that is, the advent of a granddaughter, christened Phoebe after her, who inherited those green eyes and long black lashes . . . but that is another story . . .

Nathaniel Eeles, under the Russetts' roof, met a widow, who had been left comfortably off; she had a little house in Chelsea, and she married him. For the rest of his days his shirts were washed for him (he affected a soft frill instead of a stock, and wore rather noticeable hats) and he walked about all day, or sat in his study, being very poetic indeed, to the entire satisfaction of Mrs. Eeles, who adored him.

And the little climbing boy? What happened to Ben? When Arabella came back from her visit to Arden she found that he had grown so fond of William that it would be a shame to part them; so he went back with the Welby family to Curteys Court, and lived with Hannah and William after their marriage. Arabella paid for his keep, and for his lessons at the Dame School at Curteys Percy; and then William trained him in the gardens. They never found out his true name, or his parentage; so, when he married in the grey-stone church at Curteys Percy, he signed the register, "Ben Small", knowing no better, and thus frustrating the efforts, two hundred years later, of the Linchestershire Smalls to trace their ancestry. Try as they might, they never could get back any further than that entry in the marriage register! They searched back in the records—no earlier Smalls; then they searched in all the surrounding parishes, and in the local market town of Melton, to find other traces of Ben. But no! The Smalls sprang from nowhere, they concluded at last. Not that it would have worried Ben, if he could have known of it, as he whistled and sang round the gardens, and went home to his bride, and blessed the day he had refused to climb a chimney . . .

"Well, Mr. Watts?" said Caroline, as she greeted him on one of his flying visits to Curteys Court. "How is your lady? How is my sister?" She looked at him, and noticed how well he appeared, how glowingly content.

"I have been teased out of part of my garden, to give her room to keep Leghorn hens; it is her latest craze; and it has necessitated a new straw hat, with blue ribbons, in which to feed them. If you could see her, scattering the corn . . ." and here he stopped, and laughed out of pure happiness; and Caroline decided her sister was at rest at last.

Of the three couples, the Earl and his Countess at Arden Priory, Jane and Robert Spencer in their vicarage, and Arabella and Cornelius Watts in the old chambers above Waveney and Watts offices, making their first home with the stir of London about them, it would be difficult to choose the happiest. But perhaps, as Cornelius watched Arabella pouring his coffee at the breakfast table, or when she came up behind him when he was working, and leaned over to rest her cheek against his, perhaps we can think that, of all the couples, there was none happier than our Quicksilver Lady and her not-so-very-elderly gentleman.